MW00873389

THE ENGLISH ROSE

DEBORAH E. HAMMOND

Copyright

DEDICATION

To the People of Lewes, Delaware, my home away from home; your history and your beauty are the inspiration for this story and to the love of my life Bill; thank you for your support and inspiration.

CHAPTER ONE

The gale force winds lashed the tender ship across the heaving waves which threatened to sink it at every turn. The men were told that precious cargo was on board and the men at oars knew to bring the cargo to shore safely. Why it was essential to bring the cargo to shore tonight of all nights was not explained or understood.

On arriving at the landing, the precious cargo was brought onto dry land. "Bring her to St. Peter's," was the order. The wagon headed to the church at breakneck speed, the driver following orders of Hans Van Ressller, the largest landowner in the town of Lewes, Delaware. The precious cargo on board was the bride who was the subject of the arranged marriage. Catherine Wentworth went to the altar as a lamb to slaughter. She was in this country for no other reason than to settle a debt of her uncle and the upcoming wedding was meant to resolve the matter between Van Ressller and Sir Jonathan Wentworth, uncle of the bride.

To the church and up the short path, the reluctant bride was brought to St. Peter's Episcopal Church for the quick ceremony. There would be no special gown, no bouquet of flowers, no music and no family; just the bride, groom, priest, her uncle's steward and the men of the Van Ressller businesses as witnesses. It was they who were sent on this errand this evening to meet the Trinity and collect this passenger and they who were to serve as witnesses to the hastily arranged service.

"Get it over with priest; I have a fleet to save," Van Ressller said angrily. Only at that moment was any notice taken of the bride, the precious cargo who had been retrieved on this wicked night. The dark cloak that had been obscuring her face was thrown back and the bride was visible for the first time. Her skin was as white as marble and for all the expression on her face, she could have been a statute made of it as well; the eyes were as dark blue as the angry sea from whence she had only recently been plucked. Her hair was midnight black, as dark as the velvet cloak that had just been removed. Not only the priest but the witnesses behind stared with open mouths at the immovable statute before them. She was one of the most beautiful women that any of them had ever seen. Her intended husband, however seemed strangely unaffected by his prospective wife and her other worldly beauty.

The Reverend Clayborne had been pulled from his bed to perform this hasty service. He proceeded at his richest parishioner's urging. The Reverend began the customary service but was again cut short by the groom. "Fast service priest; no hearts and flowers needed. We have work to do this night," Van Ressller interrupted a second time.

Reverend Clayborne twice chastised quickly sped through the vows. "Do you Hans Wilhelm Van Ressller take this woman to be your lawfully wedded wife?"

"I do; get on with it," Van Ressller stated again angrily.

"Do you Catherine Elizabeth Wentworth take this man to be your lawfully wedded husband?" The witnesses moved forward to hear the response and the voice of the beautiful statute come to life; "I do," she said; two words, no more; no smile, no other reaction given.

"By the power vested in me by the State of Delaware and by the Episcopal Church, I now pronounce you husband and wife," Reverend Clayborne added.

Before Reverend Clayborne could say "You may kiss the bride," the groom was down the aisle shouting orders to the witnesses. "Hayes, take the Mistress and her belongings to the house. Return her uncle's steward to the Trinity and the

2

rest of you, come with me. We have a fleet to save," Van Ressller stated again angrily.

The new Mrs. Van Ressller was left standing at the altar. She looked at the flustered priest and thanked him for coming out in such weather, replaced her hood and prepared to follow Hayes to her new home. The home was not far away which was a blessing given the night. For the second time this evening she entered into the gale not knowing the reception at her next destination or the nature of her welcome upon arrival.

The house was located but one block away. The new Mistress followed Hayes as silently as she had left the ship and began the trip to the church. Her thoughts and opinions on the hastily organized wedding were unknown to any save herself.

When they arrived at the intersection of Second Street and Shipcarpenter Street, Catherine looked at her new home and was impressed by its size and stature. Clearly her new husband was wealthy and well connected in this new land to live in such a fine home. That she noted, was one factor in her favor. Hayes knocked at the door which was opened by a stout woman in a white cap. "This is your new Mistress Mrs. Jones. The Master has gone with the rest of the lads to save the fleet from the storm. Please show the Mistress to her room," Hayes said curtly.

"Please follow me Mistress," Mrs. Jones stated as she led Catherine to her second floor room, "I am sure you will wish to rest after your long journey. May I help you change out of your gown Mistress?" Catherine removed her cloak and presented her back to Mrs. Jones for the removal of the heavy, wet gown. That accomplished, Mrs. Jones lit a candle before leaving the room. Catherine noted the room was outfitted in the newest fabrics from London. There were bed curtains on the large canopied bed, and an oriental rug in front of the fire as well as a new fire screen in front of the blazing fire. Clearly no expense had been spared in the outfitting of this room and the large curtained bed. At least I have been spared the traditional wedding night activities, Catherine thought, thanking God for that favor. Having never met her husband before the expedited wedding, she had no desire to do her duty to her new husband in the bed now standing before her.

Catherine took off her remaining layers, moved the candle to the table beside the bed and proceeded to prepare for sleep. No food or water had been brought to her so she assumed that no dinner would be forthcoming either. She quietly removed the remaining petticoats and chemise, and once undressed, placed on a simple white gown to sleep. She turned down the bed, took down her hair and extinguished the candle. Within minutes she was asleep.

The next sound that Catherine heard was knocking on her chamber door. Mrs. Jones was at the door calling her for to awaken. "Mistress, Mistress please open the door. I have important news for you Mistress," Mrs. Jones said urgently.

Catherine swung her legs to the side of the bed and tried to stand. She saw that it was light outside, but she had no idea how long she had slept.

"Mistress, I have been asked to assist you to dress and come down to the library. There is news Mistress that must be shared. May I help you dress?" Mrs. Jones repeated more urgently this time.

What a difference from my arrival, Catherine thought. What on earth is the news that is so critical? With Mrs. Jones' help, Catherine quickly dressed, brushed and pinned her hair and followed the housekeeper to the library. When she entered the room, Reverend Clayborne was present along with Mr. Hayes from the previous night. Reverend Clayborne and Hayes rose at Catherine's arrival. "Mistress, we have news for you that we must immediately share. Your husband Master Van Ressller was killed last night in the storm. All the men who left the church last night save your uncle's steward have been lost as well. Hayes did not come to you today until this news could be confirmed and the bodies found. We are sorry for your loss Mistress and wished you to have this news as soon as it was confirmed. The bodies are at the church being prepared for burial," Reverend Clayborne stated with worry.

Catherine looked from one face to the other trying to grasp the news. She had gone from a bride to a widow in less than one day. Finding her voice again, she prepared to offer refreshments to her guests. "Mrs. Jones, if you will be so kind to prepare some refreshments for Reverend Clayborne and Mr. Hayes to thank them for their trouble of the errand. Thank you for bringing this news to me as soon as it could be confirmed," Catherine stated.

Mrs. Jones left the room in tears. Reverend Clayborne then spoke. "Thank you for the kind offer Mistress, but I must provide this same information to each of the families affected by this tragedy. Mr. Hayes will accompany me on this task," he said solemnly.

Seeing the Reverend and Mr. Hayes out, Catherine asked herself what was needed in this house for food to be presented. She could not remember the last time she had eaten and would have to insist that something be prepared before she fainted on the new oriental carpet. She went in search of Mrs. Jones then in the still unfamiliar house.

Mrs. Jones was found crying in the kitchen in reaction to the recent news. "Had you worked for the Master long Mrs. Jones?" Catherine asked tenderly.

"Yes Mistress; fifteen years. I am sorry for your loss Mistress. I assume you will not want the refreshments since Reverend Clayborne and Mr. Hayes have already left?" Mrs. Jones asked.

"I believe we should have food prepared for any unexpected guests that may come to the house. I myself would like some light repast as I have not eaten since my departure from the ship," Catherine replied quickly.

"Of course Mistress; I will get you dinner in just a moment then," Mrs. Jones replied.

Dinner Catherine thought? How long have I slept? She went back upstairs to check her hair and collect her thoughts. When the door closed she went to the full length mirror. Free; I am free. I came here, I married him as I was instructed and now I am free to return to London. Should I feel remorse for the man I saw for only a matter of minutes? He treated me like the business transaction that I was. Woman arrives; check; woman married; check; onto the fleet. Well, Catherine thought the fleet got him killed didn't it. And now I am free. No more demands of Catherine by a man she did not know from another man she now despised.

She tried now to recreate the features of this man that she had been sent across the Atlantic to marry. His face was angry and unkind she remembered vividly, the eyes small and calculating, the mouth drawn into an angry line as he repeatedly chastised the priest to hurry with the ceremony. He was of medium height, appeared to be roughly fifty years old, and yes, the one characteristic that remained with her most was the coldness, arrogance and anger. She shuddered at the thought that this man would have been her husband. What type of life would she have led as a bartered bride to such a man?

Within the hour, Mrs. Jones came to the door again to let Catherine know that dinner was ready and that Reverend Clayborne had returned. Catherine came downstairs to again meet her guest.

"Thank you again Reverend Clayborne for your previous visit. Would you care to have dinner with me?" Catherine asked.

"Thank you very much Mistress; that is most kind. Mrs. Jones always sets an excellent table," Reverend Clayborne replied.

Catherine showed the Reverend into the dining room. The dining room was also well appointed. It appeared that Mr.

Van Resller set quite a store on the quality of his home. The dining table was set for dinner and there were three places. Catherine was unsure if Mrs. Jones would sit at table as well. "Mistress, I have taken the liberty of asking Attorney Thomas Wendell to come to the Manor House this evening. I hope you do not mind. There are terms of your late husband's will that he wishes to review with you immediately. He thought it would be easier for you to have pastoral support when you receive this information," Reverend Clayborne further explained.

"By all means Reverend; thank you very much for your consideration in joining me. Mrs. Jones, please be so kind to show in Attorney Wendell on his arrival," Catherine stated. Mrs. Jones showed in Attorney Wendell within minutes and started to serve dinner.

After dinner was completed and cleared, Mr. Wendell began. "Mrs. Van Ressller, let me be frank; you may or may not be aware of the terms of the agreement that brought you here to America and to Lewes, Delaware," Attorney Wendell stated.

"I am aware of only some of the facts Mr. Wendell. I am aware of a gambling debt on the part of my uncle that could not be satisfied in the typical gentlemanly manner. I also understand that Mr. Van Ressller subsequently agreed to accept my hand in marriage in lieu of payment of that debt," Catherine replied calmly.

"Ah . . . yes Mrs. Van Ressller, I regret the insensitivity of this topic for a lady of your obvious quality and breeding, but Reverend Clayborne and I both felt that you must be fully briefed on the conditions that accompanied this agreement and the terms of the amended will. Mr. Van Ressller agreed to cover all costs of your ah . . . maintenance for a period of two years. The costs of food, drink, gowns, ribbons and other items dear to a lady's heart were to be covered under the agreement assuming immediate marriage was to take place which condition was met last night. Your uncle was clear on that demand as he wanted there to be no blemish on your reputation by your co-habitation with Mr. Van Ressller outside the boundaries of marriage," Attorney Wendell continued, clearly uncomfortable with the conversation.

"That was most considerate of my uncle," Catherine stated drolly. "What was to occur after the two year period?" she asked.

"Any issue of the marriage was to remain with Mr. Van Ressller in the event that you wished to return to London at that time. But under no circumstances was cash to be provided to you. He was very specific about that provision; no cash for a period of two years. After that interval, you would then be free to return to London with a cash settlement provided by Mr. Van Ressller should you desire to do so of course," Attorney Wendell continued.

"Why were there specific terms related to cash?" Catherine inquired.

"It was thought that any cash provided to you might find its way back to your uncle therefore your expenses only were to be covered, the expenses of the household and of course the expenses of any issue of your marriage," Attorney Wendell replied.

"Obviously that is a moot point at this juncture," Catherine responded.

"Quite so madam," Attorney Wendell replied.

"There is one exception to this agreement and that is Mr. Van Ressller's shipyard. That was a recent acquisition also acquired through a game of chance by Mr. Van Ressller," Attorney Wendell continued.

"It seems Mr. Van Ressller was uncommonly lucky at games of chance gentlemen," Catherine stated drolly.

"Quite so Mistress," Attorney Wendell responded. "The shipyard business was acquired after the terms of the will and agreement was prepared so it therefore falls outside of those restricted terms."

THE ENGLISH ROSE

"What exactly does that mean in English Mr. Wendell?" Catherine asked with a touch of exasperation.

"It means Mistress that you may operate the shipyard at a profit and retain the cash of that operation for your own personal use. All other properties remain within the estate for the specified period of two years and cannot be sold until after that time period has been exhausted," Attorney Wendell explained.

At last Catherine thought; there is a loophole to gain cash and possibly return to London. "You have given me a great deal to think about gentlemen. I am sure that I will have other questions as I absorb this information. Can we expect the funeral to occur tomorrow?" Catherine inquired.

"It most certainly will occur tomorrow Mistress. Everyone in the community will be there. Your late husband was well known in the area," Attorney Wendell stated.

If not well liked Catherine thought secretly. "Thank you again gentlemen for making these issues known to me. I will be sure to forward all costs of the funeral to your attention Mr. Wendell is that correct?" Catherine asked.

"That is correct Mistress. All invoices are to be directed to me as executor of the will and executor of the terms of the agreement of marriage," Attorney Wendell replied.

"I will show you out gentleman and thank you again for taking the time to share this information with me," Catherine replied.

Catherine closed the door behind her guests and climbed the steps to her room again to think. After she had closed the bedroom door behind her, she started to pace; so I am free, but not free. I am free of a man I did not know and who appeared to be a monster to all concerned, but not free to return to London just yet. Dear God, did they think I would return to London in two years time and leave any children of my own behind me? Is that what he thought of our family? Well Catherine to be fair, your uncle signed you away for the elimination of a debt; what else must they think? Two years;

9

she was twenty-one now so in two years time only twenty-three; not the end of the world. There was also the issue of the shipyard. If she could make a go of it, she could sell the business and get the cash for her return trip before the two year interval had expired.

What did she know about ship building however; nothing of course? She had only been prepared for a life of leisure and refinement. Thankfully her Mother saw fit to permit her to study if for no other reason than she was the daughter of a second son of the British aristocracy and an education could come in useful. After her Mother and Father had died in the West Indies, all education had ended. She was a trophy to sell to the highest bidder by her uncle who was a notorious gambler and always short of cash for his countless debts. And now this, Catherine thought; how the mighty have fallen. Niece of a baronet and bartered for like a horse; or a brood mare was of course a better description. Have two babies and walk away? Is that what Van Ressller thought; the answer was clearly yes; that is exactly what he thought of her and her family.

Somewhere during the night Catherine prepared a plan of action. She would live in this house rent free, present her invoices for payment by her departed and not lamented husband and build the shipyard business with someone in the community who knew something about ship building. She would advertise tomorrow after the funeral and place her plan into action. With the plan in place she fell asleep prepared to begin her new life and the two year sentence in this new land.

The next day Catherine rose and dressed and went downstairs for breakfast. Although she knew it her right to be served in bed as a married lady, she thought it pointless to stand on ceremony in a household of two people.

After breakfast, Mrs. Jones and she walked to St. Peter's Episcopal Church for the funeral. Mrs. Jones explained that Mr. Van Ressller thought a horse and wagon a luxury not needed in this small town. Of course he did Catherine thought inwardly.

When they arrived at the church, the entire congregation had turned out to see the new Mrs. Van Ressller. She wondered inwardly how much the town knew about her predicament, but assumed in a small town, news would travel quickly. Did all of these people lament her husband or were they just curious to see her?

Catherine and Mrs. Jones took their places in the Van Ressller pew and the service began. Catherine sat emotionless through the service held for a man she had met for only a few moments and who clearly viewed her as nothing more than chattel; the resolution of a debt and nothing more.

At the conclusion of the service, Catherine spied Mr. Wendell and asked if she might have a word. "I would like to post an advertisement for a skilled ship builder and designer. I need someone to run and supervise the shipyard for me. Do you think you can do that for me Mr. Wendell?" Catherine asked.

"I can Mrs. Van Ressller and will do so as soon as I return to my office. Good day to you and you have my deepest sympathy in light of the unfortunate circumstances," he replied.

CHAPTER TWO

"He is here Mistress. You should see him. He is a real charmer and oh so tall and good looking. He is here Mistress; you must come," Mrs. Jones stated in an agitated manner.

"Who is here Mrs. Jones?" Catherine replied. The woman had the worst habit of bursting in when Catherine was deep in thought prattling on with partial information about subjects that usually were of no consequence to Catherine.

"Why the man who answered your advertisement Mistress; he is here," Mrs. Jones replied smiling.

"Please ask him to wait in the library. I will be down shortly," Catherine replied calmly.

Catherine smoothed her hair and her gown. She hoped that the faux mourning she wore could soon be ended so that she could order another gown. Well, Catherine thought, best to look serious under the circumstances. Catherine went downstairs then and prepared herself for the interview.

When she opened the library door, she saw long legs spread toward the fire. He rose at her arrival. She was met with a six foot three inch man of reddish brown hair and blue eyes which were the color of a summer sky. He was young by the look of him, perhaps twenty-five. His eyes crinkled at the corners as if he was always smiling. He was tan, muscular and extremely handsome and was brazenly staring at her from her shoes to her hair with a lingering remaining gaze at her décolletage. She felt undressed and immediately off balance which she assumed was the purpose of the exercise.

"Mrs. Van Ressller?" he asked tentatively, with just a touch of Scot burr. "Are you Mrs. Van Ressller or her daughter?" the stranger asked.

Catherine went behind the desk in the library to put some distance between herself and the stranger. "Yes, I am Mrs. Van Ressller and you are . . . ?" Catherine asked haughtily.

"I am Cameron McCullum. Forgive me for my question, but I did not expect anyone quite so young." He smiled again at the last word. Catherine assumed he smiled a great deal by the look of him.

"What can I do for you Mr. McCullum?" Catherine replied. She had seated herself to stop the inspection that continued by Mr. McCullum after his last comment. She tried to keep the blush from her cheeks as she asked the question.

"I came in answer to your advertisement Mistress. I went first to Attorney Wendell's office and he directed me here. I am a shipbuilder and designer and am here to do a job for you Mistress," Mr. McCullum replied smiling.

"I see Mr. McCullum. Do you have any references of your past work?" Catherine inquired haughtily.

"I do, as well as a portfolio of my designs for your review." Mr. McCullum handed his portfolio to Catherine and made a point of touching her hand in the process of transferring the documents. The man was maddening Catherine thought.

Catherine sat studying the designs. She knew nothing about ships, their construction or design. She had only supervised maids and never hired anyone in her life. She thought she would not let him know any of that information however.

"Do you see anything that you like Mistress?" he asked again smiling that overly familiar smile.

"This is not my area of expertise Mr. McCullum. I would suggest that I offer you the position on a trial basis for six month's time. If you are successful with your first ship we can assume you have the position permanently. Is that acceptable to you?" Catherine inquired.

"Very well Mistress; you have a deal. I can discuss terms with your attorney if agreeable to you," Cameron replied. The maddening smile again accompanied this speech.

Catherine rose to her feet and handed Mr. McCullum back his portfolio. He grasped it and her hand at the same time. He shook her hand and then kissed it. "Americans shake hands on a deal Mistress. The kiss is Scots and my own," McCullum said smiling.

"Thank you for responding to the advertisement. You have my leave to go Mr. McCullum," Catherine replied coldly.

"In America Mistress, men do not require leave to come and go. You might want to remember that in the future," McCullum said smiling but with the same maddening inspection of Catherine's form before leaving the room.

He is not to be borne Catherine thought! If I wasn't so desperate to restart this business, I would throw him out on his overly familiar ear. Stay away from him Catherine, the inner voice stated in her ear. The man is trouble and an upstart who doesn't know his own place. I may be vulnerable now, but not for long. In two years time I will be on my way home to London and back to the life that I was meant to live.

*****

The next day Mrs. Jones was all aflutter about Mr. McCullum. "He is to start at the Yard today Mistress. He has moved into a cottage on Shipcarpenter Street right down the way so he can be close to the Yard. He will be hiring lads this week. They say he has ship designs like no one in Lewes has ever seen," she stated excitedly.

"The proof will be in the pudding Mrs. Jones as my Mother used to say," Catherine replied. Good Lord, it has started already, Catherine thought. Will everyone be full of new about Mr. McCullum? Good Lord! I must talk to Mr.

Wendell regarding whatever arrangements they have agreed upon.

After dressing, Catherine walked to Mr. Wendell's office situated not far from St. Peter's Episcopal Church on Second Street. She would never become accustomed to walking everywhere she went. Van Ressller was a skin flint in her opinion and still appeared to control her every movement from the grave. Well that will not be forever Catherine, just remember that. Two years at the most and less if Mr. McCullum the miracle worker can make the shipyard successful.

"Mrs. Van Ressller; how pleasant to see you again. We have such good fortune with Mr. McCullum. He is certainly well qualified and should give a great advantage to the shipyard and the community with the hiring. We were so fortunate that he agreed to my terms as well," Mr. Wendell stated.

"What exactly were those terms Mr. Wendell; if I may ask?" Catherine inquired.

"The terms are one half of the business assuming his work is satisfactory and he has produced his first ship in six month's time," Mr. Wendell replied.

"He has been given one half of the business? I am partners with Mr. McCullum?" Catherine stated in a shocked tone. Good Lord! The idea made her physically ill. "Why would you agree to such terms Mr. Wendell?" Catherine asked aghast.

"I knew how anxious you were to re-start the Yard. He is highly qualified and can design, build and oversee the Yard. You have three men in one Mistress Van Ressller," Wendell replied cheerily.

And he will never let me forget it Catherine thought silently. She quickly regained her composure not wishing Attorney Wendell to see her true feelings. "On another topic Mr. Wendell; does the agreement between my uncle and the late Mr. Van Ressller permit me to have a hired horse and wagon at my disposal on a daily basis?" Catherine inquired.

"No Mistress; I am very sorry. Mr. Van Ressller was very clear on that point. He viewed horse and wagon travel as an unnecessary expense that was not allowable under the terms of the agreement," Mr. Wendell stated.

"Thank you Mr. Wendell. I thought that might be the case, but also thought it was worthwhile to ask. Thank you again and good day to you sir," Catherine stated. She left the office then and walked back to the Manor House. Controlled by one man from the grave; partners with another upstart of a man; traded for a debt by a third. I hate men and will count the days until I can be away from all of them and on my own again in London, Catherine thought stonily.

*****

In short order, Cameron McCullum was the talk of the community as Catherine had feared. He was described as a miracle worker who knew all there was to know about building ships, designing ships and hiring men with Van Ressller's shipyard money. Men wanted to meet him; women wanted to hear his Scots burr and see those massive shoulders. Even Mrs. Jones was not immune.

"Mistress, the shipyard is the talk of Lewes. Everyone is talking of nothing else. We are so pleased that the shipyard will be restarted again after the recent tragedy," Mrs. Jones stated.

"I am glad that the men of the community have that opportunity Mrs. Jones. I am also glad that Mr. McCullum has been so well received," Catherine replied. Now if he will just stay away from me, Catherine thought, all will be well.

Several hours later Mrs. Jones came to Catherine's room. "Mistress, Mr. McCullum is downstairs in the library asking to see you." Of course he is, Catherine thought to herself. My worst nightmare is downstairs asking to see me yet again.

"I will be down in just a moment Mrs. Jones," Catherine stated calmly. Let him wait she thought silently. She went to the mirror and smoothed her hair and gown. I will be so glad to stop wearing this faux mourning. I may order some material and have a new gown prepared. I shall need to send for some patterns from London as well. I wonder if there is a dressmaker here in Lewes. After spraying on her favorite lavender scent, Catherine determined that she was ready to face her nemesis. There, that should be long enough Catherine thought smugly.

"Mrs. Van Ressller, so good to see you again," McCullum said as she entered the library. The same head to toe gaze was completed by Mr. McCullum which Catherine met stonily this time.

"How may I assist you Mr. McCullum?" Catherine said sitting at her desk.

"I wanted to advise you that I have hired my team. We will be ready to start straight away. Since we are partners I wondered how often you would prefer updates on our venture; daily, weekly, *nightly*?" The last word was said with particular emphasis Catherine thought.

"I appreciate the information Mr. McCullum. I am not sure how you managed to sway Mr. Wendell to your favor, but I want you to understand that I will be watching you and your activities at the shipyard very closely," Catherine replied haughtily.

"Likewise Mistress of course," Mr. McCullum responded warmly. "Since your establishment is without a horse or wagon, would you prefer me to come here for your updates?" Cameron replied smiling.

"We can alternate Mr. McCullum. I am not opposed to walking whatever you may think and would like to see my investment in person as your work progresses," Catherine replied coolly.

"Very well Mistress; as you wish. I plan on working five and a half days a week at the Yard and give all men the Sabbath off. I hope you approve of that plan?" Cameron stated.

"I certainly do Mr. McCullum. Is there anything further?" Catherine inquired coldly.

"No Mistress; I will be on my way. Shall I see you tomorrow evening at the Yard then?" Cameron asked.

"Yes of course; until then Mr. McCullum. Good evening," Catherine replied.

"Good evening to you Mistress," he said smiling.

When he had left the library and the house, Catherine left out a sigh. Why must my life be controlled by difficult men? At least one was beyond controlling her in most things not outlined by the agreement of course and an ocean stood between her and her uncle. That left only McCullum to encounter on a daily basis. She would at least look forward to their verbal confrontations. She had to admit that he was intelligent and appeared to be educated when he was not being overly familiar with his celebrated charm.

CHAPTER THREE

Despite herself, Catherine came to enjoy the daily verbal sparring with Cameron McCullum. What she didn't enjoy was the man's constant appearances in all aspects of her life. On Sunday when Mrs. Jones and she attended church he was already seated in the Van Ressller pew and sat so close to Catherine that she could feel the heat of his leg through her gown. His long legs were stretched in front of him just as they had been the first day that she saw him in her library. He never fidgeted or fell asleep in the pew. When she dropped her prayer book, his hand was there before her, his eyes on her décolletage as she corrected herself in the pew.

As they walked back from church as walking was always required, Mrs. Jones invited Mr. McCullum to luncheon after church with the excuse that she had made too much food for only two to eat. Catherine rolled her eyes at that comment which was not missed by McCullum. His hand brushed hers as they walked side by side back to the Manor House; his smile too smug for her liking.

After luncheon she thought to confront him regarding this constant shadowing. "How has the work at the Yard gone this week Mr. McCullum?" Catherine inquired.

"Shouldn't you call me by my Christian name now that we are courting?" he replied with his customary maddening smile.

"We are not courting Mr. McCullum. Why would you even think such a thing? I am a recently widowed woman," Catherine asked aghast.

"I see you every day whether here or at the Yard. We sit together at church and share luncheon afterwards. Even you must admit it Mistress; we are courting!" Cameron replied grinning.

"We are not courting and do not even consider such a concept. It is most improper," Catherine replied haughtily.

"We are the most properly matched couple in age, intelligence, education and common interest for hundreds of miles," Cameron replied smiling.

"So you are saying by process of elimination that we are automatically courting?" Catherine asked frowning.

"Do you know anyone else but Attorney Wendell in this community with their own personal library? And Wendell is ancient in comparison to you and me and married as well," McCullum replied smiling.

"You have a library Mr. McCullum?" Catherine said sitting forward in her chair.

McCullum saw the spark and the movement with the receipt of that information. He didn't miss much or anything for that matter particularly as it related to Catherine. "I wasn't always a ship designer and builder Mistress. I was fortunate enough to attend University, so yes, I have a library," Cameron replied smugly.

She had abandoned her customary coldness in the heat of this recent revelation. "May I borrow a book from your library Mr. McCullum?" Catherine replied.

"You may if you call me Cameron," he answered with that maddening smile.

"That is quite out of the question Mr. McCullum as I am sure you know. When did you become a ship designer *Mr.* McCullum?" Catherine emphasized the title in her question.

"When I decided that I didn't want to ask anyone's permission to come and go whenever I pleased," Cameron answered. "I came here to build something that I wanted to build and build a life which I defined. I love this country and will share my skills to help it grow," Cameron replied.

"What type of books do you have in your library?" Catherine continued.

"I have all kinds of books; history, literature, theology, all subjects," he replied smiling.

"What part of Scotland do you come from originally Mr. McCullum?" Catherine asked.

"I am originally from the Highlands but as I am sure you know the Highlands have been all but deserted following the Rising of 1765. My Father took us to Edinburgh for more opportunities. I attended University there. It was odd living among Lowlanders and Presbyterians, but I came to adjust to it. We learn to adjust do we not Mistress? Didn't your family ever frighten you with tales of the marauding Highlanders descending on England?" Cameron asked smiling.

"They did not Mr. McCullum I suppose because the family estate was located near London. It seemed a safe enough distance from the Highlands and Highlanders for that matter. If you were a Highlander by birth, would you not be of the Catholic faith Mr. McCullum and if so, isn't it odd that you attend St. Peter's and not a Catholic Church?" Catherine asked.

"The closest Catholic church is over a hundred miles from here; besides I like the view in the Van Ressller pew," he said smiling. "Why don't you stop by my cottage and review the titles in my library on your way back from the Yard tomorrow?" Cameron offered with a mischievous grin.

"I think not Mr. McCullum. This is a small town and I am sure that all eyes are upon us. I cannot just go to your cottage without a chaperone. It just simply is not done," Catherine replied primly.

"We are not in London Mistress and besides are you saying that Mrs. Jones is your chaperone?" Cameron replied laughing.

"Of course she is and she would be in here in a moment if I called for her," Catherine retorted.

"She is asleep in front of the fire Mistress and you know it as well as I do. You needn't worry Mistress; I would never force a lady to do anything that she didn't want to do. When the time comes we will both know it and it will be well worth the wait," Cameron replied again with his maddening smile.

Catherine tried to keep the blush from her face and her gaze directly on him. "If you will be so kind to bring some books to the Yard tomorrow, I can choose among them at our daily meeting," Catherine replied seemingly unfazed by his words or actions.

"Whatever you wish Mistress. You know, it is a very intimate thing to select a book for another person; especially for a true book lover. I will try my best however. Until tomorrow Mistress; thank you for our talk. I am glad that our intentions are now clear," Cameron replied.

"What intentions are those Mr. McCullum?" Catherine asked frowning.

"Why my intention to court you and your intention to say yes of course, when the time is right," Cameron replied. "Good afternoon Mistress."

When he had left the dining room and the house itself, Catherine let out the sigh that she had been holding in for the past hour. The man was impossible and becoming far too familiar. What was wrong with this town? Was everyone trying to play matchmaker? She would not tarnish her reputation nor become involved with anyone who would keep her from returning to London; even if he did have a library.

The next day, Catherine noticed that to her own mortification, she kept checking the hall clock to see if the day would pass faster and was furious with herself for repeatedly doing so. A parcel arrived for her with fabric and patterns from London. It was a welcome diversion from the constant thoughts of Cameron McCullum. Catherine asked Mrs. Jones if there was a seamstress in town who could make up the latest designs in the fabric just received.

"Mistress, I am a seamstress," Mrs. Jones replied. "I can make up those dresses for you. Let me see the designs if I may."

Catherine showed the design to Mrs. Jones. "Mistress, this gown is positively indecent. Look at the cut of the neckline; look at the sheerness of the fabric. You would catch your death of cold in this," Mrs. Jones replied shocked.

"I have been assured that it is the newest style direct from London by way of France," Catherine answered.

"Well France; what do you expect. I will make them for you with a modesty panel over the bodice and you can wear a shawl in the summer and a jacket in the fall and your black dress in the winter," Mrs. Jones replied cheerily.

"I do not want to wear widow's weeds ever again Mrs. Jones," Catherine stated heatedly. "In fact, it is my intention to burn this dress once my prescribed time of mourning has passed," Catherine continued angrily.

"We will see what we can do Mistress." Mrs. Jones smiled to herself as she returned to the kitchen. They are courting alright. At last she wants to be out of those widow's weeds. If she made the dress like the pattern, they will be married in six months she chuckled to herself.

*****

At long last the appointed hour of the day had been reached and Catherine set off walking to the Yard. Walking again, Catherine thought. No one walked in London. If her friends in London saw her now; well what good did it do thinking about London and her friends there? They would all know that she had been bartered like a commodity to settle a debt. Maybe they were right. What would happen if she did return to London? She would certainly be considered damaged goods in the eyes of London society. With limited fortune and nothing that could be provided by her uncle to accommodate a match, what chances did she have back in London? Maybe Mr. McCullum was right and she should stay here and decide her own fate. That would be the ultimate betrayal of her original mission to return to London. With her own funds however, she could make a life for herself here. At least now she would have a real book to read at last as she decided her next move and two years in which to make the decision.

When she arrived at the Yard, the lads were done for the day. She entered the office and found Cameron sitting at his drafting table working on a new design. "Mistress how good of you to walk down; is there a reason that you do not have a horse and wagon of your own?" Cameron asked.

"It is a long story Mr. McCullum and not one that is very pleasant in the telling," Catherine replied absently.

"Why are you here Mistress?" he asked with that full gaze of his trained on her.

"I am here for our daily report and because you promised me a book if I remember correctly," Catherine replied.

"Not here in this office; here in Lewes, Delaware, in the United States of America?" Cameron responded.

"That is also a long story and even uglier than the first. I prefer not to talk about either if you will be so kind. I would like to see your drawings if I may." She thought she had adeptly changed the subject. He thought they were in yet another fencing match. Just once he hoped she would drop her guard. What have they done to you Catherine and why are you here, was his daily thought? Rather than pursue his questions further, he brought out his sketches and laid them on the table. "This is a design that I am experimenting with to enhance speed. Note the revisions in the rigging," Cameron replied. Catherine looked at the sketches with genuine interest but with no knowledge of what she was reviewing.

"They are beautiful Mr. McCullum. You are very talented. What is this?" she asked pointing.

"That's the bowsprit and is where the ship's decorative figurehead is placed. For now, this ship is tentatively called the English Rose," Cameron replied watching her intently for the expected reaction.

"The English Rose; won't the citizens here object to that reference?" Catherine asked.

"Well this country is neutral in this latest spat between England and France for now at least. I do not think they will mind. I named her for you," he replied softly.

Her dark blue eyes rose to meet his. She seemed surprised as always by his frankness and directness. "That was very kind of you Mr. McCullum. I have never had anyone name anything for me before," Catherine replied smiling.

"The face that launched a thousand ships . . ." Cameron continued smiling.

"That was Helen of Troy, Mr. McCullum. I do not think anyone would go to war for me. I have generally been in the way of others not their focus," Catherine replied wistfully.

"I cannot think why Mistress. A man would be a fool to not make you his focus," Cameron replied softly.

"So what book have you selected for me today then?" Catherine asked skirting the comment again.

"Shakespeare's sonnets; *Shall I compare thee to a summer's day* . . . ?" Cameron responded.

"You are quite the Renaissance man Mr. McCullum. Ship designer, poet . . . what other talents do you possess?" Catherine asked smiling.

"You would be surprised Mistress at the depths of my interests and talents," Cameron replied with a mischievous grin.

"Thank you again for the loan of the book. I have so missed reading since being here. The library at the Manor House is just a room. There are precious few books there and none that I would wish to read," Catherine replied.

"I am happy to loan out any of my books to a fellow enthusiast. Perhaps we can discuss them of an evening as well," Cameron suggested.

"Thank you again Mr. McCullum," Catherine replied smiling.

"I will walk you back to the Manor House shall I? Why is it again that you don't have a horse or wagon at your disposal

Mistress?" Cameron inquired as he gathered his coat for departure.

Catherine sighed this time and changed her mind in answering the persistent question. "The late Mr. Van Ressller did not approve of horses and wagons it appears for the movement of people in a small town. I am therefore still controlled by the grave," Catherine replied with exasperation.

"You can control your own destiny Mistress. That is what this country is all about; controlling your own destiny," Cameron replied earnestly.

"You may be right Mr. McCullum. Thank you again for the loan of the book," Catherine replied.

"I will escort you as far as the Manor House. It is on my way home after all," Cameron replied smiling.

*****

The following week, Cameron had a visit from the Captain of the English Rose as Cameron had dubbed her. He knew the Captain would be pleased with the design he just needed to convince him of the selection of the name and of the decorative figurehead that he had in mind.

"Captain McEwan, I am glad you found me. How goes it with you?" Cameron asked welcoming the Captain to the shipyard office.

"I was pleased to have your letter Cameron. I ken your work well and I ken if you say you have a new design, it will be worth my while to visit and see the plans," Captain McEwan stated.

Cameron laid out the plans and explained the elements of his new design and all of its attributes. "Give me all of the speed you can give me man and all of the maneuverability. Unless I miss my guess, she will go up against the British for prizes Cameron. We will be at war again soon and I expect to do some good hunting," Captain McEwan stated.

"You will have both Captain and if you are pleased, I hope you will let your fellow merchants know the same," Cameron asked smiling. "There are two things that I would ask; small things for sure but I need to know that you are on board with the suggestions before I move forward," Cameron stated.

"Of course Cameron; what would they be then?" Captain McEwan asked.

"I ask that we name her the English Rose. It is in honor of a lady who is very special to me. I would also offer that I carve the figurehead for you. I want to make the figurehead in the image of the same lady," Cameron said smiling.

"A lass is it Cameron? I have never seen you for want of the lasses. Why this one in particular?" the Captain asked smiling.

"She is like no one I have ever met Captain. She is a lady for sure and English if you can believe it, but I have made up my mind that I will wed her. I just need to convince her of that fact," Cameron replied grinning.

"English you say? Cameron, are you sure man? I am sure you could find a wee Scot lassie that will be less trouble than the prize you are seeking," the Captain said laughing.

"Aye that is true but she is the one Captain. I ken it well; she is the one and I will have no other," Cameron replied emphatically.

"Aye then; ye have a deal. Give me all the speed ye can muster and make her quick to maneuver and ye can name her what you will. I will call her the Rose anyway and if this lady is as beautiful as you say, your figurehead will be the talk of the Delaware," Captain McEwan stated.

"Aye Captain, she will be all of those things you will see," Cameron promised.

*****

The next day, Catherine walked to the offices of Attorney Wendell to provide invoices for payment by the estate. She tried to keep current by making sure that the invoices were provided on a monthly basis for payment so that none of the local shops or tradesmen would need to wait for their reimbursement. Having lived in a household of constant indebtedness, Catherine was extremely prompt on all matters of billing and payment.

When she arrived at the office, Mr. Wendell was entertaining a visitor; none other than Cameron McCullum. Of course, Catherine thought; the man haunts my comings and goings and is everywhere that I need or wish to be. "Mrs. Van Ressller, I was just meeting with your business partner Mr. McCullum regarding the activities at the Yard. I must say the town is aflutter with the work that he has already been able to achieve; I should say that you both have been able to achieve," Mr. Wendell stated smiling.

"You were correct the first time Mr. Wendell. I am merely the silent partner; Mr. McCullum is the designer and builder. The talent lies with him. I am merely the conduit to permit the shipyard to continue in operation," Catherine replied.

"That is certainly a very important part of the equation Mrs. Van Ressller. Otherwise a great many men would have been out of work and we would not be seeing the first ship take shape. Mr. McCullum was just showing me the designs," Mr. Wendell stated.

"Yes, they are quite beautiful. Mr. McCullum is a very talented man," Catherine replied. She had kept her attention on Mr. Wendell during this exchange but knew that Cameron was waiting to share that maddening smile with her if she were to meet his gaze. She chose not to do so in front of Mr. Wendell in order to staunch the rumors that the two were courting.

"Mrs. Van Ressller, we were just discussing the affairs on the national level regarding the trade bill. Whatever affects trade, affects the coast as I am sure you appreciate. The impressments of mariners by the British cannot be allowed to stand. Would you not agree Mr. Wendell?" Cameron stated heatedly.

"I would indeed Mr. McCullum. Mr. Madison may have another war on his hands if these matters cannot be addressed," Mr. Wendell responded.

"Do you have any opinion on the matter Mrs. Van Ressller?" Cameron asked.

"It is not a subject with which I am familiar Mr. McCullum, but I would be happy to do some reading on the matter if any newspapers are carrying the debate," Catherine replied.

"Well Mr. McCullum here would be a perfect example of what we were just discussing. As a native born Scot, the British Empire would consider Mr. McCullum a citizen of Great Britain even though he is now a naturalized citizen of the United States. With his knowledge of ships, their design and construction he could be impressed by the British Navy in any port on the coast. He would find himself on a British ship as quickly as you can say Jack Robinson with no say in the matter and that is the British law that we hear so touted the world over. The estimates that I have read are upwards of six thousand men who may have been impressed by the Royal Navy who count themselves as American citizens," Mr. Wendell said heatedly.

"Why that is terrible and totally unfair," Catherine replied aghast.

"Would you be bereft if I were to be carried off by an impressments gang Mrs. Van Ressller?" Cameron asked smiling his wicked smile again.

"What I mean is it would be terrible for the families of all of those poor souls who would find themselves on a ship of a foreign nation through no fault of themselves. I would very much like to read the debate on this matter," Catherine replied hastily.

"I had no idea that we had a fellow avid reader in Mrs. Van Ressller, Mr. McCullum," Mr. Wendell replied cheerily.

"Oh Mrs. Van Ressller is also a woman of hidden talents and interests. Isn't that right Mrs. Van Ressller?" Cameron replied with his maddening smile directed at Catherine.

"I certainly enjoy reading and would love to see our community have that opportunity as well. Has there ever been any discussion of a local lending library here in Lewes?" Catherine responded.

"We have an informal one composed of local private collections which are housed in various locations. I am sure that you could find some books to your liking although you would have probably already read the books available here," Mr. Wendell replied.

"Mrs. Van Ressller and I share a passion for books Mr. Wendell and we would be interested in any new volumes that you could bring to our attention," Cameron stated staring openly at Catherine.

We, Catherine thought? There he goes again talking about us as *we* and not as *he* or *me*.

"I am sure that there are a number of individuals in town who may have that interest. Perhaps we could meet at the Manor House to discuss some volumes that would be of mutual interest to the collective readers in town," Catherine responded. She looked at Cameron at that moment to make sure that he understood that she was talking about the community and not just him, not that it would have any impact on the man whatsoever and his equally maddening smile.

"What a wonderful idea Mrs. Van Ressller? Perhaps we can discuss that at our next partnership meeting," Cameron replied.

He was unrelenting in giving the impression to Mr. Wendell that they were a couple. Catherine decided to admit defeat for the moment and return to the Manor House before she betrayed her true feelings about the man in front of the attorney and she assumed the town as a whole.

"Thank you again Mr. Wendell for the information and for addressing these invoices. Good day to you sir," Catherine stated in reply.

"I will walk with you Mrs. Van Ressller as I will be returning to the Yard and the Manor House is on the way," Cameron replied smiling.

When they were outside of the office, Catherine trained her attention directly on Cameron. "I wish you would not provide the impression to Mr. Wendell and the town as a whole that we are a courting couple when clearly we are not," Catherine stated heatedly.

"Ah Mistress but we are. Have I not told you that we are perfectly matched in intellect, education, interests, age range and all other attributes?" he replied again with that maddening smile. "I saw the look on your face when Mr. Wendell mentioned impressments and me as a prime example. You know that you have the most extraordinarily transparent face. Whatever you are thinking is instantly apparent on your face," Cameron said grinning again. "Would you be at a loss if I were to be impressed Mrs. Van Ressller?" Cameron asked with a wink.

"Well the Yard most certainly would be at a loss. You have done an admirable job and I would be the first to admit it. But I am of course speaking as a partner in the venture and not as me personally," Catherine hastily added.

"Oh I think you are talking both as my partner and as Mrs. Van Ressller. The whole town looks upon us as a couple so certainly you can understand why I look upon us as a couple as well. I appreciate your kind heart and how you would miss me should the worst happen," Cameron said mockingly.

"And have I not replied that just because we happen to be two people who are single with the attributes that you mention does not by process of elimination mean that we are courting?" Catherine said blushing.

"You certainly do not want to have a lover's quarrel here in the street I am sure. That would also become public knowledge in short order, especially after we were getting along so well in Mr. Wendell's office," Cameron replied laughing.

"That is only because I did not want to kick you in front of witnesses," Catherine replied again heatedly.

"Anger is certainly a frequent manifestation of deeper feelings for another, wouldn't you say?" Cameron replied grinning.

"I would agree only if those deeper feelings reflect frustration and dislike," Catherine responded her face flushing with anger.

"I disagree. I believe anger can typically be misplaced by the party in question and taken as dislike when in point of fact, the anger may mask one's true hidden feelings for another; something for you to ponder until next we meet Mrs. Van Ressller. Good day Mistress and I will see you later this evening." Cameron left on that comment and walked on to the Yard leaving a storming Catherine behind at the Manor House gate.

He walks on as if he doesn't have a care in the world and as if I am dying for love of him. In this case anger is just anger and not masking anything further. She had to admit that she enjoyed their arguments however. At least he was an educated person and quick witted. But that was as far as she was prepared to admit.

That evening was Cameron's turn to come to the Manor House to review the activities of the day. He did not come empty handed. He had selected another of Shakespeare's works for Catherine, but this time he did so with a mixture of humor and mischief in light of their conversation from earlier in the day. He had brought the *Taming of the Shrew* as his book loan of the day and within it, had included some newspaper articles from the Dover, Delaware and Baltimore, Maryland papers dealing with the latest crisis on the national front. Since the growing tensions with Britain potentially affected their business venture, he felt she should be made aware of the potential impact. Besides, it gave them something further to talk about. He also enjoyed their daily fencing matches as she was the most intelligent person that he typically talked to on a daily basis. He also loved the fact that her eyes turned dark blue when she had flashes of anger and her cheeks had a flush of color that was immensely attractive. She was not aware of the latter two traits, but he found those reactions another part of the day that he looked forward to the most.

When he arrived at the Manor House, Mrs. Jones answered the door. "Good evening Mrs. Jones. Is your Mistress available?" Cameron stated smiling.

"She is Mr. McCullum. Please come into the dining room. Won't you have a bit of supper with us? You know I always make more than two people can possibly eat; especially since the Mistress eats like a little bird," Mrs. Jones replied smiling.

"I will be most pleased to take supper with you Mrs. Jones. You and the Mistress always set a fine table," Cameron replied.

Catherine heard the voices and immediately thought; again Mrs. Jones presumes to invite Cameron to dinner. Is everyone in this town conspiring to play matchmaker? In a moment Cameron was at the door and as always his tall frame and always present smile filled the doorway and the dining room. "Good evening Mistress. I have very kindly been invited to dinner," Cameron stated.

"I am sure that Mrs. Jones accidentally made too much dinner again and just wanted to share," Catherine replied drolly.

"Thank you as always for the pleasant invitation from the Mistress of the house," Cameron replied mockingly.

Catherine decided to let that comment pass when she saw that Cameron had brought her another book. "What book have you brought this time Mr. McCullum?" Catherine asked with eyes shining.

"One that I thought might be appropriate given our conversation earlier in the day. You may be familiar with Shakespeare's *Taming of the Shrew*?" Cameron replied smiling his mocking smile.

At that moment Mrs. Jones came in with the first course and Catherine was temporarily unable to respond to Cameron's comment. He sat smiling and immensely proud of himself for both the book loan and his tailoring to this afternoon's discussion. When Mrs. Jones left the dining room, Catherine was ready with her retort.

"Was there any reason for this particular selection Mr. McCullum?" Catherine asked casually.

"I had wondered if anyone had ever called you Kate in your past. It is merely a coincidence, but of course there are some useful points related to courtship in the *Taming of the Shrew* that I thought might be of interest," Cameron replied smiling.

"How many times do I need to tell you that we are not courting?" Catherine replied angrily.

"Oh but we are Mistress; we most definitely are." Cameron grabbed her hand at that moment and made a point of kissing it before he returned it to Catherine. The response was the one that he was hoping for; the darkening of the dark blue eyes and the flush of color that said the night's fencing match had begun. "I also included some articles for you about the events at the national level on this kerfuffle with Great Britain. It could have an impact on our own business if there are trade restrictions imposed on the United States. In addition, the matter of the impressments of sailors must be sorted in quick order. If any of our lads were to go to Philadelphia or Baltimore they could run the risk of finding themselves on a British ship without their consent. Great Britain needs to learn that this country fought one war to stop that sort of nonsense and we may need to fight a second one," Cameron replied heatedly.

"You are the first man who ever wanted to discuss anything of substance with me. I have typically been treated as an ornament by those around me. I do not think anyone ever asked my opinion on anything before now. I was always free to explore in the world of the mind, but never free to express those opinions. That was not a part of my world until coming here," Catherine replied wistfully.

"That is but one of the magical things about America. There are so many freedoms here that we could only have dreamt of in the old country. Why shouldn't you be asked your opinion? I would hazard a guess that you would have a better grasp of most issues than the majority of men that I encounter on a daily basis," Cameron replied smiling.

Catherine flashed him one of her rare smiles at the conclusion of that speech. If what he was saying was true, maybe America was worth a second look after all, she thought.

"You clearly have a hunger to read and to learn. What was the source of that do you think?" Cameron asked casually.

"I was often left alone and the one thing of value that my uncle possessed was a library. It was not collected by him of course, but by his father, my grandfather and generations before him. No one ever went into that room except to drink; apart from me of course. I could hide whenever anyone else came in for their secret assignations and continue to read. It was not a very positive reinforcement of married life or any kind of life beyond personal pleasure and gratification, but I had a whole world to explore through those books. It was truly the most wonderful thing about Edgewater," Catherine replied smiling.

Catherine didn't tell this tale of her childhood with self-pity or regret, but coolly and objectively as if trying to explain her cool detachment from the rest of the world; the quality that made her appear like the marble statute that she resembled versus the flesh and blood woman that Cameron knew her to be. Cameron felt for the first time that she was letting down one of her many guards and wondered if the mutual love of books had a hand in that decision. He approached Catherine each night like a young doe that he fed by hand, coaxing the doe more and more into the clearing and into actual life. He had come to live for their nightly chats and hoped that Catherine had come to feel the same.

*****

In short order Easter was upon them and an improvement to the weather. On Palm Sunday during their usual post church luncheon, Cameron had jokingly asked Catherine what she had given up for Lent. "My Father used to give up summer melons for Lent," she replied with eyes shining.

He saw the radiant smile then and the true glimpse of spontaneous joy that was so missing from her daily exchanges with the world. "Well we could have given up arguing Mistress Van Ressller," Cameron replied smiling.

"I doubt that very much Mr. McCullum; perhaps only on Sundays and Sunday mornings at that," she replied teasingly.

"Ah but then we do not speak in church do we?" he responded with his mischievous grin.

"Just so Mr. McCullum; I think we may have been able to manage it; at least until lunchtime," she replied smiling.

Whether she wished to admit it or not, Cameron was now a welcome presence in the family pew. It was a comfort to have him there every Sunday. He always arrived before Mrs. Jones and herself so she knew that he was not out the night before drinking, gambling or worse. He never smelled of the drink but only of his own personal scent which was a clean, solid mixture of soap and the outdoors; a distinctive scent that she came to identify as Cameron's own; not a cloying French cologne like those who were friends of her uncle's had favored, but a decidedly masculine smell that was very pleasant.

When they stood in church, he never sang, but always listened to her sing and followed along in the Prayer Book and the lessons. He never had the page marked so she felt compelled to share her Prayer book with him. When they stood side by side, she did not reach his shoulder. She would feel his eyes on her face as they stood and when she would glance in his direction, the look was not lascivious but a steady gaze instead as if he was memorizing every feature for some future purpose.

When they knelt to pray, he would always provide her his hand to steady her as she returned to her seat and the same when they took communion side by side. When he held the Prayer book, his left hand was twice the size of her small hand and the strongest hand that she had ever seen.

That was in the church of course where they did not speak and so could not disagree. Once outside the church, the usual argumentative banter returned.

"So Mrs. Jones, I was thinking that perhaps after lunch you and the Mistress might like to stroll over and see the ship as she is taking shape. What say you to that little diversion Mrs. Jones?" Cameron asked as he walked back to the Manor House with Catherine and Mrs. Jones following the Easter service.

"Oh that would be wonderful Mr. McCullum. May we do so Mistress?" Mrs. Jones asked excitedly.

"I am sure that we would not wish to turn down such a lovely invitation made to *you* Mrs. Jones," Catherine said drolly.

Cameron waited then for her to turn to him with that usual mixture of exasperation and mirth on her face. He laughed then and was happy that they would have the whole day together and not just the customary church service and luncheon.

After the meal, the threesome walked over to the Yard and he showed them the English Rose as she was taking shape. Catherine quietly took in the bones of the ship that she had seen from the very earliest stages as drawings on the drafting board. Mrs. Jones was effusive in her praise. "Why it is the most beautiful ship that I have ever seen Master McCullum. She is truly unlike anything that I have ever seen before," she said with shining eyes. Cameron glanced up then and saw Catherine some distance from them. She was viewing the ship and the horizon beyond; the sun shining on her as if she glowed from within, the breeze picking up the ribbons of her bonnet and her eyes capturing the light from the water in the canal beyond.

"Oh aye, Mrs. Jones, that is a true statement. She is unlike anything that I have ever seen," Cameron replied softly. Mrs. Jones followed his glance then and smiled to herself. Any day now, she thought, they will start courting for all to see; any day now.

CHAPTER FOUR

The next day Mrs. Jones returned from her daily shopping trip all atwitter about the newest activity sponsored by Cameron McCullum. A spring dance was being organized by Mr. McCullum. "Oh Mistress, Mr. McCullum is organizing a spring dance at the park. It will be the first dance that we have ever had as a community. He says he is doing it to thank the community for the support of the Yard and to thank the lads who have been working so hard to make the new ship a success. What do you think Mistress; the whole town is talking about it," Mrs. Jones stated.

"Well it sounds very much like something that Mr. McCullum would enjoy doing. He likes to organize things and he certainly seems to enjoy himself at community functions. We will need to ask him when next we see him," Catherine replied.

That night at their daily update meeting Catherine sought to determine if the rumors were true. "Mrs. Jones heard at the market today that you were organizing a spring dance for the community. She said it was to be at the open area next to the canal. Is there any truth to that rumor?" Catherine asked casually.

"Why yes Mistress; I thought it would be nice for the lads and of course the community as a whole will be invited. I think everyone enjoys a gathering and most people enjoy a dance. Do you dance yourself Mistress?" Cameron asked just as casually.

"I of course have not danced since coming here. It would not be seemly to dance as a widow. I certainly enjoy music and used to enjoy dancing at home. It has been a long time of course," Catherine responded.

"Well Mistress, you should put on your dancing shoes. I am sure the community would not expect you to be in mourning forever for a man that you barely knew and were married to for such a short time; just a thought," Cameron responded with his maddening smile.

Catherine wondered then how much Cameron McCullum knew about her personal affairs and assumed given that comment that he knew more than she would wish. She chose to ignore it in the thought of entertainment that she could attend if not actually partake in.

The dance was scheduled for May 1st at the open area next to the canal on Front Street. Torches would be placed on the perimeter of the property so that the dance could continue well into the night. Cameron had everything in hand as he always seemed to do. Catherine was excited despite herself at the news of the dance. She thought it an opportune time to break the tradition of black mourning that she had worn since the death of Mr. Van Ressller. By now she assumed that no one in the community would expect her to continue to mourn for a man that she did not know. She decided to select a dress that she had brought with her from England to wear to the dance. It was still dark in color, but was a midnight blue shade, designed perfectly to match the unique color of her eyes and to make her eyes appear even darker. She would wear her hair up in the front denoting her marital status but down in back denoting the fact that she was her own woman; unmarried and ready perhaps for life to start anew.

Mrs. Jones assisted her with her preparations the night of the dance. The gown was silk with a low neckline in the late 18th century fashion. Mrs. Jones pulled the stays tight that evening which provided an extreme décolletage to the gown. Mrs. Jones thought to give Master Cameron a bit of added inducement to ask the Mistress to dance. Not that she thought he would need any. His constant attention to the Mistress had not gone unnoticed by the community. Despite Catherine's statements to the contrary, everyone believed they were courting. Mrs. Jones thought this an opportune time to set the record straight by encouraging the Master to show his interest publicly for the first time.

Mrs. Jones and Catherine walked together to the dance location. Cameron had gone ahead to make sure that all of the arrangements were in order. When they arrived they saw an improvised dance floor in the center of the lot and chairs around the perimeter for those who would wish to sit and rest between dances or to await a partner for the next dance. Cameron saw their arrival and as he held a cup of punch, he raised his glass in their direction to note their appearance. Catherine selected a chair next to the Reverend Clayborne and she and Mrs. Jones engaged him in conversation. The Reverend Clayborne graciously retrieved punch for Mrs. Jones and Catherine. Cameron noticed his absence and thought it a good time to welcome the ladies to the dance.

"Mrs. Jones, Mistress Van Ressller; I am glad that you decided to join us this evening. It is a little experiment, but I hope the community will enjoy the opportunity to gather on a warm spring night and enjoy the music and the company. Mistress, I see you have selected this evening to shed your widow's weeds. May I say that I approve of that decision? You are looking very lovely this evening; very lovely indeed; don't you agree Mrs. Jones?" Cameron stated graciously.

"Oh yes indeed Mr. McCullum; the Mistress looks as beautiful as a spring flower tonight. We thank you for organizing this dance. We have not had an event like this in Lewes to the best of my memory. All of your ideas are so welcome in our community." Catherine smiled at that comment but remained quiet. She noticed that Cameron had taken in her new dress and had focused his admiration on the neckline. Well, she thought, some things do not change.

"I will make my rounds ladies and then circle again for a dance. Don't let anyone fill in your dance cards," Cameron stated with a grin.

"What do you think of that Mistress? Mr. McCullum may want to ask you to dance," Mrs. Jones stated.

"I do not know if that will be appropriate Mrs. Jones. I do enjoy dancing, but I am not sure what the community would think of me joining in since I am recently widowed," Catherine replied.

"I believe the community will understand Mistress. You are a young woman and you certainly were not married long enough to warrant long term mourning," Mrs. Jones responded.

Once the music began, Catherine found herself keeping time to the music by tapping her foot. She had so loved dancing in England in the year that she had come out into society. The music had of course been very formal as well as the location of the dances and company at that time. She had not had the opportunity to hear any music other than church music throughout her stay in Lewes. It was a great delight to just hear the music and enjoy the soft spring night and the sweetly flowering trees that surrounded the dance site. It was the first time that she felt she had enjoyed herself since coming to America. The dancers and the laughter added to her enjoyment. She felt herself relaxing and enjoying herself for the first time in her recent memory.

Cameron ever watchful and mindful of Catherine and her moods; saw the change. She smiled easily tonight for the first time in his recollection. He thought to let her relax and enjoy her surroundings before asking her to dance. He wanted to make sure that she was enjoying herself, but that she was also losing her inhibitions around the neighbors of her community. He knew that she set a great store on appearances and wanted to make sure that she was ready for the next step.

After an hour or so, Cameron had watched her become more engaged with those around her. He noticed the tapping of her foot and the fact that she smiled at her ease with her surroundings. The business members of the community who sought him out to discuss community affairs and affairs at the national level could not help but notice that his eyes were trained only on Catherine and his attention though polite was elsewhere. They were soon to discover the focus of his interests. He had had enough punch and enough enjoyment in watching Catherine at a distance to decide that the time was right to ask her to dance.

Cameron came across the dance floor in his usual authoritative manner. Mrs. Jones noticed his approach first and began to smile at him. She was unsure at that juncture if he was approaching them with the intent to dance or merely to make polite conversation. Since he did not appear to wish to sit and converse, she thought she knew the true purpose of his errand. Before he had come across the dance floor she saw him make comment to the dance master and a slow, English Country dance had started. It would be the perfect opportunity for the two to dance for the first time together and for Catherine to accept his request knowing the dance would not be too lively and unseemly for a widow on her first public outing.

When Cameron came at last to Catherine's feet, he held out his hand and asked her to dance. She looked to Mrs. Jones for a moment who slowly bowed her head as if to nod approval. Catherine looked up at Cameron then and gave him one of her rare smiles and took his offered hand. The dance was slow and stately and was accomplished with several couples standing in a line and then interweaving between the partners. The hands of the couples were held throughout the dance. Although Cameron made no comment to Catherine, the assembled guests noted that he never took his eyes from her. Catherine remained outwardly calm as she had always appeared to the world, but for the first time by standing up with Cameron she had taken the next step in acknowledging to the community that they were indeed a couple. Cameron and her neighbors noticed for the first time the slight blush to her cheeks which were usually so ivory in their appearance. As the dance commenced, the dancers would weave between partners and back around to their principal partner. Cameron was a very good dancer Catherine noticed and they took the lead as the principal lead couple to the dance. Only the best dancers took the lead role. In Catherine he knew that he had a partner who would be familiar with the steps, but would also gracefully lead the partners who followed. Tonight he found he could not take his eyes from her and from both her graceful steps as well as her other worldly beauty. At the conclusion of the dance, the partners ended by facing each other and the ladies made a deep curtsey to their male partners. The deep bow gave Cameron another opportunity to admire the extreme décolletage of Catherine's gown. If she minded his admiration, she gave no outward sign of it.

At the end of the dance Cameron took her hand and raised her from the deep curtsey, smiling from ear to ear. The dance had done the very thing that he had intended; it had signaled to the community as a whole that he and Catherine were courting and that she was moving beyond the mourning that had enveloped her since her arrival in Lewes. As she rose from the deep curtsey, she gave Cameron another of her rare smiles. The smile was seen by the community and commented on for days following. Oh yes, Cameron thought, I have accomplished the true goal of this dance; I have brought Catherine out of her self-imposed mourning and have made the community know my intentions even if Catherine has not yet accepted them herself. For the remainder of the evening, Cameron made sure that the same dance was played on an hourly basis and that he captured Catherine as his partner each time. He danced with no other partners and in so doing, Catherine was approached by no other men at the dance. Cameron had accomplished his goal.

At the conclusion of the dance, Cameron offered to walk with Mrs. Jones and Catherine back to the Manor House. Mrs. Jones was all aflutter about the dance and how it brought back memories of her youth. Catherine smiled but was quiet on the return trip to the Manor House. Cameron was lost in his own thoughts and made no comment until they returned to the Manor House. He said good night to Mrs. Jones and then taking Catherine's hand, kissed it and thanked her for the dances. Catherine smiled and wished him good night.

*****

That night when Catherine returned to her room, she was astonished at the level of her feelings. It had never occurred to her that she would not return to London as soon as the two year period had expired. London was the center of her world and the very mannered life style was all that she had ever known. Tonight, she had seen a glimpse of a world that lay beyond that mannered world of behavior. Mr. McCullum had been very gentlemanly but there was something in his eyes that she had never encountered before. His attentions to her were not just polite. In his every encounter with her, he made her feel as if she was the only woman in his world. There were other single women at the dance, but she noticed that he did not give them any attention. She was not sure what to make of that yet, but it certainly was a circumstance that she had not anticipated. Despite her protestations to the contrary, Cameron McCullum was becoming an important part of her life and she dreamed of him for the first time that night. She woke embarrassed at the thought, but Cameron McCullum had now inhabited both her sleeping and waking hours.

*****

In light of the dance, the abandonment of her widow's weeds and the approach of summer, Catherine felt the new wardrobe created by Mrs. Jones should receive an airing for the first time. There were five gowns for summer; one in the new French Empire style and the others more traditional dresses patterned on the late 18th century style. She had only been able to persuade Mrs. Jones to create one new dress in the French style and then only if a modesty panel and a shawl was part of the attire. Otherwise, Mrs. Jones proclaimed, the dress was indecent. Catherine on the basis of the patterns provided pronounced it the height of fashion. Any opportunity to permanently shed the widow's weeds which she wished burned was regarded with joy. Mrs. Jones said she could re-work the black gown but for Catherine's part, she would consign it to the back of her closet forever. It was bad enough to wear black, but especially for someone that she didn't know and who appeared to be universally hated by the community as a whole.

On the first warm Sunday in May following the evening of the dance, Catherine dressed in the new French Empire style gown. Although worn wet in France to further accent the shape of the wearer, Catherine was not sure that the St. Peter's congregation would be ready for that style advancement. Catherine inserted the modesty panel and covered herself with the shawl. She considered herself the height of fashion. How she would be perceived was another matter. As it was her first Sunday out of widow's weeds, she assumed that fact alone would garner sufficient comment by the parishioners and the community as a whole.

Mrs. Jones and Catherine walked their usual route to church. As Catherine had taken extra time on her attire, they were very close to the 11:00 hour and the start of service. Cameron was already in the pew and stood at their arrival. His face registered a mixture of shock and mirth. Shock she assumed since the widow's weeds had been abandoned for good and mirth at the new French style and the obvious emphasis on her best assets. Even with the modesty panel in place, her assets were clearly on display. Catherine caught the sideways glance by Cameron throughout the service. Her only fear was that he might assume that she had dressed only for him and not for the beautiful spring day and the release of her pseudo-mourning state.

As they returned to the Manor House for luncheon; an invitation now implied to include Cameron, she noted his glances in her direction and waited for the inevitable comment. "Mrs. Jones I believe I see your handiwork in evidence. I assume that the Mistress' new dress is all the style in London?" Cameron said addressing the housekeeper and not Catherine.

"Why yes Mr. McCullum. We have done up five new gowns for Mrs. Van Ressller. This one was of some concern to me as it is the latest style from France," Mrs. Jones replied worriedly.

"It should be practical for a summer day as it is uncommonly sheer with little fabric to speak of," Cameron replied with his full attention on Catherine now as he spoke.

"I was not aware that your design skills extended to ladies' fashions Mr. McCullum. I thought they were limited to ships," Catherine replied coolly.

The game was on and the fencing had begun for the afternoon. Cameron for one had decided that he had had all he could stomach of the unending match and intended to tell her so when they were alone. The dress was positively indecent. Without the shawl she may as well have been in her undergarments. Not that he wasn't enjoying the view of course; he just wanted the view restricted to his eyes only and not the entire community. Although he was relieved to see her out of the widow's weeds once and for all, this transition was too extreme.

"I will be down in just a moment Mr. McCullum. Please make yourself comfortable in the dining room," Catherine called to him as they returned to the house.

Cameron went through and took his customary seat at the table. Catherine was allowed to eat well through the terms of her late husband's will and the hated agreement and spared no expense in either her cellar or her larder. It was the best meal of the week for him and he genuinely looked forward to the food and always to the spirited company.

When Catherine returned to the dining room she had removed her shawl and the modesty panel. The dress had gone from indecent to downright dangerous. If Catherine was signaling a change in their relationship, that was the dress to do it in.

Mrs. Jones came in with the first course and took one look at Cameron's face and one look at her Mistress and quickly left the room. She limited her stays when bringing additional courses to the extent possible. When at last the meal was over, Catherine asked Cameron if he would like a whiskey in the library.

After the door was closed on them, Cameron turned in one fluid motion and headed for Catherine. She had nearly made it behind the desk when Cameron had her pinned to the wall. "I would like to know what you are playing at in that dress. One day you are in widow's weeds for a man you didn't know and the next day showing your assets to the entire community," Cameron stated angrily.

Catherine, to her credit met his eye and did not cower or look away. "This dress happens to be the latest in French fashion. I have the patterns directly from London. I do not remember your resume and qualifications noting fashion designer among your many talents," Catherine replied heatedly.

"I have told you before that the people of this town believe that we are courting. What do you think they are saying about your attire in light of that fact?" Cameron responded heatedly.

"I would like to think that they would regard you as a lucky man. Besides, are you not the one always telling me that we are free to live as we please in this country? Does that not extend to women and something as simple as their attire of choice?" Catherine replied.

"Do not try to twist ideas of liberty and freedom when it suits you. I do not want you as a trophy or something to only be admired. I want you as a flesh and blood woman. I have waited for you longer than any woman that I have ever wanted. I mean to have you as my wife and I will not tolerate any more verbal fencing. I want us to be free to exchange views and opinions and thoughts on all topics. I want us to build a life here in a good country where we are free to carve out our own life and not be beholden to others for leave taking and book reading and any of the things that we hold dear and I certainly do not expect you to parade your assets in a gown such as this one for all and sundry to admire," Cameron countered heatedly.

"Do you intend to force me into this marriage that you have planned for us?" Catherine replied.

"Have you not heard a word that I have said? I wouldn't defile the woman that I want to marry. I love you. I have from the first that I met you. I have never met anyone like you and I have never wanted anyone more. You do not have to perform for me in your new French style. I would love you if you were in rags or without them for that matter. If you would stop being afraid of love and afraid of a true man's feelings for you, I think that we would have a chance to be happy," Cameron responded anxiously.

Cameron had been very careful to not touch Catherine during that speech. He held her solely by the force of his height and over powering physical presence. With one hand on either side of the wall beside her head he made no attempt to touch her as he poured out his feelings to her. Now with her physical nearness so painfully close to him, he leaned in to kiss her very gently on the lips, but with no other part of him touching her. After a few moments, he pulled back to look into those bottomless dark blue eyes. She looked confused by the action. He sighed then audibly. "It would be so much better if you would help. You can kiss me back you know," Cameron replied humor at last restored.

She smiled then and when he next approached he felt her body relax and join into the kiss; first brief then more and more intense. Only when he felt her move towards him and place her hands on his upper arms did he dare place his hands around her waist. The kiss tentative at first grew more and more passionate as the pent up feelings each held for the other began to unleash. She moved closer and closer to him seeming to not want to separate from his warmth and his strength. Little did she know that very strength and self control were slowly and irretrievably slipping away. He held her closer to him and in doing so, gently lifted her up off of her tiny feet. The kiss continued, becoming more arousing by the moment. As if aware that she was quite literally being swept off her feet, she seemed to snap back to reality. "We cannot; I must not go further," Catherine said quietly, alarmed now by her feelings.

"I know love; I know," Cameron replied. He looked down at her swollen and red lips and felt very possessive and satisfied with himself. "I have only one thing more to say to you and that is this; do not keep me waiting. We can announce our wedding for July when the first ship is christened. It will be a good start to a new life; do you not agree?" Cameron replied watching her intently.

"Cameron, you understand that this is all very sudden. May I wait to give you my answer? I have much to think on and after all Reverend Clayborne will need to read the banns you know," Catherine replied cautiously.

"I know and I will be happy to tell him to do so and to stop studying my intended's décolletage on a given Sunday or at any community dance in the future," Cameron said with a grin.

Catherine did laugh at that remark. "You think everyone is studying it because you are," Catherine replied smiling.

"I am allowed to and no one else," he added possessively. "Oh and that dress you have on; please save it for our honeymoon if you will be so kind my love. I don't think my

50

heart can stand another outing until then and I am lawfully permitted to do something about it." Cameron gazed carefully over Catherine's face for signs of any misgivings. Seeing none, he placed his hands on either side of her face and kissed her more gently this time. "You will see Catherine what life is like when you are truly cherished and not just an object to be admired in a drawing room," Cameron stated quietly. He had said her Christian name for the first time and the Scottish burr created a chill that travelled down Catherine's spine.

Catherine held Cameron's gaze then and placed her hands in his which he took as the signal for one final kiss. What started as a simple sealing of their new found understanding ended with both having lost their breath and on the verge again of the loss of self control that Cameron had feared.

"I will see you tomorrow evening perhaps with a new book and other things to discuss my love; many other things. I will hope to receive your answer tomorrow evening as well. Good afternoon Catherine," Cameron replied huskily.

"Good afternoon Cameron," Catherine said quietly.

After the door to the drawing room and front door had closed, Catherine went up to her room to be alone and sort out her feelings over this change in her circumstances. Cameron obviously loved her. He was an educated man with good prospects. She on the other hand was still a captive to a dead man's agreement and a hated uncle's ill treatment. In this country she would be free to marry as she wished and free to marry for love. The thought of that was so revolutionary as to be beyond her reasoning. If she returned to London in two years, even as a widow, her status would be in the hands of another. Here she could set her own course and with Cameron's encouragement, build a life with him. What she had not expected was this outpouring of passion that she had for him. Trained to keep all of her emotions locked inside and to act only as an ornament for others to admire, she could not believe that she could have the depth of feelings that she held for Cameron whenever he was near her and now especially after he had touched her for the first time. That was the greatest surprise and not an unpleasant one. He had been patient and had not forced her in any way. That certainly would not have been the case with her marriage to Van Ressller. She shuddered at the thought of Van Ressller touching her as Cameron had just done. That one fact alone convinced her that her way forward was a true one. Her choices were to return to London and remain a pawn in someone else's game or chart a new course in this country with a man who clearly loved her and who she now admitted had lit a fire within her that she had never expected to experience.

*****

The next day she informed Mrs. Jones of the offer of marriage by Mr. McCullum. "I am so happy Mistress. Master Cameron is a good man and will be good to you. I cannot say you would have been so happy with Mr. Van Ressller. He was always fair with me, but was a hard man at heart. I know about the arrangement with your uncle Mistress. It was a hard thing to do to another human being and I am sorry for the misery that brought you here. I only hope that you will have happiness with Master Cameron," Mrs. Jones said smiling.

That night Catherine walked to the Yard as was her custom. The first ship was quickly taking shape and would be ready for christening in July. The wedding could occur the same week and would be the culmination of Cameron's twin dreams; ship building and Catherine's love.

When she came into the Yard office, Cameron looked up and smiled. "I have lost all track of time Catherine. Let me button my sleeves my love," Cameron replied.

Catherine had noticed his tan neck and arms; his shirt sleeves rolled up to expose his muscled arms. She had not seen anyone of such physical strength in her uncle's home or indeed anywhere in her life up to this point. He certainly compared favorably in that department as well as many others.

"Is that a new dress as well? I certainly approve. It is more conservative then yesterday's gown, but at least it won't cause a riot when you walk down the street," Cameron said laughing.

Cameron noticed that Catherine was unusually shy around him and wondered if she was thinking about the kisses that they had exchanged yesterday. He knew he was and had thought of nothing else since returning to his cottage last night. He decided to open his arms to her and see how she responded. He was happy with the reaction. Cameron moved to the front of his desk and sat there casually waiting for the shy deer to come to him yet again. She moved slowly towards him and he put out his hands to take hers. She noticed how strong his hands were; he noticed that she had not pulled her hands away from his. She held his gaze and did not look away. "You told me to not keep you waiting," Catherine said at last.

"I did say that Catherine and I meant it," Cameron replied firmly.

She moved closer to him coming within inches of his open arms. "I came to a decision last night," Catherine continued.

"Did you now; and what would that be Catherine?" Cameron replied casually.

"I have decided to accept your offer of marriage Cameron," Catherine replied. With the last statement she moved at last within the circle of his arms; within reach of his embrace. She had not moved away or looked away and for the first time in his memory she looked her true twenty-one years. Her hair was down around her shoulders and she had a genuine smile on her face, not the contrived smile of a

London drawing room. She moved several inches closer to him and into his open, warm embrace. His arms encircled her waist then and her arms slowly encircled his neck. At this level, with me sitting, we fit extremely well, Cameron thought to himself. Catherine just felt safe and cherished and loved for the first time since her parent's death. The tears stung her eyes and she quickly closed them so that Cameron would not see and misunderstand. Cameron bent to gently kiss her and seeing all, noticed her tears for the first time.

"Catherine, why are you crying? Are you coming to me of your own free will or because you think you must? I will not coerce you; that has happened to you before. I told you; I will not force you in this or anything," Cameron said worriedly.

"Oh no Cameron; you do not understand. I am crying because I am happy. For the first time since I was a child, I am happy because I am loved and cherished as you said. I came to Lewes as payment for a debt to a man who I had never seen. If he had not died I would have spent my life with a man who was prepared to barter me for a debt. I never expected to have happiness Cameron and you have handed it to me. That is the reason for my tears, Cameron; happiness only," Catherine replied quietly.

Cameron gently kissed her eyes kissing away her tears. He ran his fingers through her hair and cupped both sides of her face with his strong hands. She felt the calluses on his hands and had never felt such strength in two hands before. When he came to kiss her this time, they were both shaking with their need for one another. Cameron at last pulled away, taking no chance in losing his self control as Catherine had just exposed her very real vulnerability to him.

When he could again speak, he looked deeply into those bottomless dark blue eyes and whispered, "We should go see Reverend Clayborne about the reading of the banns right away. I do not think we should delay my love. Do you agree?" Cameron asked tenderly.

"Oh yes Cameron. I do agree." Catherine smiled then knowing that neither of them wanted a delay in the upcoming wedding.

Later that evening, Catherine relayed the decision reached by the intended couple on the planned wedding. "Mrs. Jones, Master Cameron and I have decided to not postpone our wedding until July. Do you think you could have a wedding dress prepared within one month's time?" Catherine asked.

"I can and I will Mistress," Mrs. Jones quickly responded. "We will not be using one of those new French designs will we?" she asked worriedly.

"Oh no, Mrs. Jones; I do not believe Master Cameron is a proponent of the new French designs. The older design may be more conservative but I think it is Master Cameron's favorite and that is all that matters. Do you not agree Mrs. Jones?" Catherine stated smiling.

"I do indeed Mistress; I do indeed," Mrs. Jones replied smiling knowingly.

Catherine felt as if she was walking in a happy haze in the weeks leading up to her wedding. She may not be marrying in a great cathedral in London to a titled nobleman, but she was definitely marrying a noble man; a good man and one who would not use her and barter away her future. Her only concern was maintaining her self control for the next four weeks. Once their flood gates of happiness had opened, keeping her emotions in check was not easy. She awoke happy, thinking of Cameron. She went to sleep happy, thinking of Cameron. She tried to read books loaned to her by Cameron, but her mind kept wandering to his lips on hers; his hands holding hers and other delights that she could not yet fathom at this juncture. Maybe Cameron would have a book on the unknown pleasures that she was yet to discover once they were married.

For his part, Cameron kept occupied pushing his men to complete the first ship as he worked with them and pushing himself so that the ship would be ready prior to the promised

July date. In the evenings, he carved the figurehead of Catherine; a perfect likeness of his English Rose. He had come to know every feature by heart, every asset which would soon be within his hands in the flesh and not his wooden likeness alone or the sketches that had preceded it. Oh yes, he decided, it was imperative for them both that the wedding be moved up.

In the mornings for the next several weeks, Mrs. Jones and Catherine worked at the wedding gown and the fittings and in wedding planning in general. Each afternoon Cameron and Catherine completed counseling sessions with the Reverend Clayborne in anticipation of their wedding.

*****

Soon the happy day would arrive and all preparations had been completed. The gown hung in Catherine's room, the flowers would be gathered from her garden on the morning of the wedding and the wedding feast had been prepared and was ready to be set up in the dining room. Cameron had at first objected to any connection to the Manor House and to Van Ressller seeing it as a dark cloud over an otherwise happy day. Under the terms of the agreement, Catherine was bound to the Van Ressller holdings. Fortunately Van Ressller had not foreseen his demise so there was no objection to Catherine's re-marriage. Cameron had only one demand; that their wedding night be spent in his cottage and not Van Ressller's house. Catherine had no objections. She had never seen his cottage for propriety sake and was anxious to see the extent of his library, among other things.

It was the *other things* that still concerned Catherine. She finally summoned her courage to ask Cameron for a book that may help her understand the intimacy that they would experience after the wedding. She knew there would be more than the kisses and embraces that they had shared, she just didn't know what. When next she went to the Yard, she summoned up her courage to ask Cameron for a book to help her understand.

"Cameron, I was wondering if you could loan me another book," Catherine asked shyly.

"Well of course my love. They will all be at your disposal soon enough. What is the topic that you are seeking?" Cameron replied smiling.

"I need a book that will help me understand . . . um . . . well . . . marital relations," Catherine replied quietly.

Cameron turned from his desk at that statement. He tried not to show any humor as he knew what courage it had taken her to make this request. "My love, you were married to Mr. Van Ressller. How is it that you need education on this of all topics?" Cameron asked with amazement.

"Cameron, I was married to Mr. Van Resseller for five minutes before he set off into the night in a full gale to save his fleet of ships. The next morning I was advised that he had been killed during the storm trying to save the fleet. I am the same maid that I was when I entered the tender ship nearly six months ago. In the circles in which my uncle travelled that was considered highly desirable for marriage purposes if for no other purpose. I know no more about marital relations than the kisses we have shared Cameron. I want to make you a good wife in all manner of ways, but I need help Cameron, I need education," Catherine replied imploringly.

She met his gaze again as she had done in the past; direct and full. There was no shrinking between them; no shyness and timidity as there would be no drawing room smiles or flirtations. That point had been made quite clear when their understanding was first reached.

Cameron grasped her hands within his and pulled her into his embrace. "When the time comes my love, I will show you the joys of marital relations as you so eloquently describe them. You do not need a book to show you what I will teach you. You have no idea how happy it makes me that Van Reseller never laid a hand on you. Anyone who would barter in human flesh to satisfy a debt had no business with a treasure such as you," Cameron replied smiling.

"I want to make you happy Cameron. I want to please you and know what to do to make you happy. I know nothing about this Cameron and it concerns me if I need to educate myself in order to do it successfully," Catherine countered.

"You do not need anything but your love for me Catherine. I am not a novice, love. It will be my great pleasure to introduce you to the joy of martial relations and so many other things that we will experience together. It is much more rewarding in the showing then in the telling or reading. Come here my love," Cameron replied.

Catherine stepped into his embrace and into the warm kisses that she had come to live for. When at last they separated, both were breathless from their embrace. Catherine may not have come closer to the mystery of marital relations but she knew that the mystery would soon be revealed.

CHAPTER FIVE

At last the happy day dawned. For once, Catherine would not walk to church as Attorney Wendell had volunteered his horse and carriage to pick up the beautiful bride. It was the least he could do after being party to the despicable Van Ressller agreement. He had felt like he had made a deal with the devil that day particularly after meeting the bartered bride herself. At least she had found happiness and he knew Cameron to be a good man who would keep to his word both for the sake of Catherine and the town with the shipyard activities.

Catherine was up and bathed; excited with anticipation of a real wedding to a man she truly loved. Had she been asked six months ago she would not have believed it possible. Mrs. Jones came to help her into her gown. She pronounced it the most beautiful that she had ever made. "It fits you beautifully Mistress. It certainly puts your assets in the best light," Mrs. Jones stated.

Catherine turned then and looked worriedly at the mirror when she heard those words fearing Cameron would be angry again. What she saw was beautiful for sure, but not in a suggestive way. There would be no argument, as Cameron would be very pleased with the results she thought. Pleasing him, she had decided had become uppermost in her mind. For the first time in her life she was truly happy and she wanted to remain that way. Having exposure to real life for the first time meant that she did not want it to be taken away for any reason.

The wedding feast had been prepared and was ready for the guests. The only thing remaining was for the carriage to arrive. Mrs. Jones called up to her when that happy moment occurred. Catherine vowed to remain calm and step out of the Manor House into her new life.

Attorney Wendell was outside of the door with his waiting vehicle. The carriage had been decorated with flowers and white ribbons had been woven through the horse's mane. It truly appeared that the entire town was playing a part in her wedding in small ways that even she was not even aware of. Cameron was looked on with respect in the town by the lads who worked with him day to day and by the townspeople who came to respect his straight forward and no nonsense manner.

Catherine had always been a mystery to them as she had kept herself closely guarded fearing that she had been shamed by the bartered bride story on her arrival. In fact, the town respected the fact that she had kept the Yard open and would be making a success of it with Cameron's help. They saw their union as commitment to each other and to the town. Besides that, everyone loved a wedding and the party that accompanied that happy event.

When Catherine boarded the carriage she was briefly carried back to her upbringing but with the knowledge that this time she would go to a marriage of love and not the marriage of convenience that she was reared to expect. She knew that Cameron was waiting for her at St. Peter's and she was warmed by the fact that today she would embark on a new life. It was a life that she knew little about, but one that she was very excited to begin.

The carriage stopped in front of St. Peter's and the happy bride descended. The contrast between the earlier hasty pairing and this wedding could not have been more extreme. Where one had occurred in the dark of night with few witnesses; with only one save the bride and priest remaining to tell the tale, this wedding included nearly all of the community's residents. This was a real wedding as Cameron continued to emphasize to all and sundry. The bride was not to be given away as she came to him of her own free will, not bartered or bought, but of her own free will for love for the groom alone.

When the wedding music of *Trumpet Voluntary* began, the doors at St. Peter's were thrown open and the marble statute from January had come to life. She was dressed from head to toe in white in order to put to rest any lingering questions about her first hasty marriage. Her veil covered the midnight black hair which at Cameron's request was left down and about her shoulders as it had been the day that she had accepted his proposal. The dress was in the late 18th century style, more conservative than her French experiment but with the same deep décolletage customary of that time period. Cameron would be watching the Reverend Clayborne closely to make sure his attention centered on his prayer book and not on Catherine's assets. The flowers were simple and from the Manor House gardens. Cameron thought no one would look at the flowers while Catherine stood before them.

The smile on Catherine's face was only for Cameron. She did not look to her right or to her left but only to her handsome groom standing at the rail. When at last Catherine arrived beside him, he took the flowers from her hand and placed them on the rail. He wanted her hands in his throughout the service. They were very tiny and cold today from nerves, but they were his and the first connection that they had ever made. By taking her hands, he had Catherine's full attention. Those dark blue eyes that he had always thought a man could lose himself in were directed only to him. Her vows and responses would be made only to him. It didn't matter if the congregation heard her responses, as in his mind they were made only to him.

The contrast between Catherine's travesty of a first marriage and this one could not be greater. Cameron understood why Catherine never wore a ring from that marriage as none had been given to her. He made sure that she had one now; one bought by him from his own labors. At the end of the ceremony, Reverend Clayborne told Cameron he could kiss his bride. Cameron carefully raised the veil, making sure his large hands did not catch in the fine material. With Catherine's eyes shining, he briefly kissed her in a perfunctory manner and then seeing her disappointment, gave her a proper kiss and a wink thereafter. Handing her back her flowers and extending his arm, they walked down the aisle, man and wife and down to the waiting carriage.

Once settled inside, Cameron took Catherine's hand and kissed it. "When I first kissed your hand, I dreamed of this moment and now it has come to past. Are you happy, my love?" Cameron asked.

"I am so happy Cameron. Thank you so much for this lovely day and for the opportunity to live a real life with you," Catherine replied smiling.

When they arrived back at the Manor House, Catherine ran upstairs to take off her veil as it would be easier to dance and enjoy the rest of the day without it. She planned on thoroughly enjoying the day and the night to come. The refreshments were to be served inside and the dancing would occur outside in the gardens. Cameron had asked Catherine if she objected to a real party as part of her wedding and she had happily agreed. She looked forward to dancing with her new husband among other things.

Cameron was having a drink of whiskey when she came back down. She had placed flowers in her hair to replace the veil. Cameron planned on enjoying the day but wanted nothing more than to be alone with his beautiful bride. Catherine came to his side then and took his hand. She seemed shy today, still fearing that the town knew her sad story with Van Ressller. He would do his best to disavow her of that notion as quickly as possible. He knew that they respected her for keeping the Yard open when she hadn't needed to and for marrying a good man to make a good life in this country versus a sham of a life in her homeland. He would encourage her to take a more active part in the community as his wife. This day would be her introduction to that wider world.

The community streamed in to give their best wishes to the bride and groom. Mrs. Jones could be seen with her apron at her eyes thankful that her Mistress had made a happy match and with a tall, good looking man like Cameron McCullum. Sandwiches and other treats were provided for the multitudes. It gave Catherine wry pleasure to know that Van Ressller's fortune was paying for the wedding feast he had previously denied her. She kept that bit of information to herself because she knew the effect of any connection to Van Ressller and herself on Cameron. It was why she had gladly agreed to travelling to Cameron's cottage for their wedding night. She wanted no connection between her feelings for Cameron and her utter disregard for Van Ressller and his dastardly associations with her uncle.

Once the guests had been fed, they moved out into the gardens and on to the dancing. Chairs had been placed outside for those who wished to sit or watch with a central area cleared for dancing. The musicians were tuning their instruments when the bride and groom came into the garden. After the May dance, this would be a second opportunity for Cameron and Catherine to dance together and the first as man and wife.

Cameron led Catherine onto the improvised dance floor. A slow number was requested by Cameron so that he could hold his bride. That generated laughs all around and blushes by the bride. Throughout the dance, Cameron never took his eyes from Catherine which intensified her blushes. The community looked on uniform in the belief that the two were meant to be and that a good match had been achieved. Catherine felt as though she were living a dream; dancing with her husband in a lilac scented garden. Could any greater happiness exist?

The dancing and refreshments went on throughout the day and well into the evening. Cameron looked for the earliest possible opportunity to slip away with his bride. As the dancing became more spirited, lit no doubt by the cellars of the Manor House, Cameron grasped Catherine's hand and led her into the darkness and down the road to his cottage. He had prepared for this night for weeks, making sure that he had the house supplied with treats for Catherine, candles for his room and a privacy screen of his own design that would give his new bride privacy for changing and bathing on her wedding night.

As they approached the cottage, Cameron opened the front door and then took his new bride into his arms. "I will carry you over this threshold, love, but not the Manor House threshold," Cameron said earnestly.

Once over the threshold, Cameron returned Catherine to her feet, lowering her ever so slowly so that their two bodies entwined in the darkness. Cameron cupped her face with his hands and gave her a proper kiss in the privacy of his cottage. He kept up his assault on her lips until he felt her relax into his arms and place her arms around his waist.

Cameron at last pulled away reluctantly. "Let me light some candles my love, so that I can see your beautiful face." He lit candles in the front room which lit her face and the red and swollen lips that he possessively had created. "Let me help you with your gown my love. I know Mrs. Jones has had that honor up to now and I will be happy to provide that assistance going forward," Cameron stated huskily.

Catherine presented her back to him and moved her hair to the side to provide him full access. As a ship designer and builder he certainly grasped technicalities in rope construction and riggings. He was temporarily confused by the lacings before him but found his footing and had her unlaced and ready for the removal of her dress in short order.

"I placed a privacy screen for you within the bed chamber love so that you could bathe and prepare for bed." He led her into his inner chamber then to show her his handiwork. He returned to the front chamber to heat some water for her for bathing. She saw for the first time the bed in the center of the chamber.

"You certainly have a large bed Cameron. I have never seen a bed quite that large," Catherine said wide eyed.

"I am a tall man love and need a large bed. I am sure your bed in the Manor House would not have fit the bill. Do you need any further help with your dress, my love?" he asked quietly.

"Oh no thank you Cameron; I will be just a moment," Catherine replied shyly.

"I will heat the water for you and bring it to you in a moment," Cameron said smiling.

Catherine lit the candles laid out for her by Cameron and was thankful for his consideration in preparing the privacy screen suspended from the ceiling by his own design. Also laid out for her were her favorite lavender soap and a nightgown from her closet. She was certain that Mrs. Jones had helped Cameron with those details. It seemed that the whole community had had a part in their courtship and now their wedding and wedding night.

Catherine stepped out of her wedding gown and placed it on a hook provided. She had been told that ladies in this country wore their wedding gowns on Sundays and special occasions. It would be pleasant to think that she would have use of the lovely gown on more than one day.

Cameron called to her from the front rooms where he was heating the water and bathing. "I have the water for you my love. May I bring it to you now? Do you have everything else that you need my love?"

"Oh yes; thank you Cameron. You and Mrs. Jones have thought of everything," Catherine replied.

Once she had properly hung her wedding gown, Cameron handed her the ewer and basin with warm water and she started to remove each of her undergarments. Shortly thereafter, Cameron had finished in the front room and had come back to sit on the bed. The unforeseen circumstance of his handiwork was that the silhouette of his beautiful wife was projected as if on a screen by the candles from the opposite side. Catherine would have had no idea of the transparency effect. Had he not been fearful of the invasion of her privacy, he would have taken his sketch pad and sketched the form that he had studied for so long. That sketch would accompany the many sketches of her that he had completed since they first met. As it was, the appearance of the silhouette had had an unexpected affect on his self control which he felt slip away by the moment. He decided it might be prudent for his young wife's sake that he wait for her under the covers. A casual conversation might also help to lessen her nerves as well.

"Were you pleased by the day my love?" Cameron asked casually.

"Oh everything was so very well done Cameron. I think everyone enjoyed themselves. Mrs. Jones outdid herself today. She will be exhausted for a week from all of the arrangements," Catherine replied.

Try as he might he could not force himself to take his eyes from the privacy screen. His beautiful wife was as graceful as a dancer with the most mundane of tasks and he was transfixed with the knowledge that this beauty was now his not only to dream of and sketch, but to love and cherish in the flesh.

When at last Catherine had completed her nightly preparations, she blew out the candles and came to the other side of the screen. The sight that met him would have been comical had he not wished to save his shy young wife from embarrassment. Her nightgown was buttoned to the neck and showed less flesh than the infamous French design which had been worn in broad daylight. If this was Mrs. Jones idea of wedding night attire, they needed to have a serious conversation Cameron thought.

Although all of the candles had been extinguished, the full moon shone brightly through the clerestory cottage windows. He was thankful for the natural light as he wanted to see her face throughout the lovemaking that would follow.

When Catherine came to the edge of the bed she saw that Cameron was shirtless. "You do not have on a night shirt Cameron," Catherine said quietly.

"No my love; I don't sleep in a night shirt," Cameron replied.

"Do you not get cold in the night?" Catherine continued.

"Not when I have my beautiful wife to keep me warm," Cameron responded smiling.

"But you did not have a wife last night or the night before that," Catherine continued.

"That is true my love. Are we going to fence again Catherine or shall I initiate you into the joys of marital relations as you so eloquently call them?" Cameron replied smiling.

"Oh no Cameron; I do not want to fence anymore, it is just that I am nervous because I do not know what to expect," Catherine said shyly.

"I know love; come here and kiss me. You like it when we kiss do you not?" Cameron asked tenderly.

"Oh yes, Cameron; I like it very much when we kiss. Shall I take off my nightgown now?" Catherine asked anxiously.

"Just come here my darling girl. We will take care of the nightgown later. Was there a particular reason that Mrs. Jones saw fit to dress you as if it were a winter night? I have seen more of your assets in your French gown you know," Cameron stated grinning.

"I am so sorry Cameron. I did not know she would be giving you one of my gowns and the lavender soap," Catherine replied.

"Ah the lavender soap; I will never smell lavender scent again that I do not think of this minute," Cameron responded smiling.

Catherine completed the remaining distance to the bed and Cameron pulled back the covers to welcome his new bride. He leaned his head on his arm as casually as possible in order to create the impression that he had all of the time in the world. The effort was a struggle for him, but he was willing to do so to calm his nervous bride. When she was settled, Cameron slowly leaned over to kiss Catherine. The affect was the one he had anticipated. Catherine very slowly placed her arms around his neck and pulled him down closer to her. The kiss became more intense at his urging. He mated his tongue with hers attempting to bring her a sense of the lovemaking that was to follow. When he released her, they both were breathless from the experience. He noticed that she still clung to him. He thought that a very good sign indeed.

Cameron whispered to Catherine then leaning in to her ear. "Why don't we unbutton some of these buttons so you don't suffocate in all of that material?" he said quietly.

"Would you like me to do it Cameron?" Catherine asked anxiously.

"Oh no my love . . . let me do it," he whispered huskily.

Cameron carefully unbuttoned each button taking care to watch her expression as he did so. The same frank gaze never left his. It was if she was trying to read his thoughts to gain some understanding of what would transpire between them.

"You know how you like it when we kiss?" Cameron asked casually.

"Oh yes Cameron," Catherine said quietly.

"I am going to kiss you now; but I am going to kiss you all over and it will be just as wonderful, I promise." When he had finished unbuttoning her gown, he traced a line of kisses from the top of the opening to the bottom. Cameron felt rather than saw her relax against him. The secret he discovered was to tell her what was going to occur so that the fear would gradually leave her.

"Now I am going to take off your nightgown my love . . . so I can touch you all over. It will be very nice indeed I promise," Cameron whispered to Catherine. Catherine helped and the nightgown was soon lying across the bed. Cameron took her into his arms again. "Doesn't this feel wonderful my love? I have dreamt of this for so long, but the reality is so much better than any of my dreams," Cameron continued.

"What was I wearing in your dreams, Cameron?" Catherine asked shyly.

"You were wearing me my love," Cameron replied grinning.

With the last comment Catherine's eyes widened and she came to fully understand his outrage at the French gown. He was thinking of this, she thought and worried that the other men of the town were thinking of the same thing.

With each new sensation, Cameron gave Catherine time to adjust before proceeding further. The result was physical torture for him, but he would do nothing to spook his gentle wife not when they were this close to their physical contentment. Cameron continued to assault Catherine's mouth, knowing that it was a sensation that she had come to like. Gradually Cameron reached down and gently stroked his wife's breasts, her stomach and her lower abdomen. As before, he was very gradual in his actions, giving Catherine time to adjust to each new sensation. At last Cameron came to touch Catherine's outer and then inner thighs. His fingers continued to gently stroke Catherine's thighs and then her inner thighs until he felt the desire begin to rise in her. Her breathing became more uneven and her hands started to stroke his back and shoulders, pressing him even more to her. Cameron continued to whisper terms of endearment to his bride. Slowly he came to touch, then stroke the inner recesses of her intimacy. At that change, Catherine's eyes were open and her gaze fully on Cameron's at that moment.

"Catherine my love; I am going to make love to you now. It will hurt at first, I cannot help that and I am very sorry, but then the pain will go away and it will be lovely just like our kissing and our touching. Do you understand?" Cameron asked tenderly.

"Yes, Cameron, I love you and only want to make you happy," Catherine replied nervously.

"I know love. I love you and love touching your silken skin. I promise it will be very nice in just a few minutes," Cameron replied.

He resumed kissing Catherine and stroking her until the passion was again visible in her deep blue eyes. At that moment, Cameron entered Catherine gently, but with the anticipated affect. Catherine cried out in pain and upset. "Shush love, I promise the pain will stop in just a few moments," Cameron stated tenderly.

"Please Cameron, please stop. You are hurting me Cameron. Please I do not think we are doing this correctly," Catherine cried in anguish.

Cameron's head dropped to her silken shoulder. He would have laughed at that last remark if it wouldn't have hurt her feelings and made her feel even more vulnerable. "Please do not move just yet my love; I promise it will get better very soon." With that statement he kissed her deeply and intensely hoping to take her mind from the searing pain.

Cameron at last felt her relax against him and gradually he started to move against her again. She didn't cry out and her hands on his shoulders started to hold him again. The strain of his stillness within her had taken its toll, but the joy of release was within sight. Cameron cried out words of love and endearment. He cherished his bride with both words and deeds until he had found his release. Cameron's head again dropped into her neck and he remained motionless for several moments drinking in the lavender scent and the silken skin. At last he found the strength to roll onto his back bringing Catherine into his embrace at his side.

When at last he could speak again, Cameron leaned down and said "Catherine, my love; are you alright?"

Catherine was quiet for a moment then answered "I do not think there is a book that could describe that Cameron," she replied softly.

Cameron did laugh then but with love and warmth. "I think you are right my love; nothing could do it justice."

"Thank you for explaining everything to me. I just did not want to disappoint you Cameron," Catherine replied quietly.

"You could never disappoint me; have I not told you so? We were meant for each other Catherine," Cameron responded tenderly.

"I was not sure we would fit Cameron, but when we did, it was lovely. I cannot imagine making love to anyone that did not love me back. That must be true torture Cameron," Catherine stated softly.

"Yes love, but you mustn't worry about that ever again. I will keep you safe and protected and I will cherish you every day of your life," Cameron responded.

"Do you think I will be with child now Cameron?" Catherine asked quietly.

"I don't know my love. Do you want to be with child?" Cameron asked tenderly.

"I would love to have someone to love completely and utterly as my own," Catherine replied.

"Like you love me?" Cameron asked casually.

"Of course like I love you; I would not have made love to you if I did not love you; were you not listening?" Catherine asked.

"Of course I was my love; go on," Cameron said with amusement.

"But how will I know when I am with child? I will need a book surely," Catherine stated.

"When the time comes love, I will get you a book; I promise," Cameron replied grinning into the darkness.

"But how will I know; how will I feel?" Catherine asked anxiously.

"Well I have never had a baby before, but having witnessed this event from afar I believe your *assets* will become larger for one thing," Cameron replied.

"Oh you will like that part," Catherine said laughing.

"Yes, I certainly will," he answered possessively.

"And what else Cameron?" Catherine asked.

"Well your monthly will stop until after the baby comes," Cameron replied.

"That will be an important clue. How do you know all of these things Cameron?" Catherine asked into the darkness.

"What did you call me before; a Renaissance man?"Cameron laughed.

"I love you so much Cameron; I just want so much to make you happy," Catherine said quietly.

"You already make me happy love; more than you will ever know. More importantly Catherine, I want to make you happy. Has anyone ever asked you before what makes you happy?" Cameron replied.

"Why no Cameron not after Mother and Father died, I do not think that anyone ever gave it a thought," Catherine replied quietly.

"Well that has changed Catherine. This is not about making me happy; our relationship is about both of us being happy and both of us making decisions together for our mutual happiness. Do you understand?" Cameron asked.

"Oh yes Cameron; what a lovely thought. I never thought it would be possible to feel this way and to know that someone was thinking of me in that way," Catherine replied placing her arm around his waist. He held her then as if he never wanted to let her go.

*****

The next day being Sunday, Cameron and Catherine both slept in. When she awoke, Catherine was sprawled across Cameron who was looking down at her smiling. "Good morning my love; did you sleep well? It seemed you did get cold overnight. That must be why Mrs. Jones dressed you for the winter freeze," Cameron said smiling. Catherine brushed back her hair, realized her state of undress and pulled the sheet up around her. "Did you sleep well?" he asked again casually. "I myself was awakened when my bride draped herself across me this morning. It was very arousing, but as she was sound asleep I thought it the gentlemanly thing to do to wait until she opened those magnificent blue eyes," Cameron stated smiling.

Catherine did smile then to hide her shyness. "I must have gotten cold this morning. I am not used to sleeping without my gown," Catherine replied shyly.

"Just so," Cameron responded. "I was glad I could assist a damsel in distress," he said grinning.

"It was very warm draped across you. I liked it very much," Catherine replied shyly.

"So did I although it was a little painful on this end," Cameron stated.

"Did I hurt you Cameron?" Catherine asked worriedly.

"Oh no love; only with pleasure," he said laughing. "So would you like to go to church this morning?" Cameron asked.

"I think I might be too embarrassed Cameron. Will they not know what we did last night?" Catherine asked shyly.

"Of course, that's why I am still smiling!" Cameron replied laughing.

"I could not possibly go to church Cameron. I could not face Reverend Clayborne for one thing," Catherine replied worriedly.

"You do know whatever we do is our own affair right? We are married my love. Married people make love and it is nothing to be embarrassed about, in fact, it is the most natural thing in the world. Do you remember yesterday's vows; with my body I thee worship . . . you do understand what that means do you not?" Cameron asked worriedly.

"I think I do now, but by next Sunday surely. Can we just stay here today Cameron?" Catherine asked.

"Of course my love; whatever you wish to do is my pleasure. We may just stay in bed all day. No one would blame me. You might get cold again!" Cameron said laughing.

"We may get hungry somewhere along the line," Catherine replied.

"I can always cook something for us," Cameron stated.

"You know how to cook too?" Catherine asked shocked by the comment.

"Of course my love; I don't always eat at the Manor House you know. Where did you think I ate the rest of my meals?" Cameron replied smiling.

"I never thought of it before. I do not know how to cook Cameron," Catherine said worriedly.

"That is alright love; I can teach you or Mrs. Jones can teach you or I can buy you a cookery book," Cameron replied.

"That would be the best. I can read it and then we can discuss it like before," Catherine said smiling.

"Maybe we should get one of those marital relations books now. We could discuss and practice each evening," he said with a wicked grin.

"But you would not let me have one before we got married," Catherine stated.

"I had a difficult enough time surviving your necklines much less discussing marital relations with you. I will make you breakfast Mrs. McCullum while you bathe. How does that sound?" Cameron asked.

"I only have my wedding dress to put on," Catherine replied.

"Well, perhaps one of my night shirts would work for you?" Cameron asked.

"I thought you didn't sleep in night shirts?" Catherine replied wide eyed.

"I have them but I choose not to wear them; especially with my new bride in my bed," Cameron replied with yet another wicked grin.

Cameron pushed back the covers and got up to bathe in the front room while Catherine would be provided her privacy screen in the inner chambers. Before she got out of bed, she reached for her nightgown making sure she was covered before leaving the bed. She was not sure that she would ever get used to being nude in front of her husband.

Cameron rethought the night shirt suggestion realizing it would come to her ankles and cover her from shoulder to finger tips. He laid out one of his shirts instead. "I have placed one of my shirts for you on the bed my love. The night shirt will clearly be too large for you," Cameron said smiling.

Catherine bathed and put on her chemise and Cameron's shirt on top. Even his shirt came to her knees and she rolled the sleeves up to her wrists. When she came to the front room, Cameron was preparing something for them both. "Do you always cook without a shirt?" Catherine asked.

"No, just cut cold meat and cheese for my bride without a shirt on," Cameron turned then and saw his bride in one of his shirts. He smiled when he realized that even his shirt came beyond her knees. He needed to remind Mrs. Jones to pack her a bag for the cottage.

Catherine sat down at the table and saw another portfolio lying across the table. She opened the portfolio thinking there would be more sketches of ship designs. She was surprised to see that each sketch was of her.

"Cameron, did you do these sketches of me?" Catherine asked with amazement.

"I did my love; do you like them?" Cameron asked.

"They are beautiful my love. I did not know you were an artist also. I did not even sit for you," Catherine replied.

"Oh but you did love; you just didn't know it at the time. I started the first one the first day that we met. If you go through you will see poses from our meetings and church and luncheons." He stood back and watched her response to the portfolio offerings.

There were sketches of her in profile, sketches of her walking beside him, sketches from church and at their meetings in the Yard and at the Manor House. One was of her hands alone.

"Cameron is there anything that you cannot do? You can design and build ships, cook and draw . . . I cannot do anything Cameron. They did not raise me to do anything but be an ornament. I will learn how to do things I promise." She was in full blown tears by the time she finished that statement. He certainly had not anticipated this vulnerability but thought it all stemmed from her uncle and Van Ressller of course; the source of all her pain.

"Catherine my love; listen to me. No one knows how to do everything. I have taught myself many things out of necessity. Your life has been totally different because you grew up in a different world. I do not remember any vows yesterday saying that I will only love you if you can do this, that or the other thing. I will always love you and protect you and you are not going anywhere Catherine McCullum. Do you understand me?" Cameron sat then and lifted her onto his lap and dried her eyes tenderly. "Tell me you understand Catherine?"

"I do Cameron; of course I understand. I promise though I will learn to do things; useful things," Catherine replied.

"Your first job is to sit for me today so that I can sketch you with your hair all about you as you are now. Can you do that for me love?" Cameron asked tenderly.

"Of course Cameron; do you want me to put on my wedding gown again?" Catherine asked.

"No, I want you to be very simply dressed just as you are now. This is a sketch for me only love, alright?" Cameron asked.

"Do I need to sit perfectly still?" Catherine asked.

"No, I want you to eat breakfast and be very natural as if I am not even here," Cameron said.

Cameron moved across the table and Catherine sat very still eating her breakfast. Cameron completed his quick sketch. He wanted to take her mind off of her fears and her vulnerabilities. He wanted her to see herself as he saw her; beautiful; a marble statute now come to life. By the time she had finished her breakfast, he had finished his sketch. In it she was flesh and blood, the marble statute no more.

He lifted her again onto his lap and showed her the sketch. It was so very life like. "Cameron it is so very well done; I feel as though I am looking into a mirror. You are so very talented Cameron," Catherine said smiling shyly.

"I have my muse, love. You are my muse as you can see from this portfolio. You didn't have to sit for me because I have memorized your every gesture, mood and look. You can see the sideways glances in church, fits of pique when you and I did our verbal fencing, your hands at rest, the infamous French gown," Cameron continued to kiss away her tears as he tenderly showed her sketch after sketch. "And now you are here with me and you will be loved and cherished. We will talk about the books we love, build a life together, a family and no more talk ever of you being sent anywhere or having to do another's bidding. Tell me your story love, the story you never want to talk about," Cameron urged.

"I assumed everyone knew Cameron. That is why I did not want to talk about it," Catherine replied.

"I believe you think they know, love. But I truly do not think anyone knows apart from you, Mrs. Jones, the Reverend and Attorney Wendell," Cameron replied.

"Well some of this you already know Cameron. My parents died when I was eight. I was in England living at the family home so that I did not go out with them to the West Indies. They hoped to get settled there and send for me. After they died I basically grew up on my own. Mrs. Harmon was the housekeeper and nanny for all intents and purposes. My uncle pretended that I did not exist and I did not exist for him until I was old enough to start to attract attention," Catherine stated.

Cameron wrapped his arms around her to encourage her to keep talking. "The year of my coming out into society, my uncle uncharacteristically spent money on my attire. I think he thought to offer me to the highest bidder. He had offers but none that were adequate to his checkbook. At some point he encountered Mr. Van Ressller. I assume it was in London because I had never seen him at Edgewater, the family home. I do not know the particulars only that uncle had incurred a large debt with Van Ressller. Knowing what I learned here about Van Ressller's dealings I assume it was a gambling debt. As you know debtors go to prison in England so it is a very serious matter. When the debt came due, the agreement must have been developed to bring me here. I saw Van Ressller for all of five minutes, was shown to the Manor House and told the next day that he was dead," Catherine said quietly.

"The agreement had stated that I could return to London in two years time. Any children of the marriage were to remain here. They actually thought I would leave children here and return to London. Given how vile they both were, I can only assume I would then be offered again to the highest bidder," Catherine stated.

Cameron had listened quietly to Catherine's story not speaking a word. He knew it was hard for Catherine to let down yet one more guard and tell him the sordid tale of her arrival in Lewes. He understood the vulnerability now that she had opened her heart to him especially since she considered herself without value; nothing more than a bartered bride.

"That is behind you now my love. I want you to understand that the town does not know and does not care. They care about what you accomplish here. You kept the Yard open when you did not have to. You and I are making a go of the Yard and they respect that. Along those lines, I would like us to do a party for the christening of the first ship like we did for the wedding. It will be a good recognition of the lads and their hard work. Will that be agreeable to you my love?" Cameron asked.

"I think it is a wonderful idea Cameron. I am so glad that the whole town does not know the story. That is why I never went out of the Manor House except to church and to the Yard of course. It was mortifying to think the whole sordid tale was known by everyone. It was shameful to think that people would have connected me to the whole business with my uncle and Van Ressller and then for them to think that I would leave a child of mine behind however detestable the Father," Catherine said quietly.

"You need to hold your head up Catherine. You have done nothing wrong. You have been caught as a pawn between these two men. That has ended. We will make a success of the Yard, I will build you a new house and all connections with Van Ressller and your uncle end this day," Cameron said earnestly.

"Cameron, I know what you think about Mr. Van Ressller. But if I can adhere to the two years of the agreement we will have money to start our new life here on our own terms. We can reach a compromise because that is what you do in a marriage; is it not, compromise? I can spend my days at the Manor House and our nights here. When we have our babies, they will still be small until you build our new house. In the meantime, I can learn how to do some of the things I should have learned growing up but did not. Does that sound like a fair compromise?" Catherine asked earnestly.

"I still do not like connections to the Manor House of any kind. If you have any correspondence from your uncle, he is dead to you. That is my compromise. Anyone who would treat a treasure like you as chattel has no right to communicate with my wife again!" Cameron said heatedly.

Catherine threw her arms around Cameron's neck. "It is so wonderful to have someone else in my life that I can talk to and dream with and plan my life to include. I am very lucky to have you Cameron. I do want to build a life here. It is a good country and we can make it even better. I love you Cameron McCullum," Catherine said with eyes shining.

"I love you Catherine McCullum. Now, I am going to take you back to my huge bed and continue our honeymoon. Do you have any objections to that plan Mrs. McCullum?" Cameron asked grinning.

"No Cameron; I do not. Now that I know what happens I am ready for marital relations with my husband," Catherine said smiling.

"I may surprise you, my love. I have many ways to cherish my beautiful wife." With that, Cameron carried Catherine to his bed. The shirt was quickly discarded. Her chemise remained on at her request. She was still hesitant and shy about that element of their new intimacy and he expected that shyness to remain for the foreseeable future. His reminder that she was in the presence of an artist accustomed to the human form had little effect. When Cameron began to cherish his wife he was surprised by her attempts at physical strength. Not wanting to hurt her he waited to see why she pressed against him with all of her strength.

"I want to cherish you as you did me last night," Catherine said quietly. Catherine knelt beside Cameron and gently kissed his neck and shoulders. She relaxed against him and cuddled towards his warmth even on a June day. Cameron cupped her face with both hands and ran his fingers through her dark hair. He realized that she liked the feeling of being draped across him as she had during the night. He decided to return the favor. He draped himself across Catherine which promptly made her start to giggle. "I cannot breathe when you do that Cameron," Catherine said laughing.

"I like to hear you laugh. While I think of it and I have you vulnerable are you ticklish by any chance my love?" Cameron asked with mischief.

"I do not know Cameron. I have never been tickled before," Catherine replied wide eyed.

"How could you have never been tickled before? Not even as a child?" Cameron asked.

"I truly do not remember, but I would have to say no," Catherine replied smiling.

As if she had thrown down a challenge, Cameron traced his fingers down her side, very slowly and deliberately. She tried to hold his glance; all the while resisting the temptation to laugh which she knew would only encourage him to continue the torment. When at last she started giggling, Cameron smiled with satisfaction. "Well that is sorted. It is official; you are ticklish and I can make you laugh whenever I choose," Cameron said grinning.

"What about you Cameron? If we are uncovering each other's innermost secrets, are you ticklish by any chance?" Catherine asked with eyes shining.

"Of course I am not ticklish. What kind of man do you know who would be ticklish?" Cameron replied offended.

"Since I have no frame of reference, I am going to have to experiment on you," Catherine replied with true mischief in her eyes now.

"Under no circumstances Mrs. McCullum will I be the source of your experiments. I cannot believe we are having this conversation," Cameron said exasperated.

"It appears that you are now fencing with me Mr. McCullum and avoiding the subject completely," Catherine countered.

"Mrs. McCullum such issues are not worthy of discussion or investigation and what are you trying to do now? You know I am much larger than you and much stronger . . ." Cameron replied.

"And if you do not laugh soon you will explode," Catherine said giggling again.

"Enough. Now we are even and on to more important secrets. Where was I; I remember; ah yes . . . cherishing my wife in yet another way." Cameron cupped Catherine's face again and gently kissed her. The chemise was removed next. Catherine's dark blue eyes watched Cameron slowly unbutton the buttons of the chemise and pull her toward him so she was resting on his massive chest. He made love first to her mouth, kissing and mating their tongues until Catherine moaned with pleasure. He then cupped and caressed her breasts until she arched her back and called his name. "Catherine, you may be tender my love from last night and I will need to be very gentle with you," Cameron said huskily.

"Cameron, I love you and want to please you always," Catherine replied. "Besides, I find that I want you very much when you touch me like you have done," Catherine replied softly. It was all the reassurance that he needed. Cameron caressed her abdomen and very slowly the recesses of her womanhood, tenderly at first and then with greater intensity. As Catherine reached for Cameron he gently entered her as he felt her arms encircle his neck and pull him closer to her. The two entwined gently at first but with more intensity as they sought and found their climax, each calling the name of the other. It was the first such experience for Catherine and even more amazing than their first love making for that reason. After he had regained his strength and his capacity for thought, Cameron rolled to his back and brought Catherine into his side. She rested her head on his chest hearing the racing of his heart that matched her own.

"Cameron, I had no idea that love could be like this; that it was possible to feel this strongly for another human being," Catherine said quietly.

"I adore you Catherine. Did I hurt you my love?" Cameron asked anxiously.

"Oh no Cameron, you could never knowingly hurt me. I know that now. You are the real reason that I came here. You are the life that I was fated to live," Catherine replied.

THE ENGLISH ROSE

*****

In the morning when Cameron saw the first rays of sunlight streaming through the cottage windows he was reluctant to leave the warm bed. His bride had found her way to drape across him again. He smiled when he thought he would need a second blanket just for her. If he didn't owe it to the lads, he would have spent another day in this bed with his wife, sharing secrets of all varieties. He extricated himself from Catherine gently so as not to wake her, quickly bathed and dressed and sat down to write two notes; one to Catherine telling her he would come to see her at luncheon and one to Mrs. Jones to ask her to come and help Catherine dress so she could return to the Manor House. Cameron kissed Catherine one last time, covered her with an extra blanket and left for the Yard.

Mrs. Jones arrived two hours later to help Catherine dress and together they returned to the Manor House. "So what do you think of married life then Mistress?" Mrs. Jones asked as they walked.

"I highly recommend it Mrs. Jones assuming you have the right partner of course. I believe I have been blessed with the right partner in Mr. McCullum," Catherine replied smiling.

Mrs. Jones smiled to herself at that answer. It seemed that her efforts and the town's efforts had been richly rewarded.

"Mrs. Jones I think we need to work out a compromise of the French style dress. I cannot ask for help dressing each morning when I spend the night at the cottage. If we took the French style gown and raised the bodice and lengthened the sleeves, it would be a dress that I could get into and out of by myself each morning and evening. Do you not agree?" Catherine asked.

"I think that might work Mistress," Mrs. Jones replied smiling.

"Also, if you would be so kind, I would like to learn how to make some simple dishes so that I could make breakfast for Mr. McCullum at the cottage," Catherine continued smiling.

"You won't be moving there full time will you Mistress?" Mrs. Jones asked worriedly.

"Oh no, but I am trying to learn compromise in order to be successful in marriage. Do you not think that a good idea also?" Catherine continued smiling.

"Compromise is a very valuable skill in marriage Mistress," Mrs. Jones replied knowingly.

"I thought so also," Catherine responded smiling.

When they returned to the Manor House, Catherine and Mrs. Jones went upstairs so that she could change out of her wedding dress and into one of the new summer dresses. When they came down, Catherine and Mrs. Jones started with an easy dish; eggs for breakfast. Catherine told Mrs. Jones that Cameron would be visiting for luncheon also. She asked if she could do one simple dish for luncheon so that she could show Cameron what she had learned thus far. "Perhaps we could make biscuits together," Mrs. Jones replied. "They are always useful for any meal and we could do them with ham for luncheon," Mrs. Jones continued.

"That sounds like an excellent plan," Catherine responded smiling.

Both the eggs and the biscuits turned out very well and Catherine gained confidence in these simple tasks. She knew it was just a start, but if she felt she could accomplish something new each day, she would learn useful skills to help her in their new life. Once they had finished their recipe experimentation, Catherine went into the garden to cut lilacs for Cameron's cottage. She did not yet think of it as Cameron and her cottage, but she had decided it was a magical place where she felt safe to share elements of her life that no one else knew. Those elements included her new intimacy with Cameron. She still couldn't grasp that she could find such incredible bliss with another person as she had with Cameron. Walking in the gardens was really just an excuse to be alone with her thoughts about him. Soon she would go in and get ready for luncheon. She decided that he would think it highly improbable that she had made eggs and biscuits and was now checking her attire and appearance just for him. What a difference a few months had made in their lives.

When Cameron arrived for luncheon, Catherine was still upstairs. She ran down the stairs to greet him. When she reached the third step, they were actually eye to eye. He kissed her then and swung her off the step. "Hello again Mrs. McCullum; it seems you have changed your hair since I last saw you," Cameron said smiling wickedly.

"I *have* changed my hair Mr. McCullum. Do you like it?" Catherine replied wide eyed.

"Personally, I like your hair down and around your shoulders," was Cameron's quick reply.

"You know that the Mistress cannot wear her hair down anymore Master because she is a married lady," Mrs. Jones explained primly as she came upon the two.

"Nonsense, I don't see why that should matter. What business is it of anyone else what my wife does with her hair?" Cameron replied.

"It is tradition Master and custom," Mrs. Jones countered.

"May I interject something here since it is my hair being discussed?" Catherine asked laughing. Cameron and Mrs. Jones both stopped for a minute to listen. "Since marriage is all about compromise, I could wear my hair up in the front and down in the back. A compromise, you see?" Catherine said smiling.

"Compromise, eh?" Cameron said smiling.

"It has been the word of the day," Catherine replied.

"And no lace cap," Cameron interjected. "I want to be able to see your beautiful hair," he replied possessively.

"I will work on a solution," Catherine said with eyes shining.

"Mistress had some lessons this morning Master Cameron. You need to ask her about them," Mrs. Jones interjected smiling.

"More surprises for me my love?" Cameron asked mischievously.

"Mrs. Jones and I experimented with eggs for breakfast and with biscuits for lunch. You will be trying the biscuits in just a moment. I hope you will like them," Catherine replied shyly.

"Whatever you make I will like. With each day of experimenting you will get better and better. That is the great thing about experimenting," Cameron replied with a wink. "On another subject; how would you like to have a longer honeymoon Mrs. McCullum?" Cameron asked.

"Oh of course I would Cameron, but how?" Catherine asked.

"I have been asked to speak to the Governor about the issue of our coastal defense and a potential blockade and its affect on Lewes. The town is quite concerned and a delegation has asked me this morning to begin discussions with the Governor. If you can be ready to be picked up by 5:00 p.m. this evening, we will set off in the evening coach for Dover," Cameron stated.

"Will there be anyone else travelling with us Cameron?" Catherine asked casually.

"No, just you and I for two days to Dover, at least one day in Dover for our meetings and two days back," Cameron replied smiling.

"I will be ready my love," Catherine answered smiling.

CHAPTER SIX

Cameron picked up Catherine and her trunk promptly at 5:00 for the evening coach. The lilacs that she had picked for the cottage she carried with her on the coach. She had not advised Cameron that she had dressed in the infamous French gown which she now diplomatically covered with a Spenser jacket cover since she had been specifically asked to retain the dress for their honeymoon.

When she entered the coach another older couple was seated on the bench seat across from them. It was not quite the romantic night that Catherine had anticipated, but the thought of a five day honeymoon with Cameron dispelled any short term difficulties. Since she had not been out of Lewes for nearly six months, the trip was just the ticket for them both. Cameron squeezed her hand and smiled as the coach progressed out of Lewes. The older couple smiled at the *young people* heading to Dover. The first stop for the coach was Milton and the older couple would only be going that far. The first planned night would be spent at a tavern in Milford.

After they had been underway for some while, Catherine asked Cameron if he had a speech for the upcoming meeting that she could review for him. "I do my love depending of course if you can read my handwriting," Cameron replied.

"I will be happy to try," Catherine responded. Although she knew she was not familiar yet with all of the subject matter, she did want to be part of whatever he was involved in. Catherine sat reading the speech and was struck again at how knowledgeable Cameron was on such a variety of topics and how well he expressed himself. Reading it made her even prouder of her husband.

"It is awfully close tonight, my love; do you not wish to take off your jacket?" Cameron asked anxiously.

"Oh no Cameron; thank you very much though. You know how cold I can get," Catherine replied.

"I do indeed," he replied with a mischievous wink.

"Your speech is quite good. I am very proud of you," Catherine responded.

The older couple across from Cameron and Catherine nodded and smiled at the young couple. "Honeymoon then?" the gentleman asked.

"Two days so far," Cameron replied then smiled at Catherine. "Are you sure you do not want to take off your jacket? You do look like you are positively glowing my love," Cameron asked concerned.

"Oh no Cameron; thank you I am fine," Catherine replied smiling bravely.

As the sun began to set and the coach became darker inside, Catherine laid her head on Cameron's shoulder and began to doze. She continued to sleep until the coach stopped in Milton so that the older couple could depart. Cameron roused Catherine to see if she would like to stretch her legs and have a comfort stop. When she was led into the ladies lounge, the first thing that she did was remove the Spenser jacket; fan herself and refresh with cool water from the pitcher. She was hot, uncomfortably so, but was not comfortable removing the jacket in the coach after the previous argument over the dress. Being uncomfortable was preferable to another row about the infamous French gown. She put it down to experience and the art of compromise in a marriage. The close quarters and Spenser jacket had certainly brought a blush to her cheeks she noticed in the mirror of the ladies lounge. She was sure that Cameron would have noticed that blush as well.

When she returned to the coach, she found that only she and Cameron would be the remaining occupants. He had settled his long legs across the coach to rest on the adjacent bench seat. Only in this way could he be truly comfortable. Catherine sat to his left so that he would not be disturbed.

"Do we expect any other passengers on the next leg of our journey my love?" Catherine asked casually.

"No Catherine; it will be us alone," Cameron replied smiling.

"Right, that is fine then. I am going to take off this Spenser jacket then," Catherine replied still casually.

"I wondered why you were wearing it when it is so very humid and close tonight. I know you get cold easily, but no one could get cold in this closeness." Cameron stopped then as he saw Catherine remove the jacket. The infamous French style dress without modesty panel was revealed beneath the jacket.

"I saved it for the honeymoon just as you asked," Catherine replied grinning with true mischief in her eyes now.

"So you did. And you kept covered up despite suffocating to avoid a row; did you now?" Cameron asked smiling.

"I did indeed because compromise is an important part of marriage," Catherine replied with the same mischief in her eyes.

"Did you figure that out all on your own my love or did Mrs. Jones help you reach that conclusion?" Cameron asked with a wink.

"It was my idea but she confirmed my opinion," Catherine replied smiling.

"I see; right then, just so. I suppose now that we are married you consider that dress as safe to wear again do you?" Cameron asked with a raised eyebrow.

"Well, if not safe, then at least agreeable if only for you and your eyes," Catherine replied diplomatically.

"I like that thought very much Mrs. McCullum. Now come here my love and let me enjoy that dress and its occupant further," Cameron replied huskily.

Catherine moved closer to Cameron's side as he cupped her face with one hand and drew her to him with the other. He traced a line of kisses down her neck and gently lifted her onto his lap. His kisses became more intense as he reached her décolletage. With his lips, he traced a line of wet kisses that began at Catherine's ear and extended to the very bodice of her gown. His breathing became very ragged within a few minutes. Catherine clung to him and began to softly moan. Cameron's mouth slanted over and over Catherine's and he began to mate his tongue with hers. Just when they thought their self control was at its lowest ebb, the anticipated summer storm beat in the coach windows with gale force. Cameron sheltered Catherine with his coat and his upper body, but to no avail. They were both soaked to the skin in a matter of minutes. Luckily the coachmen pulled into the next available roadside inn to rest for the night. Cameron wrapped Catherine in his coat to cover the dress and the soaking that she had endured. The inn was very well appointed and Cameron requested the honeymoon suite upon entering the lobby.

"Very good sir we will show you immediately to the honeymoon suite," replied the front desk attendant.

"May we also have a hot bath sent up as we were caught in the storm," Cameron stated.

"Certainly sir; it will be brought up momentarily," the front desk attendant replied.

Catherine was holding onto her smile but was visibly shaking at this point. "It hasn't been my idea of a honeymoon trip thus far," Cameron said, "but we will improve it in just a few minutes," he stated smiling at the shaking Catherine.

When they reached the room a fire had been lit as the storm had turned the temperature extremely cool for the month of June. Catherine stood in front of the fire with Cameron's coat until the trunk and hot steaming tub were brought in. When the servants had left, Catherine took off Cameron's coat and let down her hair temporarily to dry.

"I never realized that your hair was curly," Cameron said watching her brush it out.

"It is the rain and the humidity. I can brush it straight as it dries," Catherine replied.

"So does your dress have the appropriate wet texture for the French court at this point do you think?" Cameron asked gazing intently at the curves before him.

Catherine looked down to see the body molding nature of the dress so fashioned in the French court, but not appropriate for public view in rural Delaware. "I believe it is for your eyes only my love in its present state. We do not have a privacy screen Cameron," Catherine stated worriedly.

"I will shave over here at the basin and you can bathe in front of the fire. How would that be?" Cameron replied smiling.

Catherine took off her dress then and placed it by the fire to dry. The material was in pleated folds caused by the gale driven rain that they had just travelled through. Beneath the dress due to its sheerness, Catherine had on a full length slip, corset and chemise. Cameron tried valiantly to keep his concentration on his shaving in order to lessen Catherine's shyness. Once she was undressed and beneath the water, Cameron asked if she needed her lavender soap.

"I do Cameron. It is on the top of my packed items in the trunk," Catherine replied shyly.

He retrieved it and a sponge for her use. "Here you are my love," he said kissing her exposed neck. The gently curling hair was back up for the duration of the bath. "Let me know if you need any help," Cameron replied.

"Thank you darling but I am fine," Catherine said smiling.

Cameron finished shaving, quickly bathed and wrapped his torso in a towel in deference to Catherine. He spread across the bed waiting for Catherine to complete her bath. He could see her shoulders relax as she sunk into the warm waters, now scented by the lavender soap. The fire crackled cheerfully and the bath water glistened on Catherine's ivory skin. Waiting for Catherine to complete her bath, Cameron began to have thoughts of their prior assignation in the coach that had been rudely interrupted by the gale driven rains. His thoughts soon turned to new and exciting ways to cherish his bride.

"Catherine, do you need a towel, my love?" Cameron asked casually.

"Oh yes Cameron, please," Catherine replied.

Cameron casually walked over to Catherine with a large towel. He held up the towel to wrap Catherine as she rose from the bath tub. As he wrapped her in the towel he kissed the base of her neck again. She shuddered as with a chill. Cameron took the towel from around his waist then and wrapped the second towel around her. "Are you cold my love?" Cameron asked tenderly.

"Oh no Cameron; when you kiss me like that, it gives me chills," she replied shyly.

"Well, a man couldn't ask for more than that," Cameron said smiling. "I am not laughing at you Catherine, please understand. I am just happy if I can give you pleasure," Cameron stated gazing intently at Catherine.

Cameron took down Catherine's hair then and ran his fingers through the silken strands. He turned Catherine towards him and cupped her face with his hands, kissing her deeply and mating his tongue with hers. Catherine quietly moaned at the back of her throat and placed her arms around Cameron's neck. The towels slowly dropped to the floor. Cameron picked up Catherine and carried her to the bed. With his eyes, his lips and his hands he cherished his wife, whispering his love and terms of endearment. Catherine alternately laughed, cried and screamed his name, captured by a kiss from Cameron as they both reached their climax. When at last they could recover both their breath and thoughts, Cameron pulled Catherine into his side assuring that she would not get cold during the night. "Cameron, I think we are getting better at these marital relations," Catherine said smiling.

Cameron laughed then long and hard. "Catherine I believe you are right, my love. With practice comes perfection and we are coming very close," Cameron replied warmly.

"I love you Cameron," Catherine replied.

"And I adore you Catherine," Cameron responded.

*****

The next morning the pair set off again for Dover. The coach was occupied only by them for the remainder of the trip to Dover. Catherine re-read Cameron's speech by the light of day and suggested some changes that she thought might make the argument stronger. "Thank you Catherine. You see we are partners in all things. If I have you with me, there is nothing I cannot accomplish. Thank you for coming with me my love." He kissed her hand and Catherine's eyes shone in his adoration.

"Do you think they will let me come into the room when you deliver your speech?" Catherine asked.

"Absolutely; I will insist on it. If they do not listen to me, at least they may pay attention to my beautiful wife," Cameron said smiling.

"Have you ever been to Dover, Cameron?" Catherine asked.

"I have my love and New Castle, and Wilmington. I worked previously in the ship yards in Wilmington before being informed of your advertisement by Attorney Wendell. He is our true matchmaker you know," Cameron replied smiling.

"I think he has regretted his association with Mr. Van Ressller and my uncle and tried to make amends. I will need to thank him again when next I see him. He did a wonderful thing for the town and for me personally," Catherine replied.

"We will both thank him my love and the town at the ship christening," Cameron replied.

When Cameron and Catherine arrived in Dover, they were taken to the temporary headquarters of the state government. Fearing attack from the British with the escalation of tension between the United States and Great Britain, the government had provisionally moved to Dover from New Castle until the resolution of the current difficulties. The Lewes town officials had solicited Cameron's help to gain assistance by the state in coastal defenses and protection against British invasion in light of further escalation between the United States and Britain.

The coach took them to the provisional headquarters and from there would take their luggage on to the inn where they were staying. There was much activity centered in Dover given the need to move the capital there on a temporary basis. As always, activity centered on the state center of government regardless of its location.

Catherine and Cameron were shown into the anteroom of the Governor's provisional office. They were to meet with the Governor and the Special Committee on Coastal Defenses. Their wait was not long. They were shown through to a large meeting room with desks for each member of the committee and the Governor in the center. A table was set for Cameron and chairs behind in rows. Catherine seated herself in the front row on one of the audience chairs.

"Governor Haslet and members of the Coastal Defense Committee; my name is Cameron McCullum. I am here today with my wife and partner Catherine McCullum. We have come at the request of the Lewes Town Council to discuss our concerns related to coastal defense. As you know, tensions continue to escalate between our national government and the government of Great Britain. The ongoing negotiations and debate makes it clear that military solutions may soon occur if matters related to suppression of trade and impressments of seamen cannot be resolved in a peaceful manner. Those military actions could in turn impose threats to the coastal communities of our state.

"We come to you today seeking assistance to keep our coastal communities safe in support of our coastal businesses and residents. My wife Catherine and I operate a shipyard in Lewes, Delaware which employs twenty men and feeds twenty families in our community. We are but one of the businesses that will be threatened by any potential naval blockades or attacks by the navy of Great Britain. We seek this assistance before tragedy befalls our community and any other coastal communities in our state.

"We thank you for your attention today and will be happy to answer any questions that you may have. We are respectfully requesting your aid in the defense of coastal Southern Delaware."

The Governor and assembled members appeared interested in Cameron's request and genuinely touched by his eloquence. They politely asked questions of Cameron which he replied to with equal passion to his statement. A copy of the letter was left with the committee for their record. The Governor thanked Cameron and Catherine for their time and attention to the matter. They were assured that the committee would take their concerns under consideration.

When they were outside the headquarters, Catherine asked Cameron what the Governor's words had meant.

"I believe it means they will wait until something bad happens then act accordingly I fear," Cameron replied.

"That was what I feared as well," Catherine said glumly.

"The difference is that this is our government Catherine and not His Majesty's government. If they do not do the will of the people, the people can elect another. As a true son of Scotland, that fact does my heart good," Cameron replied smiling.

"Perhaps you could run for Governor one day Cameron. You could correct what needs to be corrected," Catherine replied with her eyes shining.

"With your help, love, perhaps I will," Cameron said grinning. "Now, let us get some lunch and return to our honeymoon," he said taking her hand.

When they returned to their inn, Catherine and Cameron had received an invitation to a ball at the provisional Governor's House that night. Cameron hoped to reinforce his points to whoever would listen and to enjoy himself with his new bride. She in turn was glad that she had packed her wedding gown as this definitely qualified as a special occasion to wear it. She would need Cameron's help but reasoned he was up to the task along with his other special talents.

When she presented her back to him in dressing, he laughed in response. "I have seen ship rigging easier to understand than this dress. I will need a moment to study this before proceeding; and then only with caution Mrs. McCullum," Cameron said grinning.

"I do not recall you needing a moment to study when you were getting me out of it on our wedding night," Catherine replied smiling with mischief.

"Ah . . . when one is suitably motivated, one can do almost anything, my love. I will picture removing this gown on our return to motivate me to work the lacings," Cameron responded grinning.

"This is the very reason that Mrs. Jones and I are modifying the French style so that I can dress myself," Catherine replied earnestly.

"Will these modifications keep my heart beating at a regular rate or do I risk heart failure with each new neckline?" Cameron replied grinning.

"We are modifying the neckline at your request and lengthening the sleeves. They will be sheer but long so that I do not get freckles walking to and fro," Catherine replied.

"I happen to like freckles Mrs. McCullum; at least on you," Cameron said kissing her neck.

"They simply are not the thing Cameron. You must trust me on this," Catherine replied primly.

"I trust you on all matters of style whether they affect my heart rate or not. I believe I have you done with the lacings although I believe I could rig a ship faster," Cameron continued laughing.

"And of course undue me faster," Catherine replied.

"That goes without saying, my love," Cameron answered huskily.

*****

The ball at the Governor's residence was smaller than usual due to the provisional nature of the capital. It was an honor nonetheless to be invited and provided yet another opportunity to reinforce Cameron's points of the concerns of the Lewes Town Council. Cameron was not one to miss the opportunity. He served Catherine with a drink of punch and proceeded to find every member of the committee to speak to personally.

Catherine was happy to watch the dancers secure in the knowledge that Cameron would soon return to dance once his lobbying efforts had concluded. Unbeknownst to Catherine, the Governor made a direct line to speak to her individually. "I was most impressed by your husband's impassioned plea Mrs. McCullum. He is quite an eloquent speaker. Do I detect a hint of Scot's accent there?" Governor Haslet stated.

"You do indeed Your Excellency. My husband is originally from The Highlands of Scotland but, he is passionate about this country and its opportunities," Catherine replied.

"Your accent if I am not mistaken is English," Governor Haslet continued.

"Yes Your Excellency; my family's estate is outside London. I too have chosen to make Lewes my home and America my country. We are both passionate about the opportunities available here," Catherine responded.

"Then you will have no mixed emotions if it comes to war again with Great Britain?" the Governor asked.

"I hope war may be averted of course, but if it were to occur, I will stand with my community and my new adopted country," Catherine replied.

"Thank you my dear and your husband both for your passionate belief in Delaware. You know, I have a farm in Sussex County named Cedar Creek Hundred. I am very familiar with the concerns that your husband expressed so eloquently today. I will promise that I will do my utmost to assist with the coastal defense issue," Governor Haslet replied.

"Thank you again Your Excellency for hearing our concerns and for your gracious offer of assistance. My husband will be most pleased," Catherine stated smiling.

When Cameron returned to her side, Catherine was grinning from ear to ear. "I have just spoken with the Governor again and he promised to do all in his power to assist our cause. Is that not wonderful news Cameron?" Catherine replied with eyes shining.

"There is nothing we cannot achieve if we work together. I am convinced of that my love. Maybe we should invite him to the christening of the English Rose?" Cameron replied.

"I think that is a fine idea Cameron. May I dance with my husband now?" Catherine asked smiling.

"Your wish as always is my command, my love." With that Cameron took Catherine to the dance floor for several turns before returning to their inn for the night. As predicted, the wedding dress was much easier to remove than to put on, a fact that Cameron happily shared with Catherine as he undressed her for the night.

The next day, Catherine and Cameron boarded the coach for the return trip to Lewes. They worked on a list of invitations and a refreshments menu for the ship christening and decided on July 4th as it would give the community one more reason to celebrate. Catherine was Cameron's clerk as she recorded ideas for the big day's events which they refined during their trip home. The trip included one more night of honeymoon and Cameron intended to take advantage of that night at the inn where they spent their first night of the journey.

Cameron asked again for the honeymoon suite and for a hot bath to be sent up. Upon its arrival, Cameron suggested that Catherine may like a bath before bed. Catherine searched out her lavender soap and night gown and turned her back for Cameron to release her lacings. "I'll bathe in the basin again love, you take the hot bath," Cameron stated.

"Thank you Cameron; I do love a hot bath. It is so very relaxing," Catherine replied.

"I can tell my love; your shoulders seemed to relax as you submerged in the bath before," Cameron responded.

"You were not supposed to be peeking Cameron," Catherine replied shocked.

"Oh but I was not peeking, my love. It was a full gaze from head to toe," he said smiling and winking his mischievous wink.

"I always thought you knew what I looked like without my petticoats even before we were married," Catherine replied with mischief.

"Then I could only imagine; now I have more definitive observational skills and firsthand knowledge; essential as a designer and artist; wouldn't you agree? I may have to do a sketch of you in a bath for my own collection," Cameron replied laughing. "You have your bath and I will have a shave. I have noticed your skin is so delicate that whisker burn is always an issue." With that Cameron kissed Catherine and set about his shaving as Catherine descended into her lavender bath.

When Catherine had concluded her bath and Cameron his shave and bath, Cameron brought Catherine her towels. He knelt down and kissed the nape of her neck and presented her towels as she exited the bath.

"Catherine, I believe the next thing I will make for us is a new head board for our bed," Cameron mentioned casually.

"Why is that my love?" Catherine asked puzzled.

"I think a head board makes a good support for one's back do you not agree," Cameron replied.

Catherine looked at him in a confused manner. "I will demonstrate my love," Cameron carried Catherine to the bed then and placed her across his lap.

"Is this another surprise Cameron?" Catherine asked wide eyed.

"Oh yes love; another surprise for my wife," Cameron kissed Catherine deeply and intensely. He knew that Catherine always responded to his kisses. Her passion for her husband was in evidence by her response to his kisses from the beginning of their courtship. Knowing this fact Cameron slowly ravaged his wife's mouth with his tongue and lips.

With his hands and mouth Cameron caressed Catherine's breasts and bottom. Cameron repositioned Catherine so that she was draped across his lap. She looked confused for a moment and Cameron whispered "My surprise love," into her ear.

Cameron reignited Catherine's passion with his kisses and caresses. When he knew that she had nearly reached her climax, Cameron entered her capturing her moan with a deep kiss. Catherine placed her arms around his neck pressing closer to his strength and warmth. When they had both reached their climax, Cameron kissed her eyes and mouth. Catherine clung to her husband who gently laid her beside him. When they had both regained their breath and composure, Catherine quietly snuggled against Cameron's neck. "I loved your surprise," Catherine purred into his ear.

"You see; a headboard provides excellent back support," Cameron answered. "I think our cottage needs one."

"I love our cottage Cameron; it is a magical place," Catherine replied.

"Why do you think it magical my love?" Cameron asked.

"Because you are there and all of your wonderful designs and our love for one another," Catherine replied.

"Magical indeed; I will build you a magical house Catherine; magical for you and for our children. This is just the start of our life together," Cameron replied.

*****

The next day, Cameron and Catherine arrived back in Lewes. Cameron advised Catherine that he would brief Attorney Wendell on their meeting with the Governor and then join her back at the Manor House for dinner.

"How did the meeting go Cameron?" Attorney Wendell inquired.

"The meeting was well received but I am unsure how successful our immediate results will be. The Governor and Coastal Defense Committee were very receptive to our concerns. Catherine and I will invite the Governor to our first ship christening and perhaps it will give us another chance to demonstrate the problem first hand on the ground," Cameron replied.

Mr. Wendell as always was impressed by Cameron and his passion for his adopted country. "Cameron I want to tell you how impressed I am with your commitment to our community. We are very lucky to have you and Mrs. McCullum here in Lewes. I want to give you something that was given to me by my prior client Mr. Van Ressller. I deeply regret my involvement with that despicable agreement and its affect on Mrs. McCullum. This miniature was sent by your wife's uncle as the negotiations were beginning. I would like you to have it Cameron. I know you will treasure it as you love and respect Mrs. McCullum. That is apparent to all who see you together, if I may be so bold to express it on behalf of us all," Mr. Wendell stated.

"Thank you Mr. Wendell for your confidence and your apology. I consider it a great honor that you selected me for my position and brought me here where I have been fortunate to meet Catherine and contribute to this town. I hope that you will join us for the christening of our first ship to coincide with the July 4th holiday. We want to offer a party for the town and recognize the lads for their hard work. Thank you very much for this miniature. I can certainly understand how this image would have influenced Mr. Van Ressller's decision to bring Catherine to America," Cameron replied sincerely.

Cameron placed the miniature in his pocket and walked to the Manor House. After dinner they would walk to the magical cottage as Catherine referred to it. Wherever his treasure was found would always be magical to him regardless of her location. Catherine was his true treasure and it mattered little to him where he rested so long as Catherine was beside him.

*****

Catherine proceeded the next morning to work from her invitation list to prepare for the July 4th christening. She completed invitations to all of the dignitaries that they wished to invite and a notice for Reverend Clayborne to include in the church announcements for the next few weeks. She and Mrs. Jones would work on the menu and this time as part of her training, she would assist Mrs. Jones in the food preparation. After completing her list, Catherine went upstairs to pack a small bag for Saturday night and Sunday to be spent at their magical cottage. Cameron would come to meet her shortly and they would spend their Saturday evening, Sunday and Sunday evening at the cottage. This Saturday evening unlike her wedding night she would not have her winter expedition nightgown among her items for inclusion. She had seen to that herself.

CHAPTER SEVEN

The July 4th celebration and the ship christening plans were well underway in just a matter of a few short days. Catherine was proud of the role she had played in the event planning. She felt it was her first real test in taking on a project for Cameron and seeing it through from start to finish. She felt with each new task that she undertook a confidence building to take on new tasks and see them through as well. She knew the house they would build together would be a major challenge and test of her new skills and rather than shrinking from the thought, she looked forward to that challenge as well.

One further surprise that Cameron had kept to the last minute was the figurehead that he had carved for the English Rose. In order to keep the secret from Catherine, he had moved the figurehead to the Yard and worked to finish her during the daylight hours as the magical cottage as Catherine called it was no longer off limits to her.

He laughed when he thought how something as simple as the cottage could be considered magical to Catherine. In his mind, she had made it magical as she made everything magical that she touched. He reached in his pocket and pulled out the miniature sent to Van Ressller in advance of Catherine's arrival in Lewes. If he had not been moved by the beauty of this miniature and prepared accordingly for this treasure, than his heart was made of stone. Catherine's true value had been reserved for Cameron and him alone. He chose to recognize that treasure and he was pleased to know that she had bloomed in just the short time that they had been married. As he had told her on the Dover trip, there was nothing he could not accomplish with Catherine at his side.

*****

At last, the great day arrived. The Governor could not join them, but all of the town would be there for the festivities at the Yard, the refreshments at the Manor House and fireworks to conclude the day. It would be a day to remember and a day the entire community could participate in.

The ship's christening was the starting point for the day. Cameron had asked Catherine to break the ceremonial bottle over the bow of the English Rose. It would be at that moment that Catherine would see her likeness on the carved figurehead for the first time. He hoped that she would be pleased.

The next stop would be the Manor House for refreshments. Mrs. Jones and Catherine had worked all week to prepare the refreshments. Although she was an apprentice to Mrs. Jones' experienced hands, Mrs. Jones was pleased to inform all who inquired that the Mistress was instrumental in the success of the refreshments. The whole community would be agog at the Mistress' new skills.

The fireworks would conclude the evening and would take place over the shipyard reflecting in the waters of the canal.

Cameron helped Catherine to dress in her new French gown, a revision created by Catherine and Mrs. Jones. She had a large picture hat to protect her skin from the sun and lace gloves to protect her hands. The long sleeves were made of the sheerest material to cover the skin, but provide coolness on a July day. Cameron pronounced her the belle of the day and the treasure of his heart. That was the highest compliment that she could hope to receive. The dress was alluring but not provocative; the height of fashion, but practical for one so fair skinned. No freckles for her however sweet Cameron found them to be.

Cameron had been asked by Captain McEwan to say a few words at the ship's christening ceremony and Catherine was happy to review and perfect the speech for him. With the town gathered together, he thanked everyone for attending and for supporting the efforts of the shipyard. Lastly he thanked his beautiful bride Catherine and asked her to come forward to christen the English Rose. Catherine came forward and for the first time, came face to face with her own image on the bowsprit. Cameron took her hand, kissed it and handed her the bottle for the official christening. Catherine mouthed the words thank you with her eyes shining and proceeded to christen the English Rose and to bless all who sailed upon her.

Captain McEwan was all smiles with the delivery of his ship. "Ye did what ye set out to do Cameron. She is a beauty of a ship and she is charmed by the beauty of the figurehead. Ye have my congratulations lad on achieving both of your accomplishments. Ye always set out to do what ye set your mind to and ye have done a good day's work here Cameron. I will be sure to tell all of the merchants of my acquaintance and I will send them to ye for their ships. Well done lad!" Captain McEwan stated. Cameron introduced him to Catherine and Captain McEwan winked at him for accomplishing his dream of marrying Catherine as well.

The community then walked to the Manor House for refreshments and for musical entertainments in the gardens. Cameron took Catherine's hand and walked with her to the house. What a difference six months had made to them both; they were married, the shipyard was a success and they had been recognized by the community that they both loved and hoped to see prosper.

When they arrived at the Manor House, Mrs. Jones was busy telling all who asked how her Mistress had helped her with the refreshments and was becoming quite the talented cook. Catherine beamed at Mrs. Jones' praise and all of the ladies asked for copies of recipes. Cameron walked through the dining room like an already proud Father. His two missions in life; marriage to Catherine and the first ship had been accomplished. New goals lay before him; a new house he would design for Catherine and for the babies they hoped and planned for and the next ship as well as work on the coastal defense project. Much had been done; but there was much more to accomplish.

Like their wedding day, Catherine and Cameron had arranged for music and dancing to be shared in the garden. It was another note of appreciation that Cameron and Catherine had extended to the larger Lewes community. Catherine's promise to learn useful things was being borne out by the success of the event and the acceptance that Catherine felt by those in attendance.

Captain McEwan joined both Catherine and Cameron in the gardens and asked if they would like to slip away for a short sail on the English Rose. Catherine's eyes lit up at the opportunity. "Oh could we Cameron; just a short sail?" Catherine asked.

"Of course my love; I want you to see how she handles and not just how she looks," Cameron replied. The threesome set off for the Yard and Captain McEwan and his men unfurled the sail and set off. Catherine sat next to Cameron until he rose to stand at the bow of the ship. She thought then that Cameron's long ago Viking forebears must have looked just the same when they came into a port in England or Scotland during the Viking Age of exploration. He was the master of all that he surveyed and in his element on the deck of a ship. She sat taking in the day and his joy in the accomplishment of the ship's design.

"She is a dream lad; ye have done well just as I knew you would. Did ye give me all the speed I asked for then?" Captain McEwan called out.

"She is all that you asked for and much more. You will not be disappointed Captain; I can assure you," Cameron replied.

They sailed on then, out and around Cape Henlopen. Catherine only briefly allowed herself to think of the terrible night that she had been brought out in the tender ship from the Trinity in a full gale to land on Lewes' shore. It seemed now like a nightmare, as foreign to her current life as the drawing rooms of her uncle an ocean away. Sitting on the deck of the English Rose watching her husband in his element in a design of his own, Catherine thought it was not possible to be any happier. When he turned to check on her his face held all the joy of a small child's at Christmas.

He came to her then and sat across from her on the deck. "So Mrs. McCullum;" he said with all earnestness, "do I have the job now Mistress?" he said smiling at last. His thoughts then were of the day of their first meeting in the library. Catherine instantly captured the same thought.

"You do sir; you do have the job. We are partners Mr. McCullum and I am told that in America, we shake hands on a partnership," she replied smiling.

"Aye then Mistress; partners in work and in life," Cameron said. "The shake is American Mistress; the kiss is Scots and my own," Cameron said grinning. "You made all of my dreams come true today Catherine," Cameron said earnestly.

"We will have new dreams then Cameron; new dreams that we can experience together," Catherine replied.

*****

The crowning feature of the day was the fireworks. They meant America to Cameron and to share that gift with Catherine was another lasting memory of the day. Her eyes shone in the reflected light of the firework display. "I am so happy Cameron. Thank you for all of this; the figurehead, the acceptance by the community and most importantly your love and the life we will build together," Catherine said smiling.

"Let us go home Catherine to our magical cottage. It is magical Catherine because you are there. You make everything you touch magical my love," Cameron said tenderly.

When they arrived at the cottage, Cameron showed Catherine the miniature that Attorney Wendell had given him. "It was sent to Van Ressller from your uncle my love. Mr. Wendell is most anxious for you to know that he regrets any association with Van Ressller and your uncle and the pain it caused you. The return of this miniature is his way of making amends. I will keep this on my desk in the shipyard office if you are in agreement. To me my love, this is the face that would have launched a thousand ships had I ruled the world," Cameron said smiling.

"I never knew it had been made or sent. It must have been prepared from a sketch that was taken the year of my debut into society," Catherine replied.

"Today signifies to me exactly what we have planned; the town embraces you; the shipyard is a success and to me, our life together is everything that I could have ever hoped for. Are you happy my love?" Cameron asked.

"I am so happy Cameron. Everything that you said would happen has come to pass. Thank you so much for making me so very happy," Catherine responded.

With that said Cameron cupped Catherine's face with his hands. Catherine kissed both hands and placed her arms around his neck. He lifted her up slowly until she was pressed closely to him. "Thankfully we don't have complicated riggings tonight," Cameron whispered.

"No Cameron, only a slip, corset and chemise." Catherine replied. Cameron undid the tie belt and pulled the gown over her head and pulled the pins from her hair. He gently threaded his fingers through the silken strands. The slip and corset were next. Cameron took her hand and led her to the bed with the new headboard that he had made for them. "You see; we have good back support going forward," Cameron said winking.

"When did you have time to make this?" Catherine asked.

"I have been very busy Mrs. McCullum making our cottage more magical for you at each and every visit. Consider it a labor of love. You have only to make your request and it will be my pleasure to design and build it for you," Cameron replied huskily.

"You are so very clever Cameron." She kissed him then, not waiting to be kissed as was normally the case. She slowly unbuttoned his shirt, pulling it slowly from his breeches and kissed his neck and chest as she did so. Cameron lay back on the bed and when he did so, she kissed him from his neck to his waist. Cameron gently rubbed her back and bottom as she did so.

"Oh my love; what you do to me when you kiss me in that way," Cameron said huskily. Cameron slowly unbuttoned her chemise. He mimicked the same path of kisses from her neck to her abdomen and beyond. Catherine's eyes widened at Cameron's gentle ravishing of his wife. He teased her arousal and she arched her back and moaned gently. Cameron gently straddled her legs over him and his arousal. Capturing her sigh within his kiss, Cameron entered his wife, mating with both his body and with deep kisses. Both sighed and moaned with the pleasure of each other's bodies. Catherine reached her climax first and Cameron shortly thereafter. It had been a magical day for them both; their first July 4th together and the culmination of both their dreams.

*****

On the next week, Catherine received a letter from her uncle in London. Recognizing the seal and the handwriting she left it on the library desk until Cameron's arrival at the Manor House for luncheon. They had already had the discussion concerning her husband's opinion of her uncle.

She wanted to make sure that he was still of the same opinion on the matter before opening the letter.

When Cameron arrived at lunch, Catherine asked him if he would come into the library for a moment. "What is it my love; what can I do to help?" Cameron asked anxiously.

"I have had a letter from my uncle. We knew this time would come Cameron eventually. I just wanted you with me when I opened it my love," Catherine replied anxiously.

"Dearest Catherine,

It is my understanding that you have been left a widow by the demise of your late husband Hans Van Ressller. If this is indeed true, you will need to ask the solicitor Wendell for an advance for a return passage to London. I have had inquiries about you by a number of your old prospects including Captain Sir John Beresford of His Majesty's Navy. I am certain on your return that I could be assured of a match with Captain Beresford and a settlement in the neighborhood of 2,000 pounds per annum. Please respond at your earliest possible opportunity so that the necessary marriage contracts can be prepared.

I remain yours,

Jonathan Wentworth, Baronet"

Catherine looked up at Cameron with the old look of worry coupled with fear. "My love, this letter belongs in the fire along with any other correspondence received from your uncle. You are loved, cherished and adored Catherine McCullum and respected in this community. Your uncle cannot touch you. I will not allow it and neither will anyone else in this town. Let us go through and have lunch my love and you put it and him out of your mind forever," Cameron stated heatedly.

*****

By November, Catherine had confirmed what she had suspected for some time. She was with child and so very happy that she would have someone, as she had described, to love all her own totally and completely. After some thought, she had decided on the best way to share the information with her husband. He had been working on preliminary designs for a new house. She intended on making some suggestions today relating to a nursery with the hope that he might take the hint. He had been working hard on ship orders received after the launch of the English Rose, so she knew he was very pre-occupied with work. She hoped this news would be happy news for Cameron and that he would be as pleased as she about the coming change in their status.

Cameron walked up for dinner to the Manor House and swung Catherine off the third step as was their custom. "You look like you just swallowed the canary Miss Cat. Do you have something to tell me?" Cameron asked with one eyebrow raised.

"What would make you think that Cameron?" Catherine replied smiling innocently.

"Oh, let us say I just have a hunch and of course there is that delightful blush to your cheek and the transparency of your face. I have told you before my love that I know what you are thinking at a glance have I not? I know it is not sun creating that blush as you never go out of the house without your hat," Cameron replied. Busy or not, Catherine thought he never misses a thing.

As they walked to the cottage that evening, Catherine mentioned that with autumn upon them, they would need to carry a torch when they walked to the cottage at night. When they arrived, Catherine asked to see his sketches for the new house. "You see this my love; this is called a *widow's walk*," Cameron stated.

"Oh I do not like the sound of that one bit Cameron," Catherine said frowning.

"No my love, you misunderstand; with this feature you can see me come home for lunch and dinner without checking from one window to the next," Cameron replied grinning.

"And do you think that I go from window to window to watch for your arrival Mr. McCullum? I think that the height of arrogance on your part," Catherine stated haughtily.

"I know this for a fact as I have inside sources you remember?" Cameron responded grinning.

"Hmm; I shall have to have a talk with Mrs. Jones," Catherine replied coolly.

"She only has your best interests at heart my love. She knew your heart before you did and she certainly knew my heart from the first day that I saw you," Cameron responded.

"And what is this room Cameron?" Catherine asked casually.

"That is the nursery my love; why do you ask?" Cameron asked smiling.

"Oh . . . I am just interested in your plans and of course I want to know where everything will be located when the time comes of course," Catherine replied with eyes shining.

"By the time, I assume you mean when our baby is born?" Cameron replied knowingly.

"How did you know Cameron? I have not told a soul!" Catherine asked shocked.

"I notice things love, especially anything related to you. Are you happy Catherine?" Cameron asked tenderly.

"I am so happy Cameron. I think I am about two months pregnant," Catherine replied.

"That would be consistent with my calculations as well," Cameron replied with a knowing smile.

"Your calculations; do I have any secrets?" Catherine asked grinning.

"None at all between you and I; did I not say so from the beginning?" Cameron replied tenderly.

"Yes Cameron you did indeed. You also promised me a book remember?" Catherine responded smiling.

"So I did my love. We shall order one straight away. We need to know everything we will need for the new nursery and the cottage until the new house is built and everything you will need for a healthy delivery. This is another joint project Catherine. You are not alone. I will be there with you every step of the way," Cameron replied.

"I think the midwife may have something to say about every step, Cameron," Catherine responded worriedly.

"Well, maybe not every step of the way, but as far as I am allowed," Cameron replied laughing.

"So, have you noticed any difference in my . . . assets, Cameron? I believe you told me that was one of the signs I could expect," Catherine asked grinning.

"I believe a closer inspection may be necessary Mrs. McCullum. As your husband and your own personal sketch artist I will need to make a closer determination before I can answer. Do you have any more questions about the house my love?" Cameron asked.

"No, Cameron, I do not," Catherine answered smiling.

"Then I propose we retire to the inner chamber Mrs. McCullum. I intend on cherishing my bride and letting her know how happy I am about her news. I love you Catherine. You have made all my dreams come true," Cameron replied.

*****

The next day Catherine shared her news with Mrs. Jones. Mrs. Jones was over the moon with Catherine's baby tidings. "Was the Master happy Mistress?" she asked.

"Oh he was so very pleased. I have been dispatched to meet with the local midwife to gather as much information as I can. Of course Cameron will build any furniture that we will need, like the baby's cot," Catherine replied smiling.

"You will need a birthing chair Mistress. The Master will want to build one for you also. I will have Mrs. Bennett come and meet with you so that you can make a list of everything that you will need," Mrs. Jones replied with authority.

"Thank you so much Mrs. Jones. I know the Master will be pleased also," Catherine replied.

That evening Catherine shared the list with Cameron of everything that she had learned thus far. "You know we will need a cot for the baby but have you ever heard of a birthing chair, Cameron?" Catherine asked wide eyed.

"I have not my love, but if I can see one, I can reproduce it for you," Cameron replied.

"When I meet with Mrs. Bennett I will get our list prepared and ask her about the birthing chair. Perhaps she has one that you can sketch. Why are you smiling Cameron?" Catherine asked.

"I am smiling because we are having conversations about birthing chairs. We are going to be parents Catherine. I will build us a house with room for many children. Can you see our life ahead of us my love?" Cameron asked with shining eyes.

"I can my love and it is not one that I ever expected to live. It is the life that I have chosen Cameron and not one that was foisted upon me and I love it," Catherine said smiling.

CHAPTER EIGHT

1812

With the personal happiness that Cameron and Catherine had enjoyed since their wedding, the wider world of French and British warfare and their affect on the United States and Delaware in particular had taken a back seat for them both. The wider world was about to intervene in a much more real sense in the weeks and months to come. The meeting that had taken place with the Governor and the legislative committee on coastal defenses had resulted in enhancements to Lewes' defenses. The townspeople had not wished to interfere on the happiness of Cameron and Catherine, but the tensions escalating on the national level were soon to have a direct impact on all residents of Lewes.

The townspeople supported by their Governor's initiative had decided a local militia was in order to provide protection to the community. Petitions began for volunteers to place the community on alert if British ships were seen in the Delaware Bay. The town leaders were aware that Catherine was with child and knew that Cameron would want to stay close to home until she delivered their first baby. Attorney Wendell was dispatched to talk to Cameron and brief him on the town's volunteer outreach. They knew as a leader in the community he would wish to participate.

"Cameron we wanted you to be informed of the volunteer watch that the town has begun. We are concerned this business with Great Britain will not end well. We want to be trained and ready. We know Cameron that you will have a blessed event upcoming and we could not be happier for you both. We only hope that once the baby is born that you will be agreeable to joining us Cameron," Attorney Wendell stated gravely.

"You can count on me Mr. Wendell. I will do all I can do to help. I will ask that you keep these concerns for now from

Catherine. I will be sure to brief her on the activities once the baby is born. For now, I will try to keep her calm and contented until the baby has arrived. Thank you again for briefing me on the planned program. I can certainly participate during the day with my volunteer portion of the planned watch," Cameron replied.

Cameron left the Yard uncharacteristically early that day so that he could go and check on Catherine. She was due in May and he was keeping a close eye on her. The midwife had met with Catherine and the birthing chair had been reproduced by Cameron and was presently at the Manor House. Despite his objections to the house and its associations with Van Ressller, Cameron wanted Catherine to have company during the day while he worked. With the short days of winter, the Yard closed early and Cameron was able to leave and watch over his wife.

Mrs. Jones had been insistent that the Mistress should have the baby at the Manor House. She had successfully argued that there were fire places in every room and besides, Mrs. Jones would be there to see after the Mistress and bring the midwife when the time came for the baby to make his appearance.

This ongoing debate was thankfully carried on out of earshot of Catherine. She was so happy about the pregnancy that she walked around with a perpetual smile on her face. Cameron was nearly as bad. His smile had rarely left his face since the previous June when they had been married. As he had promised when he asked for her hand, Catherine was the center of his life. The news of the upcoming birth only enhanced their happiness for them both.

"Hello my love; did you have a good day?" Cameron asked as he swung her from the third step as was their custom.

"I did Cameron. You are home early my love; is anything wrong?" Catherine asked worried.

"You never miss a thing Catherine. How is our little fighter today?" Cameron asked. He placed his hand on her abdomen as he asked the question.

"He is kicking up a storm, Cameron. He will either be a great dancer or a great walker. It will not be long now my love. Everything is ready for the big day. Mrs. Bennett tells me that everything is progressing nicely and on schedule. Along those lines, I need to discuss a strategy with you after dinner," Catherine said with a mischievous grin.

When later Catherine and Cameron were in the cottage for the night, Catherine shared with Cameron the midwife's solution to bringing on labor. "She says that some believe there should not be physical contact between the wife and husband during pregnancy. Her belief is that marital relations should continue unabated to keep the wife, and I am using her terms and not my own, limber and ready for childbirth. She also says that physical intimacy in the last month will help bring on labor. What do you think of that Cameron?" Catherine asked with wide eyes.

"I think that Mrs. Bennett is brilliant my love. The whole scheme has my complete and utter approval. I am still waiting for you to look like you are pregnant however. Other than an enhancement to your assets, you have one tiny bump and that is all," Cameron said grinning and patting her abdomen.

"Mrs. Bennett also says that many times women with child will gain weight the last month of their confinement so we shall see. Why were you home early this evening Cameron? You never leave the Yard early so something must have happened," Catherine asked worriedly.

"I was going to spare you this until after the baby was born, but you know that we do not keep secrets from each other and I obviously could not keep one from you if I tried. You are too smart for your own good Mrs. McCullum," he said smiling. "Come here and let me rub your back while I tell you about my visitation today," Cameron stated.

Catherine settled onto the bed with her back against Cameron so that he could rub her lower back. "Attorney Wendell visited me today at the Yard to tell me that a volunteer militia is being formed from among the townspeople. The goal of the militia will be a community watch to make sure that there are no visitations from a certain foreign power that we do not have prior knowledge of," Cameron stated.

"By a certain foreign power, you are talking about the British navy aren't you?" Catherine replied.

"Yes my love; again, you are too smart for your own good. You know about our trip to Dover and our discussions with the Governor and legislature. Well so far assistance has been forthcoming in the form of militia support. We will need to make sure that as a community we train and prepare ourselves for the possibility of unpleasantness from the British navy. If we are prepared, nothing will come of it. If we are not prepared, one can only guess what could occur. So that was the reason for my early visit to pick up my wife and see her beautiful face and the tiny bump which is our son. You are not to worry. A few of us will volunteer to keep close watch on the Bay and we will prepare ourselves for an event that will never occur, I am sure of it," Cameron replied.

"I hope you are right Cameron. I knew that you would want to volunteer and help the community in whatever way that you could. Please promise me that you will stay safe my love. I cannot raise our son by myself and I cannot live the life I was supposed to live if you are not a part of it," Catherine replied worriedly.

"I told you not to worry and I meant it. All will be well as we are working together to assure that is the case. Now that your back is feeling much better, do you not think we should practice our marital relations my love? I am willing to do my bit to keep my wife limber and ready for the big event. It is the least that I can do as the husband and Father," Cameron said with a wink.

*****

The volunteer community watch gathered on a daily basis to keep watch on the Delaware Bay and to keep abreast of the latest developments on a national level. Cameron had joined with the river pilot's volunteer militia as no one in the community knew the waters better than they. As a community, Lewes had decided that its best defense was preparedness and they took that preparation seriously. The winter months were generally quiet months for conflicts throughout the world, but they were good times to plan, to drill and to start the community program which would take on special importance in the months and years to come.

Cameron played his part in this community effort as he had promised. Because work at the Yard was also slowest in the winter months, he had more time to participate in the daily watches and to drill with the other community volunteers.

Catherine spent her days reading and watching for signs of the upcoming birth. She found it hard to fathom that nearly one year earlier she had landed on these shores against her will to marry a man that she did not know and could not possibly love given his reputation for ruthlessness. As she had told Cameron many times since, her true fate was to meet and fall in love with him and to make Lewes her home both for her husband and for the children that they would bring into the world.

Cameron was considering the purchase of a lot located on Front Street near the canal. His plans for the house were also a winter month project as he continued to modify the designs with input from Catherine and from the latest publications that they ordered from London. This house would be a labor of love for them both. Catherine continued to focus on 1813 as the year that she could sell real estate and plan for the future home that they would build together. Her 1812 project was the upcoming birth.

*****

At last the great day dawned. Catherine had awoken to cramping which she thought might be the start of labor based upon Mrs. Bennett's predictions and the books that she had read throughout her confinement. She did not tell Cameron although his assistance she believed had brought about the start of labor just as they had discussed and as he had so willingly volunteered. He had taken to walking with her to the Manor House each morning as he did not want her to fall in her last month of pregnancy. She decided to keep her suspicions to herself until she had more proof that today was the day her son would come into the world.

When she arrived at the Manor House she informed Mrs. Jones that she might be starting her labor. Mrs. Jones insisted on contacting the midwife and in having the Mistress eat as much breakfast as she was able because she would need her energy and strength to bring the young Master into the world. Catherine had especially requested that Cameron not be informed until they were sure that the labor was not false labor as she did not want him to worry unnecessarily. Catherine also knew that Cameron was insistent that he wanted to assist her in any way possible during her labors and she knew that they might meet with resistance from the midwife and Mrs. Jones as Cameron's plans were revealed. Catherine decided to sit in front of the fire in the kitchen and enjoy the remaining peace before the house exploded with activity.

Her labor seemed to be primarily focused in her back for now and she knew that one of Cameron's back rubs would not come amiss. He had given them to her throughout her confinement and she longed for one now. She still was concerned about pulling him from his work until she knew for sure so said nothing knowing that Cameron would soon be home for lunch and she could then make him aware that this was the day that their son would make his appearance.

When Mrs. Jones arrived with the midwife, they both insisted that she go upstairs to her old room and prepare for the labor. She wanted to walk as long as she could and the midwife was an advocate of that plan. That was positive as Catherine did not want to become a prisoner of the bed or of the birthing chair until absolutely necessary.

When the labor continued until the noon hour, Mrs. Jones knew that the Master would not be far behind for his daily luncheon. She decided to greet him at the door so that he would not be concerned that Catherine was not at her usual location when he arrived. Mrs. Jones had pulled together a quick meal between her visits to the Mistress' room to make sure that the Master had his meal while he waited. She knew him well enough to know that he would not be returning to the Yard until his son made an appearance in the world. As if on cue, the Master arrived at the door at five minutes past noon. When Mrs. Jones greeted him at the door, he made quick work of the steps and was at Catherine's side in a matter of seconds.

"Master McCullum, I do not allow Fathers in my delivery rooms if you please. You must know the protocol that will be followed. You will be called when the baby has arrived and all are ready for your inspection and not until then," Mrs. Bennett stated haughtily.

"Mrs. Bennett, although I appreciate your supervision of the birth and of all things related, the lady in question is my wife. I have sworn to be at her side through all things as we are partners in life and in business. I will be happy to walk with the Mistress while she continues her labors and to rub her back as I have done for the nine months of her confinement. You have my promise that I will vacate the birthing room when her labors become necessary for her to take her place in the birthing chair. Until then Madame, I expect to stay at my wife's side as I have planned from the beginning," Cameron responded adamantly.

Mrs. Bennett appeared shocked by that speech and relented only slightly on her earlier demand. She was adamant that the Father was to wash his hands if he was to be in close contact with her patient and must leave as soon as the labor was at its most critical. She also advised him that not all patients liked to be touched in her experience and that Mistress Catherine may wish to be left quite alone.

Catherine weighed in at that moment and asked that Cameron be allowed to walk with her and to rub her back as he knew exactly where she had been vexed during her pregnancy and how much pressure to apply. Cameron gave his wife and the midwife his widest and most gallant smile, bowed to Mrs. Bennett and proceeded to walk the long hallway with Catherine, stopping only to rub her back when the pain would come to her. "I believe a nice warm bath would relax you my love," Cameron interjected.

"I do not know if it is allowed Cameron. But it would be lovely," Catherine replied smiling bravely.

"I will ask Mrs. Bennett," Cameron replied. He hurried into Catherine's room to consult.

"I have never heard the like of it Master. Who would give birth in a pool of water?" Mrs. Bennett replied horrified.

"With respect, I am not talking about giving birth; I am talking about the warm water relaxing Catherine so that she would be more comfortable giving birth," Cameron replied. "My wife takes an evening bath every night and has found relief from the back ache that has vexed her with the warmth of the waters. I am only asking to determine if we can achieve the same relaxation whilst she waits for the birth," Cameron stated adamantly.

"I will check Mrs. McCullum and render my opinion after she is examined," Mrs. Bennett replied haughtily.

Catherine was brought into her old room, the door closed promptly on Cameron and the examination completed. After completing her examination, the midwife agreed to the warm bath to relax Catherine's back muscles. At last Cameron had a mission in this process. He hurriedly went to the kitchen, warmed sufficient water and brought containers of warm water to fill the bathtub for Catherine to enjoy in front of the fire. He even brought her lavender soap, a pile of towels and her chemise and robe for after the bath. For his troubles, he was shown the door again by Mrs. Bennett, but at least he knew that he had assisted Catherine in finding some relaxation while the labor continued.

When she had completed her bath, Cameron continued his hallway long walks with Catherine. The relief on Catherine's face was payment enough for his battle with the midwife. He would make a note of this suggestion for the next baby when that time came.

By dinner time, the labor had increased to the point that Cameron was sent from the second floor to wait in the library. He followed the same practice of many expectant Fathers pacing the floor and consuming ample supplies of the house whiskey while his wife labored above stairs. He knew that she was in good hands, and a very healthy young woman, but his heart told him that he did not want to contemplate a life without Catherine in it. Although they had not yet been married a full year, Catherine was the center of his life as he had told her she would be. The baby would only add to that joy, but his time alone was a time of worry about the fate of both his wife and the new baby.

After what seemed like a lifetime to Cameron, Mrs. Jones came to the library door with her apron at her eyes. He knew her well enough to know that this meant good news and that she was crying happy tears. She was the first to tell him that he was a Father and that he had a healthy boy just as the

Mistress had predicted. He had to wait until both baby and the Mistress were ready for visitors, but both had come through the delivery unscathed although the Mistress was very tired. When Mrs. Bennett as the sergeant major of the labor room advised that the Master could come above stairs again, Cameron took the stairs two at a time to greet Catherine and the new baby.

Catherine was lying in the curtained bed looking too beautiful for one who had just given birth. Her face held the wonder of her confinement coupled with the joy of the new life in her arms. When she saw Cameron, her smile was from ear to ear. "Cameron, my love, you are a Father and we have a beautiful new baby boy," Catherine said smiling. Cameron sat on the bed beside her and marveled at the new life in Catherine's arms.

"So this is the tiny pugilist who has been kicking his Mother for months? Oh, well done Catherine. He is a fine wee lad indeed," Cameron replied smiling.

"I think he looks just like you Cameron," Catherine replied. "He is small yet but he has the whole world to grow in," Catherine replied with shining eyes.

"How can he look like anyone, my love; he has just been born?" Cameron replied laughing with the release of the day's tension.

"Oh no Cameron, he looks just like you. He may be little now, but he won't stay that way for long. He will be just as tall as his Father," Catherine replied with shining eyes.

"I love you so much Catherine. You have done so well at everything that you have taken on my darling girl. I am so very proud of you," Cameron stated. He kissed her on the forehead then and picked up one tiny hand of his new son. The baby's finger curled around his Father's large, callused finger. Cameron beamed from ear to ear.

"You see; he already knows his Father. What shall we name him my love?" Catherine asked smiling.

"I was thinking James for my Father. What was your Father's name Catherine?" Cameron asked.

"My Father's name was William; James William McCullum; that sounds like a beautiful name Cameron. What do you think?" Catherine asked.

"I think it a fine name my love. Are you alright? Are you in any pain?" Cameron asked worriedly.

"So long as you are here with me; I am fine. The bath was heavenly my love. It was just what I needed. Thank you so much for fighting for me," Catherine replied.

"Did you want me to stay with you darling girl?" Cameron asked tenderly.

"I know how you feel about this house darling, but I have never been parted from you since we married. If you do not feel comfortable sleeping here in this bed, we could move the mattress down next to the fire and sleep there all together. What do you think?" Catherine asked.

"I want you to get your rest and I want to be close by in case the baby needs us. I will make an exception for tonight," Cameron replied tenderly.

"Did you know that this was the guest room Cameron? It was not Mr. Van Ressller's room; that was further down the hall. I do not know if that changes anything in your mind, but I wanted you to know. Mrs. Jones told me today," Catherine replied searching his face with her eyes.

"That does change things, my love. But the important thing is keeping you warm and keeping little James William McCullum warm and safe. That is all that matters," Cameron replied.

"Thank you so much for suggesting the warm bath. It did help immensely. The back rubs were wonderful also. I am sorry you had to fight so just to be part of the baby's arrival. You were wonderful though; firm but fair as always. I am so glad you were here through most of the delivery," Catherine stated smiling.

"Was it terrible my love?" Cameron asked worriedly.

"I just kept focused on the baby and seeing your face when you first saw him. I knew it would be a boy and I was right," Catherine replied.

"We have so many wonderful memories in store for us my love. Can I get you anything? I am going to go and pack a bag from the cottage and will be back before you know I am gone," Cameron stated.

"No thank you Cameron. I have everything that I need here in my arms and in this room with me," Catherine stated smiling.

Cameron floated down the stairs and into the kitchen to tell Mrs. Jones that he was packing a bag to stay the night. "You know that the Mistress' room was the guest room Master. In case you did not know that, I wanted to make sure you know now. I understand your feelings about Mr. Van Ressller and the Mistress and I understand why you have those feelings," Mrs. Jones replied firmly.

"Thank you Mrs. Jones. Catherine told me the same. I just want her and little Jamie to be safe and warm. That is my only concern. I will take care of them with my life; I hope that you know that. I can swallow my pride for one night or as many as it takes to keep them both safe and warm," Cameron replied.

"That is spoken like a true Father. Congratulations Master. The Mistress did a wonderful job at one more thing that she has undertaken," Mrs. Jones stated proudly.

"You are correct about that Mrs. Jones. This has been her biggest production to date. I will be back shortly. I am packing a bag to stay the night," Cameron replied.

Catherine made herself comfortable in the canopied bed, content in the fact that Cameron would shortly return to her and together they would spend their first night with their new baby. James was swaddled and comfortable sleeping in his Mother's arms. Catherine stated over and over that she could not believe that she could be as happy as she had been on her wedding day and yet with the addition of their little Jamie to their world, her happiness was now even greater.

Cameron returned to the cottage and thought about all of the changes that had occurred in their life in one short day. He had been lost in thought about the joy that Catherine had brought to him. During those hours when he was alone in the library his only thought was that Catherine would have a healthy delivery and return to him happy and healthy. What a difference one short year had made in his life. He decided as he gathered a bag to stay at the Manor House that his family would remain there for as long as was needed. He did not want to be selfish any longer in his resistance to the Manor House. He wanted Catherine safe and comfortable and more than anything he wanted Jamie to be safe and warm. He could swallow his pride and stay in the Manor House with trips to the cottage on Saturday nights and Sundays. He needed to place Catherine's needs and those of the baby's before his own. They could remain at the Manor House until their new house was completed and then he, Catherine and the baby could move into the new house. He must not forget Mrs. Jones as well. He needed her to understand that she was a part of their new life as she had been a major part in the courtship, marriage and now their new life as parents. He would relay all of this to Catherine in the morning but for now, he needed to let her rest, regain her strength and prepare for their next adventure.

When he returned to the Manor House, he quickly went upstairs and removed the now sleeping Jamie from his Mother's arms. She was sleeping as was the baby. He placed Jamie in his bassinette and covered Catherine as she slept. He knew from experience that she was always cold and he needed to make sure that he kept her safe and warm. He tended the fire before unpacking his bag and settling in for the night. There was much to commend in the Manor House and he was glad that he had arrived at his decision for them to remain here until the new house was built. He wondered again at the nature of fate that had brought him first to this new country and now to the Manor House in Lewes, Delaware. Here he had met the love of his life and here they had started their business and now their family. In the months and years ahead he would remember this moment and how everything that he had ever wanted had presented itself in one very special place and with one very special woman.

Cameron released the bed hangings around them and in so doing created their own private world. The bed as it turned out was also quite large, it looked smaller only because the rich canopy and bed curtains. With the bed hangings loose around them, they were in their own private world again. Cameron took Catherine into his arms and held her while she slept, the exhaustion and worry of the day bringing release to them both.

As promised, the next day Cameron relayed to Catherine his plans for the Manor House and for the family. She at first was reluctant thinking that he had only reached this decision because he thought her somehow dissatisfied with their magical cottage as she called it. "Oh no, not at all my love. It was one thing when you could walk back to the Manor House in the morning. Then when you became pregnant; I started to worry about you walking back in the morning and possibly falling with our precious boy. Now, well I see that I was just being selfish Catherine. You need to be warm and safe as does Jamie. I cannot have you carrying him back here every morning worrying about all of his supplies. What if the weather is bad or what if you were to fall or a dozen other what ifs? I am responsible for you and for our Jamie. I need to know that you are both safe and warm each day when I leave for the Yard and I know that Mrs. Jones is always here to look after you both and to get word to me if either of you should need something," Cameron replied passionately.

"I just do not want you to think that you need to do this because I cannot manage. You know that I can manage Cameron. I have learned so much in the past year and can manage so much more than I ever could in the past," Catherine replied.

"Of course you can manage my love! Have you not just achieved your finest accomplishment to date? Just look at our perfect son and how you look far too beautiful to have just given birth. Not one bit of it Catherine; this has nothing to do with you not being able to manage. This is just me being practical and wanting nothing more than my family to be comfortable until I can build you the house of your dreams," Cameron said holding Catherine.

"I know Mrs. Jones will be pleased. She will love nothing more than being able to spoil our Jamie. I can see that already Cameron. It will be a lovely life Cameron wherever we live. It makes no difference to me. I just want to be with you and with Jamie in our lovely life," Catherine said smiling.

"Good; it is settled now and we can always go to the magical cottage on Saturday night and Sunday night; assuming of course that the weather is fit," Cameron replied.

*****

Six weeks from Jamie's birth, the christening was scheduled. That date also coincided with the first year anniversary of Cameron and Catherine. Catherine came down the stairs that morning holding Jamie. She was dressed in a new lilac silk dress with an ivory bonnet with an ivory veil and matching gloves. Cameron thought she looked very much like a bride which was fitting as today was their wedding anniversary. "Are you ready my love? You look as beautiful as a bride you know," Cameron said proudly.

"I am ready Cameron and thank you for the lovely compliment." Catherine held Jamie proudly and they left the Manor House heading for St. Peter's. Catherine continued to hold Jamie in the church with the smile of the Madonna on her face. Now that Jamie was in the pew, they alternated holding the Prayer Book and holding Jamie. Jamie's small head was covered in the cap that Catherine had crocheted for him, his christening gown made by Mrs. Jones. Beneath the christening cap was the same reddish brown hair of his Father, his eyes the same sunny blue color and as Catherine had predicted, he was the image of his Father. His ears were like tiny perfect shells, so pink and delicate that Catherine could stare at them for hours. He rested now on Catherine's chest as if he had been there his entire six week life.

Cameron's steady gaze now took in the beauty of his wife and the great gift of Jamie added to their life. When called by the Reverend Clayborne, Catherine, Cameron and Mrs. Jones rose to the front of the church and the now sleeping Jamie slept through the entire procedure right until his christening cap was removed and the christening itself commenced at the baptismal font. His eyes opened quickly when he felt the water of the baptism on his head and just as quickly Reverend Clayborne returned him to his Mother who placed her little finger into his mouth, ending his anticipated cry. His blue eyes opened widely and he looked up at his adoring Mother and smiled for the first time. Mrs. Jones had her hankie to her eyes and Cameron smiled as the proud Father of the tableau. The congregation quietly applauded and the group resumed their seats in the Van Ressller pew.

One year before they had walked down this same aisle, Catherine to her Cameron, pledging their troth. One year later, wee Jamie was christened as a representation of that same love.

When they returned to the house, Catherine put Jamie in the dining room cot while they ate their luncheon. She took him back in her arms as soon as they had finished the meal. "I will take him up now and get him settled Cameron," Catherine said smiling.

Mrs. Jones came in to clear the table and shook her head with disapproval at the departing Catherine. "The Mistress will spoil the lad Master. He should be left to cry himself to sleep when it is his nap time," she stated with authority.

Cameron smiled then undisturbed by the criticism. "I reckon it is the same with all new Mothers Mrs. Jones. She loves the wee lad so very much," Cameron said wistfully.

"Aye Master, she is a fierce Mother," Mrs. Jones added.

Fierce Cameron thought smiling; and she as tiny as a wee girl. Before joining her upstairs, he went outside then and into the garden to cut a lilac bough for their room. It was a reminder of their wedding and of their one year anniversary.

Cameron came into the nursery where he found Catherine rocking the now sleeping Jamie. His little eyes were blinking closed as she looked down at his dear face.

"So I hear there has been a kerfuffle about the rocking of our wee Jamie. Spoiling him are you now lass?" Cameron asked smiling.

"He is so young Cameron and he sleeps so well when I rock him. I cannot bear to hear him cry all alone in his little cot. It is a very frightening thing to come into a new world all on one's own," she said looking again at his sleeping face.

"Aye lass; I ken it well," he replied knowing she spoke of herself as well as Jamie.

"Besides, he will not be small for long Cameron. He will be as tall as his Father one day," she said with shining eyes.

"And he has a fierce wee Mama to fight for him," Cameron said smiling, "one who does not come to my shoulder," he said chuckling softly.

"That is only because you are unnaturally tall," she responded back with mischief in her eyes.

"Unnatural is it?" he retorted with one eyebrow raised.

"Well magnificently tall then," she replied smiling.

"You know the lilacs are in bloom again my love," Cameron said quietly.

"And it is our wedding anniversary. Can you believe that so much has happened in one short year Cameron?" Catherine replied smiling.

"I have cut some lilac blooms for our room Catherine. When we have put down the wee Jamie for his nap, I have things I would say to you my love," he said softly.

"I have things I would say to you as well Cameron," Catherine replied softly.

Cameron stood then and took the now sleeping Jamie from her arms, kissed him on the forehead and laid him gently in his cot. He tenderly pulled up the light blanket and patted his stomach, the look of total, unconditional love now on his face in the process. He turned then and taking her hand, led her to their room; her hand around his waist, and his around hers. Their anniversary and Jamie's christening all in one day and the lilacs the symbol of their wedding day and all that had gone before this day.

When they returned to their room, Cameron closed the door. Catherine walked over to her dresser and took off her jewelry and turned to Cameron.

"Are you well my love?" Cameron asked.

"I am right as rain Cameron; thank you for asking," she replied softly.

"And . . . all is well then Catherine? You have been assured that it is so? I would not have you hurt in anyway," he asked worriedly.

"Oh yes Cameron; all is well, you must not worry. It has been six weeks now my love since Jamie's birth and all is well," Catherine said beaming. "Am I . . . much altered in the past year Cameron?" she asked worriedly.

"Oh yes my love but not in the way that I think you mean. You have the beauty that comes from being cherished by now two generations of McCullum men. And you have the assurance that your course is the right one in the raising of young Jamie. Do not let anyone sway you on what you know to be the right course my love in this and all things. Jamie knows he is cherished and he responds accordingly. You know you are cherished and it shines in your eyes. I thought last year when we married that I could not possibly love you more than I did when I saw you come down the aisle to me. I was wrong Catherine. When I saw you today in the pew holding our wee Jamie to you, I said, I love her more every day," Cameron replied tenderly.

"That is just what I thought Cameron. Seeing you hold our own darling Jamie I thought; how could I love him more than I did last June and yet here I am, loving you more and wanting you more because I understand it all so much more do I not my love? I understand the joy of having the love of my life beside me in the pew at church and in the dining room each day . . . and now in my bed," she said shyly.

He went to her then and put her face in his hands and then reached up and took out the pins from her hair. She turned her back to him and he unlaced her new dress carefully, and pulled it over her head. He went to the bed and pulled the coverings back. She stood in her shift, looking slightly shy since they had not shared intimacy since Jamie's birth. Cameron sat on the side of the bed removing his boots. He reached out his hand to her. Catherine came to him and pulled the shirt from his breeches, and sitting on his lap, kissed his neck and shoulders. "Oh lass, what you do to me when you kiss me like that," he said softly. She unloosened the bed hangings then and lay across him.

"Our own little world Cameron; safe from the rest of the world; you, me and Jamie, but you and I first Cameron; always you and I," she said quietly.

"Happy anniversary Catherine; thank you for my wonderful life," Cameron said kissing her deeply.

"And thank you for mine Cameron my love and for my beautiful lilacs," she said smiling. They spent the afternoon together and the carefully rocked Jamie slept until dinner.

CHAPTER NINE

The decision by Cameron to relocate his family to the Manor House could not have been made at a better time. Later the same month of June, the country had again been plunged into war with Great Britain. The War of 1812 which was declared on June 18, 1812 had significant repercussions for the coastal states and the safety of Delaware's residents was again called into question. The militia from the state had taken up residence in Lewes along with the local volunteers who continued to keep watch over the Bay awaiting the sighting of any British ships of war. At first Cameron and Catherine were concerned that their shipbuilding business would be negatively affected by the war. In reality the demand for ships grew at a far greater pace than ever before. Merchants were outfitting their mercantile ships as privateer ships in the absence of a competitive United States Naval presence. Cameron saw orders for ship construction that far outstripped his Yard's size and personnel. An additional twenty men were added to the operation to assure that the demand for ship construction and outfitting could be met. In order to assure that Cameron could stay focused on the design and construction end of their business, Catherine volunteered to take over the accounting portion of the business which she offered to complete from the library of the Manor House.

"I worry that you will be overdoing my love by this new undertaking," Cameron stated worriedly.

"Nonsense Cameron; I shall have my little Jamie here beside me in his little cot and I can keep all of the accounts for the business as well as keeping payroll going for you. If I am able to complete these functions for you, we shall have more time together and with the baby. You simply cannot work day and night and accomplish all of your other goals and commitments my love. I need to be able to see you some part of the day if only to tell you how much I love you and to make sure that you are getting your necessary meals and rest," Catherine replied smiling.

"So you are telling me that this offer to complete the accounts for the business is to assure that we have time together? Is that the motivation my love?" Cameron asked with eyes shining.

"Of course my love; I can easily accommodate these functions along with the household accounts and relieve you of this burden. We have no idea how long this horrid war may continue Cameron. I simply cannot have you working day and night and have no chance to see you or for you to see the baby. He will be growing before your eyes and you will not have the chance to see it my love," Catherine replied passionately. "Besides, how will we ever find the time to expand our family if I never have the chance to see my husband," she replied mischievously.

"As always my love, you find the ideal argument to confirm your position. I bow to your excellent intellect. The opportunity to expand our family is an ideal argument for your latest venture Mrs. McCullum. How could a gentleman deny such an argument to such a beautiful lady? I am a thrice blessed man with a bonny wife, a bonny son and a growing business. If we are to endure this horrid war as you call it, at least it is with the knowledge that our business will not suffer," Cameron replied.

"Excellent my love; I will start with the business accounts straight away. If there are any other tasks that I can assume for you, I will be only too happy to do so. Mrs. Jones takes such excellent care of the house and the kitchen. I can take care of our lovely boy and the business accounts as well. That way we are truly working together in partnership in the business my love," Catherine said smiling.

"Capital idea Mrs. McCullum. I shall have time to devote to the business and the volunteer militia work as well as ensuring time for the expansion of our family," Cameron said with a wink.

*****

The anticipated first sighting of British warships in the Delaware Bay was a daily cause of concern for all in the community. Cameron was thankful yet again for his decision that Catherine and Jamie spend all of their time in the Manor House. It was a sturdy residence and the constant movement back and forth from the cottage needed to cease while the war continued. Cameron would take no chances with the safety of his young family. He had the always nagging worry that one of the British warships could carry members of the British aristocracy who would be known to Catherine. Although he did not share his concerns with Catherine, the letter from her uncle had remained uppermost in his mind since its first receipt. The thought of a plan to abduct Catherine and return her to her uncle was a nagging fear that haunted him. If the British Navy was flagrant in its impressments of men into their fleet, then it followed that members of the British aristocracy would have no qualms in kidnapping the niece of a baronet should her whereabouts become known. Besides that fear was the knowledge that one of her uncle's planned suitors for Catherine was Captain Sir John Beresford. Should he receive word of Catherine's whereabouts, anything was possible.

The work on the ships at the Yard was now doubled by the second crew brought to work on the expanding list of orders. The privateer ships had proven their value to the syndicate owners and Cameron had an impressive list of back orders for new ships and the outfitting of current mercantile ships. Catherine was as good as her word and completed all accounts for the business freeing Cameron for time to complete his volunteer militia work and to spend time with his family which was always a great joy to him.

On returning home from the shipyard one day, he had a proposition that he wanted to share with Catherine. One of the new crew members taken on to complete orders had approached him about buying the cottage and Cameron was considering the offer now that they were nearly permanently located at the Manor House.

"Catherine, one of the new lads approached me today about purchasing the cottage. I wanted to discuss the suggestion with you and obtain your thoughts my love," Cameron asked tentatively.

"Well Cameron, it is true that it has been a special place for us both, but to have two houses within blocks of one another is hardly practical. I know that I did not grow up in a practical household Cameron, but I try to be very frugal in my expenditures as I am sure you have noted," Catherine said proudly.

"I thought only Scots had a reputation for frugality my love, but yes, I certainly see your point. Having two houses within blocks of one another particularly when we only use the cottage on Saturdays and Sundays does not seem practical. As the family grows, we will certainly not fit into the cottage much longer," Cameron replied.

"Besides my love, if we build the new house some day, we certainly will not need three houses in one town. In the meantime, if we need to build an addition onto this house for additional rooms for the children, we can certainly do so," Catherine replied smiling.

"So are we expecting to need additional room for children yet?" Cameron replied with eyes shining.

"Not at this moment no but I certainly would expect more children. I was an only child and I know how lonely that existence was for me. You were an only child and well, I would love to give Jamie brothers and sisters in the future," Catherine said smiling.

"So would I my love. I am glad that we are of a similar opinion on that topic as well," Cameron said smiling. "So it appears that we are of one mind on this suggestion as we are about most items," Cameron replied.

"I know that we will need to pack up your remaining items. May we have a last visit there Cameron; I mean you, Jamie and me; may we spend one last visit there?" Catherine asked.

"Of course my love; it is where our marriage began after all. I may need to take some additional sketches of my favorite subject whilst there. The light is outstanding for that purpose you know," Cameron said grinning.

"Would your favorite subject be me or Jamie?" she asked with mischief in her eyes.

"My favorite subject will always be my first subject and that is you Catherine my love," Cameron said kissing the top of her head. She placed her arms around his waist and thought with joy of the final visit that she would plan for the three of them.

That Saturday afternoon all three headed to the cottage. Catherine had packed for herself and Jamie and thought that she could always return to the house again if she needed any additional supplies for Jamie. Cameron carried Jamie's little cot so they were ready for the visit.

When they arrived, Catherine became immediately wistful of the place where they had spent their wedding night and so many other blissful nights together. She placed her packed items in the changing area that Cameron had created for her. So many memories she thought and all of them wonderful because they were shared with Cameron.

"I never told you the story about the decorative screen and our wedding night did I?" Cameron asked with mischief in his eyes.

"No you did not my love. I know that you designed it for me as I remember you telling me that. But I do not remember you telling me a story about it," Catherine replied. She had placed Jamie on the bed while Cameron made himself comfortable stretched out beside him. She was seated next to him on the edge of the bed.

"Well it seems that my design had one flaw, or at least a potential flaw; from the viewpoint of the viewer, it was perfect. When you lit the candles on our wedding night, the screen very vividly displayed your silhouette on the other side. I did not mean to intrude upon your privacy, but the screen that I had so carefully designed had that very effect," he said grinning.

"And you never told me this fact until now?" she said with her dark blue eyes growing darker by the moment.

"I did not my love but I thought it only fair to share that fact with you as this would be the final time that we would be spending the night in the cottage." He had by this time taken her hand and was very lovingly caressing the back of it as he spoke.

"I see Cameron; well, I suppose as soon as I put Jamie down for the night, I will start preparing for bed shall I?" she asked holding his gaze. "And I will be lighting candles Cameron as I prepare for bed, behind the screen that you so very carefully designed for me. I thought I would let you know that my love," she said grabbing up Jamie and looking at him with the same look of mischief.

"I appreciate the information my love. I will then very hurriedly prepare for bed in the front room and return here to wait for you while you prepare for bed shall I?" he said grinning up at her.

Saturday night was so blissful for them both that they decided against going to church on Sunday morning. They slept in and spent the entire day together as a family, leaving only to take a walk to the Yard and down Front Street in the summer sun. It was a wonderful visit for the three of them and Cameron though practical in his resolve to sell the cottage, also felt the same wistfulness that they would not spend similar visits in the future.

*****

A second letter from her uncle was received by Catherine the following week. As she had done previously, she did not open the letter until Cameron's return to the Manor House for luncheon. She had the customary feelings of fear in seeing the stationary and seal of her uncle. She was amazed that he had not written before, but wondered if the war had created the delay. When Cameron returned from the Yard at luncheon, she asked him to step into the library before they began.

"What is it my love? Is Jamie ill?" Cameron asked worriedly.

"Oh no my love; Jamie is as bonny as ever. No Cameron, I have received another letter from my uncle. I wanted you to be by my side when I opened it," Catherine said worriedly.

"Of course my love; let us open it together. You know my opinion on the last letter and I will not have relented one bit. Let us see what he has to say to you this time," Cameron replied.

"Dearest Catherine:

I am mystified by your apparent disregard for family commitments. I have waited anxiously for word from you regarding the passing of your husband Mr. Hans Van Ressller. As I cannot fathom an emotional attachment to the man, Lewes, or to America, I can only assume that my first letter did not arrive to your attention. The war has now intervened and I fear that you may need to remain in America until its conclusion. Trust that I continue to work in your best interests. I continue my communication with many suitors of your past knowledge including Captain Sir John Beresford who has been dispatched to the Americas until the conclusion of this latest unpleasantness. I request that you write at your earliest convenience to assure receipt of this letter and your intention to return to London as soon as safe passage can be arranged for you. Let me assure you that your beauty and refinement will mark you for a marriage of distinction. You are in no way tainted by your association with the Americans of your acquaintance.

I anxiously await your response to my latest correspondence. May God keep you until I am able to arrange your expeditious return to these shores and to the arms of your family.

I am your devoted uncle,

Jonathan Wentworth, Baronet"

"The man has no qualms to send you to America and then to request your immediate return so long as a union benefits him. He is simply appalling Catherine and if I had the misfortune to meet him personally, I would call him out for what he did to you. Again Catherine, my advice to you is to destroy this letter as we did the last one. Your uncle lost all privilege of your company and regard when he sent you in a ship to cross the Atlantic in order to resolve a gambling debt. His hold on you has ended Catherine. You are cherished and adored by your husband and by all of your acquaintance. Think no more of it my love as I assure you that I will have no thought to your uncle or his continued plans for your re-marriage," Cameron said heatedly. "Now my love, again to luncheon and then I believe we will take a stroll through the gardens after luncheon. I would like to show you my plans for the planting of a rose garden in your honor. You will always be my English Rose Catherine. What do you think of that idea?" Cameron said smiling and gathering Catherine in his arms. The letter was placed in the fire grate as had the previous letter from Catherine's uncle.

*****

The first sighting of British warships in the Atlantic off the coast of Lewes was a cause of alarm to the community as a whole and to Cameron in particular. He had kept his ongoing concerns to himself regarding Captain Sir John Beresford. Although he knew from Catherine's letter that the Captain was in the Atlantic, he also knew that the Atlantic was a large body of water and the chances that he would be in the same part of the world as Cameron and Catherine was remote indeed. By the spring of 1813, his concerns would become magnified.

January of 1813 brought more news of a private nature for Catherine and Cameron. Catherine had discovered that she was expecting again and expected the happy event to occur in September. 1813 was also the year in which she was allowed to divest herself of real estate under the terms of Hans Van Ressller's estate. Cameron's recommendation was that they wait for the end of the war as he would still need to build them a house to replace the Manor House and the work at the shipyard coupled with his volunteer work with the militia had prevented that design and construction from continuing. He also believed given the uncertainty of their world that a delay in those plans would best be served until the war was over. The horrid war as Catherine had called it had resulted in a full blockade of the states of the Eastern seaboard at the present time. Cameron began each day with the sick fear that one of the ships of the blockade could hold Captain Sir John Beresford. By March, his worst fears were realized.

Attorney Wendell came to the shipyard unexpectedly on a cold damp day in March 1813. "How may I help you

Attorney Wendell. Has something happened that requires my attention?" Cameron asked worriedly.

"The Town has received a letter from a British captain Cameron. I have a copy here as the original has been sent onto the Governor for his response. We believe that a parlay of peace may be in order. This British Captain is demanding supplies from the Town of Lewes. We simply do not have the stores needed given the state of the blockade. Our fear is what will occur if we do not comply with his demands," Mr. Wendell stated worriedly.

"May I see the letter Mr. Wendell?" Cameron asked anxiously.

"Certainly Cameron; we thought perhaps a parlay meeting here in the shipyard would be appropriate as soon as the Governor can join us of course. We do not have meeting space large enough in the town and thought that yours would be a good head to assist in the negotiations as well," Mr. Wendell stated worriedly.

Cameron was provided the letter and read through the list of demands made by the British.

March 16, 1813

"His Britannic Majesty's Ship Poitiers in the Mouth of the Delaware

The letter was addressed to the first magistrate of the town of Lewes:

Sir:

As soon as you receive this, I must request you will send twenty live bullocks with a proportionate quantity of vegetables and hay for the use of his Britannic Majesty's squadron, now at this anchorage, to be immediately paid for at the Philadelphia prices. If you refuse to comply with this request, I shall be under the necessity of destroying your town.

I have the honor to be, Sir Your obedient servant

J Beresford, Commodore Commanding the British Squadron in the Mouth of the Delaware"

Should the town submit to these demands, there was no way of knowing how many other ships would make similar demands upon the town and its resources. Cameron knew that his advice was to deny the request and take the chances that the militia would be here in sufficient numbers to address whatever was to follow. It was only when he read the name at the bottom of the letter that he had cold chills. The letter had been sent by none other than Captain Sir John Beresford of His Majesty's Royal Navy. There could be no other. This was the same Captain Sir John Beresford who had sought out Catherine's uncle repeatedly for her hand in marriage. Cameron's worst nightmares were coming home to him. His first thought was to deny the Attorney's request for a meeting at the shipyard. His second thought was to do anything possible to keep Catherine safe and to keep her out of the clutches of a man who could easily demand her return to England with a warship to back up that demand.

"Of course Mr. Wendell; a meeting of parlay with representatives of this ship will be in order. You may feel free to hold the meeting here of course. Please let me know when you wish this to occur and we will try to hide all evidence of our ongoing work here at the shipyard. It would not do for the enemy to see the number of ships that are being commissioned and outfitted to come against His Majesty's Navy. In fact, a meeting under cover of darkness may be the best thing for all concerned," Cameron added worriedly.

"Very good Cameron; I will advise the other members of the Town Council and we will prepare accordingly as soon as we learn of the Governor's schedule. We are asked to give a response to this letter which is being prepared by the Governor's staff. After that I think the best response will be to suggest the meeting that you have graciously agreed to host. That way we will have more time to prepare and to hopefully move more militia into place as well as to have the Governor here to see the condition of things on the ground," Mr. Wendell stated anxiously.

"Very well Mr. Wendell. I will prepare the Yard accordingly and prepare our men to cover all work that we currently have in progress or move those ships that are seaworthy out to an undisclosed location," Cameron added.

On his return to the Manor House at luncheon, his mind was racing with thoughts for Catherine and Jamie's safety. He felt that he could not keep this secret from Catherine as they had always shared each of their concerns. It was bound to come out anyway with a presence of British navy men coming into town. He was not sure if Captain Sir John Beresford would come himself as part of this parlay or if a representative would be sent. Regardless, he needed to make sure that Mrs. Jones and Catherine were on high alert and kept out of sight for the duration of the crisis. The weather at least meant that Catherine would not be out and about as was her custom in the gardens of the Manor House. He needed to make sure that she was inside throughout the upcoming days.

When Cameron arrived at the Manor House, he knew that his worries would show on his face. He was correct about that assumption. "My love; what has happened?" Catherine asked worriedly when she and Jamie met him at their customary third step on the front stairway.

"You will want to put down the baby my love. I need to talk to you about something that has happened and the potential implications to us both," Cameron said worriedly.

"Let us go into luncheon Cameron. All is ready and you look as though you could do with a strong whiskey. You can tell me after luncheon my love. All will be better after you have eaten and given yourself a strong drink," Catherine replied worriedly. Cameron kissed her then and laid a hand and a kiss on Jamie's small head. He looked up at his Father then as if even he could sense the tension in the air.

The threesome went into luncheon and Catherine placed Jamie in his customary high chair for luncheon. The three sat in silence relieved only by Mrs. Jones' visits to the dining room between courses. When at last luncheon had concluded and Cameron had had two strong whiskies, Catherine laid Jamie down for his nap and joined Cameron in the library. She went immediately to his side as he sat beside the fire.

"What is it my love; what has happened?" Catherine asked worriedly.

"I have had a visit by Attorney Wendell this morning Catherine. It seems the town has received a letter from a British warship and the attached squadron under its command. There is a written demand for supplies my love and a threat which now hangs over the town. I have been asked to host a meeting of parlay between the town representatives, the Governor and representatives of the British warship," Cameron replied anxiously.

"Should we just give them the supplies that they need Cameron in the hope that they will just go away?" Catherine asked worriedly.

"If only it were that simple my love. If the demands of this warship are met, how are we to deny the demands of the next warship and so on and so on until the town is bereft of supplies? If the blockade continues to tighten my love, the town could be without food. There is much more Catherine which I have not yet told you," Cameron said worriedly.

"What is it Cameron? You know that we do not keep secrets from each other. I do not want you to carry these worries alone," Catherine replied anxiously.

"The officer who wrote the letter Catherine and who is making these demands is none other than Captain Sir John Beresford. You will remember that name no doubt from your uncle's letters," Cameron replied searching her face intently.

"Good Lord Cameron! He is here in these waters?" Catherine replied anxiously.

"Yes I fear so my love. He is here in these waters and is now making demands of the very town where you are found Catherine," Cameron replied. His worry was palatable now as he knew that he could no longer keep his long held fears from her. Should this officer get it into his head to abduct Catherine and return her to England, everything that they had built during the past two years would be lost. Cameron's worry must have shown on his face at that moment.

"Cameron, if the town would wish me to meet with him personally and to reason with him, I am sure that he would not do anything to harm anyone here if for no other reason than my long ago association with him and that of my uncle's of course," Catherine offered tentatively.

"I cannot take that risk my love. Were he to know that you were here . . . I have never shared my fears with you Catherine on these very points. I thought it highly unlikely that he of all officers would find himself in these very waters so close to where you are . . . but I cannot take that risk Catherine. I cannot take the risk that you would be carried away from Jamie and from me. And now with the new baby on the way, I simply cannot take that chance Catherine. I believe our plan is sound. We will meet with Captain Beresford or his representatives at the shipyard. I have already advised Attorney Wendell that the meeting must take place under cover of darkness as I would not wish any of His Majesty's navy to see the number of ships under construction nor the number that are being outfitted as privateers. We will cover that work to the extent possible, move everything seaworthy to an undisclosed location and let darkness cover the rest. We will attempt to reason with them as business men and explain that it is simply not possible for our small town to outfit every warship that comes into these waters. We will have the militia here and we will continue to keep the Governor apprised of the threat. He himself will be responding to the letter and will be here at his earliest convenience for the parlay. Surely he will also be keeping Mr. Madison informed as well. We are not that far from the nation's capital my love. Security must be paramount at this time for all concerned," Cameron replied.

"Of course Cameron; you are right of course. My only thought was for the safety of the town as a whole. You are quite correct about the baby however. I could not do anything that would risk our new little one and I simply could not live without you and Jamie. I will make sure that we stay hidden here at the Manor House Cameron. I will not go out until this matter is sorted. Please hold me now my love. I find that I am shaking at the thought of your very real fears Cameron. I need to feel your strong arms around me," Catherine said looking up at him.

Cameron pulled Catherine onto his lap and held her, stroking her back and kissing the top of her head. "We will weather this newest threat my love. We just need to keep security uppermost in our minds. Thank the Lord we decided to stay here in the Manor House. This is a sturdy house with many rooms. You will have rooms to choose from Catherine until this whole sorry affair is over and done with. I am so sorry that you need to stay cooped up inside, but at least the weather has not yet broken so you will not be tempted by beautiful weather to venture outside into the gardens. Please know that I love you more than anything in the world Catherine. I will not let anything happen to you or to our little family. I too could not live without you Catherine. We will see to this matter and return to our life my love, you will see. Come kiss me my love and let me kiss you. I feel I need to hold you every bit as much as you need to be held," Cameron said huskily. The two sat beside the fire for the remainder of the afternoon. If Cameron was to return to the shipyard and his worries, he needed to be buoyed by the love of his wife and son in the interval.

*****

Attorney Wendell provided word to Cameron that the Governor was responding to the letter as anticipated and that they would be told of the date of the meeting to coincide with the Governor's visit to Lewes to oversee defense preparations. Cameron thought then about his visit to Dover with Catherine and how the concerns expressed then had borne fruit. They had all hoped that confrontation could be avoided, but they had planned for it and now they needed to place those plans in action.

The Governor responded to the letter by Captain Sir John Beresford on March 23rd

"Sir:

As Governor of the State of Delaware and as Commander of its military force, I improve the earliest time afforded me, since my arrival at this place, of acknowledging the receipt of your letter of the 16th instance, directed to the chief magistrate of Lewes. The respect which generous and magnanimous nations, even when they are enemies, take pride in cherishing towards each other, enjoins it upon me as a duty I owe to the State over which I have the honor at this time to preside, to the government of which this State is a member, and to the civilized world, to inquire of you whether upon further and more mature reflection, you continue resolved to attempt the destruction of this town. I shall probably this evening receive your reply to the present communication, and your determination of executing or relinquishing the demand mentioned in your letter of the 16th instance. If that demand is still insisted upon, I have only to observe to you that a compliance would be an immediate violation of the laws of my country and an eternal stigma on the nation of which I am a citizen; a compliance therefore cannot be acceded to."

Attorney Wendell brought a copy of the letter received by the Town Council to Cameron's office for his review. "The Governor is here now and has provided this Beresford fellow with his reply. This letter is a copy for our records. I assume upon receipt by the British navy we will be informed of the time for the planned parlay. It appears that such diplomatic overtures typically involve an initial demand, a response, a counter demand and then hopefully peaceful resolution. If not Cameron, we may have to put into practice the very emergency plans that we have been preparing since the outset of the war," Attorney Wendell said worriedly.

Cameron reviewed the Governor's letter and smiled at the comment *upon more mature reflection.* "Did the Governor assume then that the Captain wrote the letter in a fit of pique and upon more mature reflection would change his mind?" Cameron asked.

"I noticed the same term Cameron and hopefully Captain Beresford will not be offended by that term of art. I have learned in discussing the matter further with the Governor and with Colonel Davis of the militia that there is an Article 56 of the Articles of War which states that whosoever shall relieve the enemy with money, victuals, or ammunition, or shall knowingly harbor or protect an enemy, shall suffer death, or such punishment as shall be ordered by the sentence of a court martial. Good Lord Cameron, the man had to know that we could not violate these Articles without finding ourselves in mortal danger under a court martial proceeding. Perhaps that was the reason to the reference upon more mature reflection in the Governor's letter. Perhaps the Governor believes the request was made in a fit of pique as you say or perhaps more correctly in a fit of hunger if their supplies are so severely reduced," Attorney Wendell stated.

"We shall continue to be vigilant Thomas as we have very little alternative at this point until one side or the other blinks. I do not see the American side doing so as from what you have told me, we would violate Articles of War if we were so inclined and I know from our prior conversations that we are not. Certainly the Town's objection to outfitting each and every warship that happens into these waters is also a sound point. We have neither the population nor the wherewithal to do so and would certainly not do anything that would provide succor to our enemies," Cameron stated heatedly.

"You are quite right as always Cameron, quite right. I am going to show the Governor our defenses to date along with Colonel Davis of course and then I will keep you apprised of our suggested parlay date and time as matters move forward," Attorney Wendell stated.

"Thank you Thomas; I will keep praying that an alternative presents itself in the meantime," Cameron replied.

That night Cameron briefed Catherine again on the ongoing dilemma. "Certainly Cameron the man must see sense. We cannot take action that would be contrary to the Articles of War. Why the Governor himself would be in violation if he bowed to such demands," Catherine said worriedly.

"I fear it is just another example of saber rattling my love and in this case, the Captain may be surprised at the resolve of the State to deny the request. We will stay focused on a positive resolution as it is not in our hands my love," Cameron said wearily.

The next day Cameron learned of the response to the Governor's letter which was quick in coming. Upon receipt, Beresford had sent his reply.

"In reply to your letter received today, by a flag of truce, in answer to mine of the 16th instance, I have to observe, that the demand I made upon Lewistown is, in my opinion, neither ungenerous nor wanting in that magnanimity which one nation ought to observe with another with which it is at war. It is in my power to destroy your town, and the request I have made upon it, as the price of its security, is neither distressing nor unusual. I must therefore persist, and whatever sufferings may fall upon the inhabitants of Lewes must be attributed to yourselves by not complying with a request so easily acquiesced in."

The letter from the Governor had been responded to and there was no budging on the part of the British. If anything, the tensions were increased in the receipt of the reply by Captain Sir John Beresford.

Colonel Davis had the unfortunate task of informing the Governor and the town officials that Beresford was not backing down and that in fact an attack appeared imminent. Colonel Davis wrote:

"This evening the Belvidere and two small vessels came close into Lewes and commenced an attack by firing several thirty-two pound shot into the town, which have been picked up; after which a flag was sent, to which the following reply was returned:"

"Sir,

In reply to the renewal of your demand, with the addition for a supply of water, I have to inform you, that neither can be complied with. This, too, you must be sensible of;

therefore I must insist the attack on the inhabitants of this town is both wanton and cruel.

I have the honor to be your most obedient servant

S.B. Davis, Colonel Commandant"

The initial shots of the attack had apparently been one last attempt at intimidation of the residents of Lewes and all concerned by the British.

One final attempt at mediation was attempted in the planned meeting of parlay scheduled for that evening at 7:00 p.m. Cover of darkness would mean that not all of the work at the Yard would need to be removed for the anticipated parlay. There was no moon which further assisted in the necessary camouflage. Mr. Wendell stated that Captain Sir John Beresford was not expected at the meeting personally. He would be represented instead by his executive officer on the HMS Poitiers. That piece of news was welcomed by both Catherine and Cameron. "If it is not he himself Cameron, I know you will be able to keep calm and reason with the gentleman. You are quite correct when you say that we cannot possibly outfit every warship that happens into these waters. Were that to occur, we would find it impossible to get through the year and as you pointed out, what about the next ship and the one after that? Why it would never end and we could not possibly keep all of them outfitted. Good Lord, when will this horrid war ever end? Can they not see that they cannot keep their supply lines open with this amount of distance? It is the exact problem that they encountered during the War of American Independence and look how that ended? Besides, how can they expect to be at war with America and France at the same time? It is simply madness," Catherine stated pacing.

"My love, you must promise me that you will try to keep yourself calm. I know that the worry is ever present, but I cannot have you placing your own health and the health of the baby in jeopardy. Please promise me you will try to stay calm for all of our sakes," Cameron asked pleadingly.

"I will my love of course for your sake and for the baby's sake of course. Perhaps Mrs. Jones can give me a task in the kitchen that will keep my hands busy or perhaps I can work at the accounts. That always helps me to remain calm," Catherine said smiling bravely.

"I believe that we both need to go above stairs Catherine. I think we need to find something to occupy both our minds until this evening. Come my love; let me give you one of my back rubs. That will help you relax," Cameron said with a weak smile.

"I do not believe my back has yet vexed me Cameron, but I also think one of your famous back rubs would be just the thing right now. Perhaps we can find something else to relax us as well my love," Catherine said smiling.

*****

That evening as planned, the anticipated meeting between the Lewes Town Council, the Governor and Captain R. Byron representing the Commodore Beresford was scheduled to occur. The Town Council members and Governor had met the prior day and they had compiled their points of argument in defense of a final denial of the letter of demand. As they had eloquently stated, it was simply not possible for a town Lewes' size to meet the demands of every British warship in these waters. Were that to occur along with the shortages caused by the blockade, the city would run out of supplies and be woefully short for the next winter. The outfitting of every British vessel in the vicinity would be ruinous to the community. It was also pointed out that one war had been fought against such high handed treatment on the part of His

Majesty's government. They hoped to refrain from that argument if at all possible. Lastly the violation of the Articles of War was the most compelling of all arguments.

Cameron decided to keep a muted approach to his involvement in the meeting. He was serving as the host and the ongoing work of the Yard had been camouflaged or relocated to the extent possible so that the British contingent would be unable to see the ongoing work to both construct new merchant ships and to outfit existing ships as privateers. It was not prudent for the enemy to see the number of ships that were being prepared to come against His Majesty's Navy.

Captain R. Byron would represent Captain Sir John Beresford in the planned parlay. The Governor and Town Council hoped to explain reason to His Majesty's representative without creating unnecessary anger over the main points. The stage was set for the meeting.

While Cameron prepared himself at the Manor House for dinner he was clearly focused only on the upcoming meeting. He only absently kissed Jamie's head when he was presented by Catherine. She could see the strain on Cameron's face and hated the thought that she was one of the causes of the added stress. "My love you simply must put all such thoughts from your mind. You are the innocent pawn in your uncle's game as we have discussed on numerous occasions. You had no part in his ongoing marriage negotiations for you and the endless intrigues for your hand. My worry focuses not only on the impact to you, but the very real impact to the town as a whole. I feel there is no further option for us and I feel my hands are tied by this whole situation," Cameron stated dejectedly.

"Your thought process is sound on this matter my love as is the town's as a whole. We can only hope that the additional militia sent by the Governor will be sufficient to the task," Catherine replied worriedly.

THE ENGLISH ROSE

*****

At last the planned parlay with Captain Byron was upon them. Cameron had determined that he would take a very quiet approach during the meeting. Although his sentiments were well known by the Governor and members of the Town Council, he did not wish to inflame the situation further with his very real concerns about the central party in this negotiation; Captain Sir John Beresford. Captain Byron arrived under a flag of truce and was extremely gentlemanly in his behavior and was warmly welcomed by the Governor and Town Council along with his small detachment of men who served as escorts to the meeting. Governor Haslet took the lead in the opening salvos of discussion.

"Captain Byron I am your servant sir; I have been asked to speak on behalf of all concerned in the matter of your requested supply letter. While we are cognizant of the very real issues of supplying warships at such a distance from Great Britain, we must also ask that you understand we are unable to supply every British ship which comes into our waters. Were that to occur, the coast would shortly be bereft of supplies. The tightening of the blockade by His Majesty's Navy only makes that possibility more likely," Governor Haslet stated.

"In addition sir as I am sure you are aware, aiding and abetting the enemy in a time of war is contrary to the Articles of War. I as Governor cannot act in a way contrary to the very standards established by our federal government for the conduct of such wars. We fear that we must respectfully deny the request by Captain Sir John Beresford for the needed supplies," Governor Haslet stated.

Captain Byron listened attentively to Governor Haslet's argument. "Whilst I understand your position, Your Excellency, I am sure that you must appreciate the need for a navy to keep supplied. Our men must have the necessary foodstuffs in order to survive. We are too far from England to meet our needs and they must be met by the locals that we encounter. You mention the blockade sir. The blockade is there for a reason and that reason is the ongoing misunderstanding of the proper place of the United States of America in the global stage. It is essential that the provisions be provided or else you and many like you could very well be speaking French in the near future. You may not regard His Majesty's Navy as a service, but our very presence in these and other waters assures that English interests are protected wherever the flag flies," Captain Byron replied.

Cameron had an immediate response to the question of English interests, but had agreed at the beginning of the parlay to keep his own private concerns quiet. He was providing the meeting place and he had given his support to the Governor and Town Council's position. He had committed himself to the fact that his own views would remain mum during this conversation for his sake and for Catherine's.

"Again Captain Byron, although we have great respect for you and for the important role that you play in His Majesty's Navy, I must remind you that the American people fought a war to assure that American interests were uppermost in these and other waters and not the interests of His Majesty's government. Although we hold many of the same democratic ideals, obviously we cannot be compelled to supply each and every warship which enters these waters. Were we to do so, the needs of our own citizens would suffer. Since we are duly elected to protect the needs of the people of Lewes and the State as a whole, our focus must be to protect them first. Again sir, let me state with respect that we are unable to comply with the demands of your Captain and must respectfully decline the request for supplies," Governor Haslet stated firmly.

"I must then assume sir that we are at an impasse. If our ship is unable to secure the supplies needed by our men, then Captain Beresford will have no choice but to fulfill his ultimatum. You can expect bombardment of the Town of Lewes within twenty-four hours as a certainty sir. On that point, the Captain is firm in his position," Captain Byron replied.

All of the parties involved in the parlay stood at that moment. The Governor had been seated behind Cameron's desk during the discussion. As he arose from his desk, his hand accidently knocked to the floor the miniature of Catherine taken during the year of her debut into society. The miniature fell at the feet of Captain Byron who picking it up from the floor, gazed at it before returning it to its original location.

"Sir, I must inquire where this copy of the miniature was obtained. I have seen only one other and it rests on the desk of Captain Sir John Beresford himself. The lady rendered in this miniature is the intended of Captain Sir John Beresford. Again sir, I demand to know who gave leave for this miniature to be exhibited on this desk," Captain Byron stated heatedly.

Cameron stood at that moment. He had the Captain by at least one foot in height and nearly six inches at the shoulder. His hands were outstretched for return of the miniature, and the look on his face had taken on an ominous appearance. The Captain had unwittingly used the one word that was like a red flag in front of a bull where Cameron was concerned. No one had given him leave to exhibit the painting; he exhibited the miniature of his wife in his own office at his own bidding and no other.

"Sir, I respectfully request the return of the miniature in your hand. The miniature is of my wife Catherine and I was not given leave to exhibit it, I exhibit it as her husband married nearly two years to the lady in question. Again sir, I request the return of my property immediately," Cameron said calmly but firmly.

Captain Byron became visibly white at the tone, towering height and statement by Cameron. The Governor and members of the Town Council moved one step away from the Captain who continued to hold the miniature of Catherine in his hand. "This changes everything sir. Not only has this town seen fit to deny our request provided in a gentlemanly manner, you hold captive in this town the niece of a baronet. I can only assume she is captive against her will. My Captain will hear of this outrage and your town will be given no quarter in the bombardment that will follow. That I can guarantee sir," Byron replied heatedly.

"Again sir, I respectfully request the return of the miniature in your hand," Cameron repeated. He had not taken his gaze from the Captain since making his first request. The Captain reluctantly returned the miniature to Cameron's outstretched hand and then retaining his dignity, turned to move towards the door to join the remainder of his men waiting for the conclusion of the meeting.

At that moment Cameron let out the sigh that he had been holding in for the past hour. The Governor and members of the Town Council looked at Cameron and saw the weight of both this meeting and the secret that he had withheld throughout the negotiations. Not only was the town under the threat of attack, Cameron personally had the fear that Catherine continued in danger so long as Captain Sir John Beresford held control of the British warships lying beyond the town in Delaware waters.

"Cameron we had no idea. Tell us what we can do to assist you in keeping Catherine safe," Attorney Wendell stated.

"I have advised her to keep to the house so long as these issues remain outstanding. I have feared from the outset that this Captain Sir John Beresford could threaten Catherine given his associations with her uncle and his repeated efforts to negotiate for her hand in marriage. I can only look to divine intervention to help us all at this juncture," Cameron said wearily.

The Governor and members of the Lewes Town Council thanked him then for his hospitality and left Cameron's shipyard offices shortly thereafter. Cameron closed and locked the office door and set off in the night for the Manor House. Unless he was very much mistaken, bombardment of Lewes was imminent. He hated the fact that he must now return to Catherine and give her the grim news which every member of the Town would soon be privy to. His only hope was to look to the almighty to keep the town safe and all of its inhabitants. At this juncture, not only did he intend on advising Catherine and Mrs. Jones to keep to the house, he would request that they stay above stairs until this horrible business was at an end.

As he returned to the Manor House, Catherine had been waiting for his return. She came from the library and placed her arms around her husband's waist. One look at his face told her everything that she needed to know. "Will it be bombardment then Cameron?" Catherine asked anxiously.

"I fear so my love; I am very sorry to tell you that we can expect a siege of the town within twenty-four hours. Our mission has failed but we can see no other compromise that can be met. We must defend the long term needs of the town and we cannot give in to His Majesty's Navy each and every time that a demand for supplies is made. In addition, we simply cannot defy the orders of the federal government under the Articles of War. We cannot give aid to our enemies in the time of war. I would like to meet with you and Mrs. Jones if you will be so kind. I want to make sure that you have all of the supplies that you need here in the house. I want you both to be as safe as possible until this horrible business is at an end," Cameron said wearily.

"I will go get her my love and then you can talk to both of us and share your concerns and thoughts," Catherine replied anxiously.

Within minutes, Catherine and Mrs. Jones were gathered in the library. Cameron had poured himself a whiskey and was pacing when they arrived. "I wanted to talk to you both at the same time and let you know what we can expect for the next day or so. We believe that Lewes will be under bombardment in short order. I would request that you both stay above stairs once the shelling begins. Whatever food stuffs that you may need should be taken with you so that you can remain above stairs for the duration of the attack. Once the siege begins, I will join the militia and we will do our utmost to assure the safety of the town and all of the citizens throughout the bombardment. I ask that you both stay in the house at all times and we will all continue to pray for the safety of the town and all of its citizenry. We are now in God's hands until this misery is at an end," Cameron said gravely.

Catherine and Mrs. Jones looked at each other and they all dropped to their knees to pray for the safety of the town and all of its citizens. Mrs. Jones stated that she would return to the kitchen and prepare sandwiches for the Master and for the whole family so that they would have sufficient food to withstand the length of the bombardment. Thoughts of invasion were uppermost in all of their minds, but they also remembered the presence of the militia in their midst and the private militia of concerned citizens who had joined to watch the bay and any ships coming into these waters. They all prayed that it would be enough to keep their town safe.

One final piece of correspondence was received following the parlay from the British contingent. It was addressed to S. B. Davis, Esquire, Colonel Commandant:

"No dishonor can be attached in complying with the demand of Sir John Beresford to Lewes in consideration of

his superior force. I must, therefore, consider your refusal to supply the squadron with water, and the cattle that the neighborhood affords, most cruel, upon your part, to its inhabitants. I grieve for the distress the women and children are reduced to by your conduct, and earnestly desire that they may be instantly removed.

P.S. The cattle will be honorably paid for."

The letter was received by Colonel Davis who responded that the ladies had been taken care of by the militia.

The attack immediately commenced upon delivery of the final correspondence by Captain R. Byron.

CHAPTER TEN

The family was wakened to the sound of the bombardment. The threat by Captain Sir John Beresford had come to pass and they could only hope that divine intervention and the support of the state's militia would be sufficient to keep the town and its citizens safe. As soon as he heard the sound, Cameron was up and preparing to join the men of the town. Catherine was awake and helping him to make sure that he had all of his equipment and food to carry with him. She said not a word, but her eyes told him all. She had told him the prior day when they had made love that she could not lead the life she was intended to lead without him. She brought a sleeping Jamie from his bed so that Cameron could kiss them both goodbye. He held them tightly to his chest and then he was gone having made her promise that she would stay above stairs as she had agreed to previously.

Mrs. Jones had stayed in another of the guest rooms the previous night so that she too would be above stairs as soon as the bombardment began. She came to the door just as Cameron was leaving and waved goodbye. Catherine and she exchanged glances and proceeded to dress to meet the day. Little Jamie went back to sleep which Catherine regarded as a blessing. If he could remain unaware of the kerfuffle during the day, it would help her to remain calm as well. She had her household to be concerned about as well as the new baby growing inside of her. She had to remain strong for everyone now until Cameron's safe return.

Mrs. Jones and she took their breakfast in front of the fire in the room used by Catherine and Cameron. They spoke in hushed tones hoping against hope that Jamie would sleep as long as possible. It would be a very long day indeed.

*****

Cameron met the men of the town and took directions from the officers of the militia. They were prepared for the siege and for any possible invasion that could occur of the town. The militia cannon were pointed in the direction of the HMS Poitiers and they scanned the horizon hoping for the best. All had the same haggard look of worry for the families that they had just left behind. Not having the knowledge and experience of the professional soldiers, their only thought was protecting the town and their families and the hope that they would live to see the night and the next morning.

To date, the cannon fire that had been sent from the HMS Poitiers had hit nothing but the waters of the canal. They did not know if the ship would change position during the day and with that the location of the cannon fire. They only knew that they would take the bombardment one hour at a time and the defense of the town in the same manner. Trenches were dug in the park area which had once been the scene of the spring dance that Cameron had organized before Catherine and he were married. Each area of the town now brought on a special significance to him as so many happy memories permeated each space. Cameron wondered then if he should have sent Catherine, Jamie and Mrs. Jones to St. Peters to wait out the attack. But what if a church was one of the first places overtaken by an attacking army? Wouldn't there be worse risk of capture in a gathering place such as a church? What if he should have sent them on the road toward Dover? So many what ifs and yet, the fate of them all was in the hands of one beyond their midst. The fate of all was now in the hands of God.

*****

Catherine and Mrs. Jones both did their best to keep Jamie entertained after he had woken for the morning. He looked from one face to the other and must have thought it strange that his Mother and Mrs. Jones were both on the floor playing with him. The two central parties in his life were always busy with accounts or with cleaning the house or making meals. Today they were both on the floor in Mama and Da's room and they were both playing with him and keeping him contented. Fortunately, that contentment was working as neither Catherine nor Mrs. Jones knew what they would have done had he experienced a fussy day and the bombardment continued. Their nerves were already stretched to the breaking point and the day was but a few hours long. They both decided when Jamie went down for his nap that they too would try to lay across the beds and rest. They knew that sleep was not in the offing, but rest would be welcome if only the shelling would stop and the endless sound of the cannon would cease.

*****

Cameron and the members of militia were proud of the fact that they had stayed cool in the face of the siege and imminent attack. Only one cannonball had hit a target thus far and it was a house not far from the park. The Rowland house and its current occupants were with Cameron and the other men that day. Gilbert McCracken and his son Henry were river pilots swelling the number of volunteer militia that day and had the misfortune to see their house hit. The cannonball had landed in the house and had not exploded. Cameron was thankful at that moment that the lot that he had considered purchasing near the canal had not yet been transferred into their ownership. This day's work had made him reconsider purchasing any property in close proximity to the canal. The risk was now too great that a warship would arrive on one's doorstep and do untold damage to property and the occupants. The thought of Captain Sir John Beresford or his men on the doorstep of the Manor House was an image that would haunt Cameron for the remainder of the siege. Be brave my love, he thought hourly as he considered his little family as he referred to them. Dear Jamie; his first born son and now the new little one still carried by his Mother. He had many blessings from the moment that he first arrived in Lewes. Today they all would be sorely tested, but he would never disavow his love for America and for Lewes and for the love of his life; his Catherine. Their family would continue to grow God willing and he wanted to be here to see it. Focus Cameron on the work ahead and on the days ahead and not the madness of the moment as he watched his town under siege.

*****

Catherine and Mrs. Jones both laid down when Jamie took his nap. As Mrs. Jones reminded Catherine, she must remain strong, but she must also take care of herself for Master Cameron's sake, little Jamie's sake and the sake of the baby that she carried. The strain on an expectant Mother was more than should be borne, but Catherine was determined that they would all three come through this experience strong and be even more reliant on the values of this country and of the life that they had chosen to live here. Catherine's thoughts returned again and again to Captain Sir John Beresford in the waters off the coast of Lewes. Surely a man responsible for his ship and crew and two other warships, would not risk placing his men against a militia and a volunteer militia set to defend the town. He would have no idea where she was located and would need to search house by house in order to find her. Her mind continued to be haunted by the needs of

Jamie and the fact that she was now with child again. Would a man risk all for the sake of a woman who had no claim of affection upon him? Catherine's mind raced at the many what ifs. How could she go on without Cameron and Jamie and how could she give birth to her second son in a land that was no longer her own? Rest Catherine; rest is what you need. Your mind will continue to race to possibilities that you cannot control and that you can only imagine. Rest your mind and your body for the return of the love of your life to his home and family when this terrible attack is over at last.

*****

The siege continued, but the town had experienced neither damage nor injury to the militia or volunteers. The officers were of the opinion that the bombardment was part of a strategy to intimidate the locals to reconsider their decision to outfit the HMS Poitiers and other ships of the fleet with the requested supplies. They were of the belief that an invasion if one were to occur, would have happened by now. In addition, the bombardment fell well short of its true goal; the buildings and occupants of the Town of Lewes. All homes along the canal had been abandoned and the residents sent to St. Peter's for the duration of the attack. Cameron was glad again that he advised Catherine and Mrs. Jones to stay in place at the Manor House. It was a fine home, sturdily built and Catherine and Jamie could remain as comfortable as possible on a day in which their home town was under siege. Cameron's primary thought throughout the bombardment remained the safety of Catherine, Jamie, and Mrs. Jones and of course the new baby. Please Lord, let them remain safe and let the siege be the worst that they have to offer the town. Let any plans for invasion pass us by.

*****

Jamie slept well beyond his usual nap time and Mrs. Jones and Catherine were stretched out in their respective rooms to try to rest.

They both knew that sleeping was beyond question so long as the relentless sound of cannonballs being propelled to the town from the HMS Poitiers was taking place. They did have the chance to at least rest their legs and backs and to try to rest their minds. For Catherine, the rest of her mind was the most impossible task of the day. She laid on the bed remembering every memory shared with Cameron from the first day that he arrived at the Manor House; handsome, provocative, charming and outrageous with his head to toe examinations of her person that she found so maddening at the time and yet so characteristic of Cameron's character once she came to know him. He was attracted to her like a magnet to metal from the very first and made no apologies for it. She was the one who had to be convinced of his true worth. She had been so cold and aloof to him and why, she asked herself now; because he didn't have a title or an estate and would not be considered a *catch* in the view of the aristocracy of her uncle?

In reality he was the most honest, straight forward, lovable man that she had ever met. One did not ask Cameron McCullum a question unless one expected an honest answer. He would work his fingers to the bone for something that he believed in like this town and this country and the life that he shared with Catherine. He was the only man who had ever encouraged her to share her true beliefs and insights and oh how they had verbally fenced when first they met. That was also testament to the fact that she had done her level best to keep him at arm's length, all the while denying her true growing feelings for him.

Could she ever forget that day when the infamous French gown had sent him into a rage and an instantaneous attraction that he could not deny both at the same time? From the moment that he kissed her that day for the first time, all of her resistance became futile. She knew that she had been pushing him away for months on end and that kiss told her the true feelings that she held for Cameron McCullum. After that, she wanted nothing more than to be the wife of the man that she could not wait to see each day, the man that every woman wanted and that only she would possess.

Had she told him that she loved him enough times? Lying on the bed and thinking of him in harm's way, her first thought was of telling him that she loved him and that she wanted to spend every day with him for the rest of her life. And what about dear Jamie; the thought of being separated from her dear boy for one moment gave her such alarm that she had to calm herself if for no other reason than the sake of the new baby that she carried even now; the second son conceived of her love for Cameron.

So many thoughts crowded through her mind on that horrible day, but each memory of her time in Lewes centered on Cameron and the joy that he had brought to her life. Returning to a life of emptiness and loneliness; her former life in London was now so unthinkable as to seem like another world. She could not wait to see Cameron again so that she could tell him all of these things and so that she knew he was safe once again, in her arms and back with his family where he belonged.

*****

By mid-afternoon, the officers of the militia were of the opinion that the bombardment could not last much longer. For one thing, the ship was bound to expend their supplies of cannon shot in short order. For another, the ship had not changed its location and all cannon fire to date had fallen well short of its intended target; the center of the Town of

Lewes. Whether the reason was a stand of trees that blocked the view of the gunners or the range of the cannons, Cameron was encouraged by the talk of the military men who knew and understood such things. As for him, he was there in support of his town and to defend the woman he loved, but warfare was not his occupation. He wanted nothing more than to return to the shipyard and continue outfitting the privateers who were beginning to make a dent in the pride of the British Navy. America may not have a truly competitive Navy at this point, but it had ingenuity and pluck. He considered himself part of that vast array of ingenuity which had thus far kept the greatest Navy in the world at bay while boasting very few fighting men and even fewer sailing vessels. So long as the supply lines of the British continued to be interrupted by the privateer ships, they had a true chance against the greatest military known in the world of 1813. If only the British would return back to their own sphere of influence and allow the Americans to chart their own destiny he thought. He hoped by the time that wee Jamie was a grown man America would be able to stand on its own two feet and look any country of the world in the eye and not blink.

He remembered the night of the parlay and the outrage on the face of Captain Byron when Cameron had defied him and his charge that Cameron did not have leave to exhibit a miniature of his own beloved wife on his own desk in his own office. That type of arrogance would be the downfall of the British Empire he was sure. He remembered the anger that he felt at that moment and was relieved that the Town Council members were close at hand to prevent the violence that he felt for the Captain who after all merely stood in place of his true nemesis, Captain Sir John Beresford. The thought of Catherine in the hands of Beresford was more than he could stomach and the memory of that outrage fueled his appearance today with the militia. Lord let them be safe was his constant prayer of the day.

*****

By dusk, both Catherine and Mrs. Jones were of the opinion that the bombardment could not long continue. They had seen no flames nor heard any sound of volunteers out dealing with fires. In fact they had heard no one out during the course of the day at all and seen no one out of their homes. Perhaps the residents of the town were as frightened as they and only hunkered down waiting for the horrible shelling to end.

Wee Jamie as Cameron called him, was as fit as a fiddle and had not cried all day long. He seemed to revel in the fact that both of his caregivers were spending the day on the floor with him and was only too happy to move from one to the other to be kissed and held and generally loved. Why they were all above stairs for the day as a whole was something that he had not grasped, but he was happy for the playmates and the chance to have his Mother's undivided attention for an entire day.

As the long shadows of evening began to stretch, Catherine hoped that Cameron would soon be home and that she could have the chance to tell him all of the things that she had been thinking about during this long day of absence. She was used to seeing him at least once during the day when he came home for lunch, but of course this was no normal day either for her or for the people of Lewes. Lord let him be safe and let him come home to us soon, Catherine thought.

*****

By the next morning, after the endless darkness of night, the continual shelling ended as quickly as it had begun. Cameron stayed at the site for as long as the militia viewed it necessary. With the suspension of the siege, the civilians were released to return to their homes. The lads from the Yard who had remained with the company for the full twenty-four hours of bombardment were released as well. Cameron told them to go home and spend time with their families and take a well deserved rest. He would get word to them if there was any change but otherwise would see them on the following day. On the way down Front Street to the Manor House, he stopped by the shipyard and saw everything in the same condition that he had left it when they departed the ill fated parlay that had ended in the twenty-four hour bombardment of the town.

His weary steps led him from the Yard to the Manor House, his family and to refuge. He was exhausted, but felt so blessed that he was alive, the town saved from this invasion at least and that Catherine, Jamie and the baby were safe.

He arrived at the door of the Manor House and Catherine opened the door, throwing herself into his arms. "Thank the Lord Cameron," Catherine said crying. She had her arms around his waist and held him sobbing. "Thank the Lord that you are safe," she said through her tears.

"Hush now lass; you know you must not upset yourself like this. You must think of the new baby. I am fine my love; just tired and hungry," he said kissing the top of her head.

"I am so sorry Cameron, come in and let us fix you breakfast and whatever else you may need," Catherine said smiling weakly. "Mrs. Jones," Catherine called out, "the Master is home," Catherine said again through tears.

"Let me wash my face and hands Catherine," Cameron said smiling. "Then I will be back and you can cover the table with food as I haven't eaten since yesterday morning," Cameron said laughing.

Catherine went to the kitchen, tears still in her eyes. "He is safe Mrs. Jones and home with us again," Catherine said smiling. "I think he may eat everything we can place on the table," Catherine continued laughing now through her tears.

Catherine and Mrs. Jones worked together to create a banquet for their conquering hero, a scene no doubt played out in houses throughout Lewes on this day. Cameron returned to the dining room and took his son from his high chair and placed him on his knee. To see his dear face again after the worry of the past twenty-four hours was a joy so great that he was rendered speechless. He kissed his dear head and held him to his chest in gratitude. Jamie placed his chubby arms around his Da's neck and Cameron drank in his baby scent and his strong little form. Catherine came back into the dining room then carrying eggs and cider with the promise of more food to follow. She kissed Cameron's forehead as she passed and ruffled the baby's hair. Jamie looked on in blissful ignorance of the fear and anxiety shared by his parents for over twenty-four hours during the town's siege.

More food followed; bacon, sausage, homemade bread; all good things started as soon as the bombardment had come to an end. They sat down as a family and Cameron took Catherine's hand and gave the blessing for the meal, for the safety of all the militia, volunteers and the Governor and for the safety of the town and its occupants.

After they had eaten, Catherine asked Cameron to tell her all that had occurred at the canal and all that he had seen over the past twenty-four hours. Cameron, clearly tired, gave her a brief summary of events. She knew he needed to talk more, but did not press him as she also knew he needed rest and escape from the past day's events.

"Would you like a nice hot bath my love to help you relax and sleep?" Catherine asked.

"That would be wonderful Catherine; thank you. I think the last day's events have kept me going up to this point, but I am just beginning to feel the effects now," Cameron stated wearily.

"We will heat the water for you my love. You will not be going to the Yard today will you?" Catherine asked anxiously.

"Oh no my love; I have told the lads to spend today with their families. We all need to take a day to spend with those who matter the most to us. Our efforts to outfit the privateers can take one day's rest," Cameron continued.

Once heated, Cameron carried up the containers of water and filled the bath in front of the fire in their room. Catherine came in behind him planning on pampering him to the extent possible. She had already laid Jamie down for his nap, so her full attention would be directed to Cameron.

"I plan on spoiling you today my love so prepare yourself for a day acknowledging your hero status," Catherine stated smiling.

"I am not a hero Catherine; only a man who did my part to assist the town in its time of need." After seeing her dejected face he then added, "However, I am very happy to be pampered by my beautiful wife and spend the day with her as I rest from the past twenty-four hours. Would you like to rest with me? It would be very beneficial to the baby, do you not think?" Cameron said with a wink.

"I think it would indeed be beneficial to us both. Would you like me to wash your back?" she said smiling mischievously. "And then perhaps I could give you your shave while you bathe. You always mention my sensitive skin . . . so I thought you might like a shave as well," she said smiling with mischief.

Cameron eased into the bathtub, letting the warm waters wash away the aches of the past day's anxieties and worries. "Here is a cider my love. I would bring you a whiskey but it is only 11:00 in the morning," Catherine said smiling.

"Did I hear something about a shave and when pray did the time of day ever matter to a Scot when the question of whiskey versus cider was on the table?" he answered with a mischievous smile.

"Would you like a whiskey then while I shave you Cameron?" she asked wide eyed.

"I would love one Catherine. The time of day does not matter under the circumstances I am sure you will agree," he said smiling.

She left him then momentarily in search of the whiskey decanter and a glass. Clearly his wish was her demand today of all days. She was back at his side in no time, pouring a whiskey for him and handing it to him as he relaxed in the warm bath. "Would you like me to shave you now Cameron?" Catherine asked hesitantly.

"I think that would be the height of luxury my love," Cameron replied with closed eyes.

Catherine secured his shaving mug and the straight razor, soaped the brush and applied the shaving soap to his face and neck. Once she had opened the straight razor, she noticed that her hands were shaking rather badly, a testament to the past day's anxieties and her excitement at Cameron's safe return. When he opened his eyes he saw the nervousness as well. "Why don't you hold the mirror for me my love and I will make short work of it. Are you ill Catherine or is it just nerves over the bombardment?" Cameron asked anxiously.

"I think it is actually a combination of things Cameron. I was so frightened for you and I have not slept since you left the house. We did everything to keep dear Jamie entertained and he was such a lamb through the whole horrid affair. I was just so relieved to have you home Cameron and I think perhaps I did not realize just how fearful I was until you were back with us and I could stop thinking about all of the horrible things that have been plaguing me for the past day. I am sorry Cameron, I truly am. I do not mean to be emotional but, well there are so many things that I want to say to you and so many things that I was afraid I would never be able to say to you again and well . . . I seem to be quite a mess suddenly and I am sorry again for that. I do not want you to be more upset seeing me in this state," Catherine said sobbing again.

Cameron set down the razor and took Catherine's small hand in his large one. "I am fine Catherine. You are just terribly tired and agitated as is to be expected. What we all need is a good rest which we shall have shortly my love. Let me finish here and you wipe your tears. I am fine Catherine truly; just tired," Cameron said tenderly. He took his hand then and tenderly wiped away her tears and held her face in both hands as she knelt at his side and kissed her tenderly. She smiled then a weak smile, but a smile that told him she was finally relaxing from her own personal terror of the past day's events. "Why don't you start getting yourself ready for a rest my love and I will be just a moment, I promise," Cameron said smiling.

Catherine rose to her feet then and started to fold back the covers on the bed, close the blinds and undress. Cameron rose from the bath shortly thereafter and dried himself on the waiting towel and then came behind Catherine to untie her dress and bring it over her head and each of the petticoats underneath. By the time she had reached her shift, she lay down in the bed and Cameron removed his towel and covered her with his body warm from the bath. She giggled then as he draped his tall frame across her tiny one. "Are you giggling because I am crushing you," he asked quietly.

"No I am laughing because you are so warm from the bath and the fire. You know how I love you to keep me warm Cameron," Catherine said looking deeply in his eyes.

"I do know that my love. Now, what are these very important things that you need to tell me that you were afraid you wouldn't have the chance to tell me?" he continued softly.

"Well some of them are silly and well . . . they are still important. I never told you that the first time you said my Christian name . . . with your Scots accent . . . well you gave me chills down my spine," Catherine said suddenly shy.

"Well that is not silly at t'all . . . Catherrrrine," he purposely emphasized the *r* in her name and she started giggling again as much from the relief of his presence as from the things that she so wanted to tell him once he was with her again. "I believe you have gooseflesh my love. This is an important thing and you never thought to tell me this after nearly two years of marriage? I could have given you gooseflesh from the very start of our courtship if only you had told me this important fact," he said laughing. "What else my love; what other important things did you have to tell me Catherrrrrine?" he said purring now into her ear.

"I needed to know that I have said it enough times to you Cameron," she bit her lip and looked at him with tears in her eyes again. "I needed to know that I had told you how much I love you and how much I need you and that I could not live without you or Jamie or the new baby when he comes," Catherine continued. He wiped away the tears again and she smiled weakly trying to continue. She was just too tired and yet so relieved that he was home that she wanted to keep telling him those important things that she had thought of, but could only cry each time she tried.

"Well shall I tell you that every time I had a spare moment from that God awful siege I thought, Lord let them be safe," Cameron said quietly.

"I said the same thing Cameron; Lord let him be safe and come back to me so that I can tell him all of the things that I want him to hear; all of the things that he needs to know. I know that I was so cold and aloof when you first came here my love. I wanted nothing so much as to go back to London. Why I truly do not know now, but it seemed important at the time. I kept pushing you away but you kept coming back," she said smiling weakly again.

"Of course I kept coming back and I will always keep coming back for you Catherine. You are my life; you and the wee Jamie and the new baby when he appears. God love her, even Mrs. Jones; you are all my life and we will never let anyone take this life away from us Catherine. Not your uncle, not Captain Sir John Beresford and all of his men, no one will take our life away from us; I promise," he said smiling. "Now are there any other important things that you need to tell me before I make love to my wife and take a long needed rest?" Cameron asked.

"Only one more thing Cameron; I have no more defenses; you have broken through all of them," she said hesitantly.

"You need no more defenses my love. You are loved and cherished. When I hear your laughter and I hear you giggling, I say to myself, I want her always to live at her ease; to greet each day with joy. I swore that you would have that every day now that you are mine to protect and love," Cameron said earnestly. "Now my darling girl; is there anything else that you need to tell me most urgently," he asked softly.

"No Cameron; I think that is all for now," she said smiling.

"Alrrrrright then lass; come here and welcome home your husband from the wars. I am not a soldier Catherine; I know that for sure. I would fight for you against anyone who tries to take you away from me whether he is family or foe. I can outfit ships for the war and hopefully we can make a dent in the enemy's supply lines, but for now, I need my wife and I need a wee rest before we go back to it," Cameron said wearily. He kissed Catherine then and she threw her arms around him and they made love and slept, woke and made love again. By the end of the day, they had said all of those things to each other that they had held inside for the past twenty-four hours of the bombardment and they knew that they would continue to fight this war on the banks of the Delaware or wherever it affected them. They also understood the value of each to the other and of the life that they had forged in this new land. Come British warships or baronets, no one would take away the life that they had made in this new land.

CHAPTER ELEVEN

The next morning Cameron gingerly moved to his side to leave the bed and begin the day's work. Catherine's arm came tightly around his waist. "I take it you are already awake my love. You should rest after the stresses of yesterday," Cameron said quietly.

"I want to have breakfast with you and lunch and dinner," Catherine said smiling. "I thought of one more thing that I wanted to tell you yesterday," she said quietly.

"Does it have anything to do with my accent Catherrrrrine?" he said chuckling.

"And this is why I didn't tell you about that nearly two years ago," Catherine answered giggling. "No, it is not about your beautiful accent my love. When all of this horrid war is over, will you do a sketch of yourself like the miniature that you have of me?" Catherine asked.

"I cannot do a sketch of myself love," Cameron replied.

"Of course you can; I can hold the mirror for you," Catherine replied.

"We will see my sweet girl; any other deep, dark secrets that you want to share with me?" Cameron asked grinning.

"We will see generally means no; I know you Cameron McCullum. What about a sketch of our darling Jamie then?" Catherine asked.

"Now that is a wonderful idea. I will start on that straight away and then one of you and the lad in the garden sitting below the lilacs when they are in bloom. I promise my love," he said kissing her. "Now did you say something about breakfast?" he asked smiling.

After breakfast with Catherine and Jamie, Cameron left for the shipyard for the morning. She walked him to the door. "Please stay inside again today my love. The weather hasn't broken yet so it shouldn't be too much of a challenge for you," he placed his forehead on hers and looked her deeply in the eyes. "I love you Catherine McCullum," he said smiling.

"I love you Cameron. Be safe my love and I will see you at luncheon," Catherine said kissing him goodbye.

On his return at lunch, Catherine had another idea that she wished to broach to Cameron. "Cameron, do you not think it would be a good idea for a Ceremony of Thanksgiving to be held at St. Peter's in light of the salvation of the town? Do you think the Reverend Clayborne would be in agreement with that suggestion?" Catherine asked.

"I think that is an excellent idea my love. I will go by the church on my way back to the Yard and broach the subject with Reverend Clayborne myself." He covered her hand with his own then. "Do not worry Catherine; you will not be shut up here much longer. I just want to make sure that the HMS Poitiers is clearly out of these waters and does not return before you start moving about the town again. The weather will soon break and you and I and Jamie will be in the garden again beneath our lilac bush," he said kissing her hand.

"I know Cameron; it is no trouble at all as you point out, the weather is still cold and we are planning our darling Jamie's first birthday party. Just think Cameron, at this time next year, Jamie will have a new brother or sister at his party," Catherine said smiling.

"So many blessings and all of them begin and end with you my love," Cameron said kissing her hand again.

"All my blessings began with you Cameron," Catherine replied.

*****

Reverend Clayborne was in total agreement with a service of Thanksgiving and relayed to Cameron that he would plan it for this coming Sunday. As Cameron returned to the Yard that afternoon, he thought more about his idea to abandon the purchase of the lot adjacent to the canal.

The Manor House may have begun as a bone of contention between Catherine and himself, but looking back now, the best moments of their life together had occurred there. He first met Catherine in the library and fell in love with her almost instantly. The wedding feast was held there and their bonny lad Jamie was born in this house. He would discuss it with Catherine of course, but perhaps remaining in the Manor House would be a good thing after all for the entire family.

On returning to the Manor House that evening, Cameron laid out his thoughts about the abandonment of the lot located adjacent to the canal.

"I think that is a very sound idea my love. You know, I have never lived in this house with anyone but you. We had all of our best verbal matches here before we wed and of course the wedding feast was held here and the birth of our darling Jamie," she said smiling.

"I know my love; besides, we never know what the future may bring, but we know we have a sturdy house within walking distance of the Yard and the church and the shops downtown," Cameron stated. "I do not want to take you away from your lilacs also," Cameron said. "Jamie and his brothers and sisters will love our yard. It is one of the biggest in Lewes," Cameron said proudly.

"I do not care where I live Cameron so long as it is with you and Jamie," Catherine stated firmly.

*****

Cameron, Catherine and Mrs. Jones walked to the service that Sunday with Jamie in tow. Catherine had worried about keeping Jamie entertained throughout the service which was bound to be longer than usual, but as all wished to attend, he was in their company. Jamie was in good spirits that morning and could always sleep if the service ran overly long. Once in the pew, Catherine and Mrs. Jones kept him occupied much as they had done during the day of the siege itself.

The Reverend Clayborne included in his homily for the day the tally of actual damage from the twenty-four hour bombardment. "I have in my hand the tally of damage experienced from the twenty-four hour bombardment by the British Navy. Were his Majesty to hear the sum total of the town's damage, he may view the expenditure of funds to have had very little return. We here in Lewes view it as yet another example of the divine intervention which has protected our town and our country throughout this war. There were no human fatalities or injuries during the course of the twenty-four hour bombardment. There was building damage which can be repaired and for the limited amount experienced we are truly grateful. The estimates range in the amount of $2,000 to some local buildings and we are assured that the Governor will assist the property owners so affected. There was one chicken fatality to be reported and one injury to the leg of a local pig which we will include in our prayers for the day," Reverend Clayborne concluded. The members of the congregation laughed at that report and were all thankful that it was the sum total of the damage from a siege that no one in that room would soon forget. "Let us pray for the continued divine protection of our town and for a quick cessation to the war in general," Reverend Clayborne stated.

Looking from face to face that day, Reverend Clayborne could give thanks to those who had risked all as part of the volunteer militia to protect the town and its inhabitants. He read from a list of parishioners who had volunteered on that fateful day. "Gilbert and Henry McCracken we give thanks for your contributions and are thankful that the cannonball that landed in your house did not explode but will instead serve as a reminder of this town's perseverance during this and all future wars in our nation's history," Reverend Clayborne stated.

Cameron's name was on that roster for the day. When his name was read and his ongoing work at the shipyard recognized, Catherine looked at her husband and beamed with pride. Those in the church that day no doubt also thought about the history of this young family from their vantage point in the church. The first time they had seen the Mistress was on the day that she appeared as a one day bride, then widow for the funeral of Hans Van Ressller. Then Cameron had arrived on the scene and sat in the Van Ressller pew from the very first and the town watched the progress of the courtship between Catherine and Cameron. They had been present for the wedding of the young couple and the arrival and christening of their first son Jamie. Many noticed on that day the bloom to Catherine's cheeks and must have wondered if perhaps a brother or sister would soon join them in the same pew.

Jamie of course was not impressed by the adult thoughts and concerns of the day. As he began to grow heavy in slumber, Cameron took him from Catherine to place him on his shoulder. The same friends and parishioners saw the identical reddish brown hair on the shoulder of his Father. Jamie's loud snores were soon echoed by several adults in the congregation before the Reverend Clayborne brought the Service of Thanksgiving to a close.

Cameron rose with the now deeply sleeping Jamie on his shoulder and they left the church into the bright, sunny day, the first warm day so far in April.

Catherine and Mrs. Jones asked if they could see the unexploded cannon shot in the house adjacent to the canal, as well as the scenes of the battle itself. Their steps travelled to Front Street so that they could see the locations for themselves, the first time that Catherine and Mrs. Jones had ventured outside of the house since the siege.

Cameron carried Jamie and they made their way to the house adjacent to the canal on Front Street to see the unexploded cannon shot and the trenches dug during the day of the attack.

"It seems so unreal that the war would come in this way to Lewes. I suppose that everyone feels the same way until the war arrives on their own doorstep. Thank you Cameron for being so brave to face them on this spot," Catherine said eyeing both the house and the field of battle. "Someday we will be able to hold a dance here again Cameron. It is something to hope for at least," Catherine said smiling.

Cameron smiled at her warmly. "Let's get this young lad to his cot. His Father is ready for his luncheon as well. Reverend Clayborne kept us all from our meal much longer than usual today. It is a good thing that the lad here inherited his Father's loud sounds of slumber. His snores were loud enough to end the sermon or we would still be in church," Cameron said laughing. Catherine and Mrs. Jones giggled and exchanged glances nodding their agreement. They all headed back to the Manor House and their long awaited luncheon.

After the meal, Cameron came to the library to check on balances on the company accounts. Catherine now took care of all payroll and payments to vendors. Her records were so exact and so neat that he wondered how she managed everything to the penny given the huge amount of work that they had taken on during the war years.

Catherine came to the door then to check on Cameron and to answer any questions that he might have. "Thank you so much my love for taking over the accounts. I have never seen such a tidy ledger and such perfect sums. It would take me all of Saturday afternoon and part of Sunday to do this each week. You were so correct my love. By your work we have Saturday afternoon and Sunday together and I can watch my son grow first hand and not at a distance," Cameron said smiling. "Thank you Catherine, truly, thank you for taking on this work. It is not too much for you with Jamie's care and now the new baby?" Cameron said worriedly.

"Oh no of course not Cameron," Catherine said coming into the room. "I am happy to help in any way so that we may have true family time together after your labors are over for the week," Catherine answered smiling.

Cameron closed the account ledger then and noticed a small journal on the desk below. He opened it and saw the same tidy handwriting within. "Is this yours my love?" Cameron asked.

"Yes Cameron. It is my diary. I started it when I left Edgewater," Catherine replied softly.

"Catherine you never told me the story of your departure from Edgewater," Cameron said.

"It is not a pretty story Cameron. That is why I never told you," Catherine said quietly. She looked down studying her hands then not making eye contact with Cameron.

"I cannot imagine any story related to your uncle being a pretty story Catherine. Come here lass. Do you remember the day after our wedding when I asked you to tell me your story? I held you then and I asked you to tell me what had happened. Come here Catherine and exorcise the past once and for all. Tell me and leave it behind you forever," Cameron said anxiously. "Come to me my love," Cameron said holding out his hand to her.

Catherine went to him and he pulled her to him to sit on his lap. He held her tightly until she was comfortable again in talking about the full story of the time leading up to her arrival in Lewes.

"I remember my uncle came to my room as I was preparing for luncheon. That in itself was a warning sign as he rarely rose before 3:00 in the afternoon after gambling the night away. My maid was behind him. I asked him if I could be of assistance. Yes Catherine, he said; please prepare for a journey. Your maid here will pack your things," Catherine said.

"Panicking inside I said calmly; where am I to travel to uncle? Am I to go to London for another ball or perhaps to

Bath to meet with yet another potential suitor? No Catherine, he said, you are to go to America. It has all been arranged. You will go there for a short time, meet your intended and then you will return to an even more glorious future here in London," Catherine said anxiously.

Cameron's arms tightened around Catherine as he felt her tremble at the memory. "I told him I would not go. I would not marry someone that I had never laid eyes on much less met and what did he mean that it was only for a short time? He told me I had two choices; I could leave the house like the lady that I was or I could be trussed by the footmen and carried from the house for all to see and comment upon. He said that he could not afford to feed and clothe me and not expect some type of return for his investment. At the conclusion of that speech, I packed all of my things and an hour or so later, I left the house with my uncle's steward bound for a ship in London," Catherine stated quietly.

"I was told to remain in my cabin until we reached America. I had been brought on board under the cover of darkness with my cloak hiding my face. The steward was housed in the cabin beside me. He was there you see to assure that I was not . . . well . . . disturbed in anyway. I was not to be brought to America as . . . um . . . damaged goods; that was made very clear on both sides of the horrid agreement," Catherine said quietly.

"I stayed in my cabin for the duration of the voyage. When we arrived here in Lewes, they put me in a tender ship with all my possessions in the middle of a gale. I was brought to St. Peter's in a wagon with my things. Reverend Clayborne had been roused from his bed to marry us. Mr. Van Ressller was there and his men as witnesses. He kept interrupting Reverend Clayborne to make the ceremony quicker. The Reverend finally finished and Van Ressller went out into the night again and the gale to save his fleet and he and all of his men save the one who took me to the Manor House perished in the storm. A man named Hayes and

Reverend Clayborne came to the house the next day. I must have slept the whole day as Mrs. Jones said it was nearly dinner time when she came to wake me to take me to them in the library here. They told me then that Van Ressller was dead," Catherine continued.

"Attorney Wendell and Reverend Clayborne came back later in the day to tell me the terms of the accursed agreement and the rest you know," Catherine stated meeting Cameron's eyes for the first time.

"When you arrived in Lewes, I had made up my mind that I would return to London in two years time without fail. You were right at the time of course; I continued to push you away and your love for me because I simply could not trust anyone, least of all another man," she said smiling weakly.

"And then you wore the infamous French gown," Cameron said softly "and I swore that morning that I would either turn you over my knee and paddle you for the tease I thought you were, or else kiss you because I thought no one had ever given you the love that you so richly deserved," Cameron said taking her face in his hands. "I chose the latter course and I have never looked back," he said tenderly.

"Have I told you today that I love you?" Cameron asked quietly. "I promised I would love you and cherish you all of the days of your life; do you remember?" Cameron continued.

"I do Cameron; I always remember that," Catherine said with tears in her eyes.

"How is it love with the new baby? Is all well Catherine with all that you have been through this past week?" Cameron asked anxiously.

"I am fine Cameron. I feel exactly the same as I did when I carried Jamie. I do not know if that means another boy or not, but I am fine my love," Catherine replied smiling.

"I have a bonny wife, a bonny son, a baby on the way, a booming business and all my blessings began with you Catherine. I promise I will always be here for you and you

188

will never fear me love. Your uncle, that way of life, even the Captain Sir John Beresfords of the world are all in your past Catherine. You are loved by your husband more each day and you will be surrounded by your bonny children all the days of your life," Cameron said.

"You have kept all of your promises Cameron," Catherine said laying her head on his shoulder.

"And I always will Catherine," Cameron said tenderly.

CHAPTER TWELVE

On the first Sunday in June, Catherine placed a vase of lilac blooms on the Sunday luncheon table. It was a reminder to Cameron of his promise. Cameron had been making sketches of Jamie's face as he ate at the table, during his bath time and even during sleep, knowing that he would be unable to keep him still long enough on Catherine's lap for the sketch he planned to complete. This sketch would result in a work in oil paint for Cameron's library and would consist of a painting of Catherine and Jamie in the garden beneath the lilac bushes.

After church and luncheon, Cameron brought down his sketch pad, charcoal and pencils and led his two subjects to the lilac scented garden and the bench beneath the flowering lilac bushes.

Cameron made himself comfortable on an adjacent bench and placed his tools together in readiness. Catherine placed Jamie on her lap with a variety of items designed to keep him still while his Father completed the desired sketch. She had also brought a blanket to place him at her feet for the inevitable play that Jamie would desire after he lost interest in the proceedings.

Once settled, Cameron came to the bench with Catherine, sat down and one by one, took the pins from her hair, bringing the rear portion down and around her neck and shoulders as was his preference. "I could have done that for you Cameron," Catherine said smiling.

"Half of my joy is in preparing my subject exactly as I want her," Cameron replied with mischief in his eyes. He lifted up Jamie and placed him at the precise location that he had envisioned on her lap and took her face between his hands and kissed her intensely. When he pulled away from the kiss, he smiled and said "That is the exact look that I was seeking. I may have to keep kissing you to assure it," Cameron said smiling. Jamie looked up at his Da and

Cameron ruffled his hair, smiled down at him and resumed his place on the adjacent bench.

Catherine sat quite still trying to maintain the look that Cameron had created as well as keeping Jamie still for as long as possible.

The scent of the lilacs carried her back to their wedding day and the dancing that had occurred in this very garden as well as the lilacs that Catherine had cut for their trip to Dover. Before Jamie and the new baby that she carried, it had only been Cameron and Catherine; two newcomers to America and to Lewes. That was the look on her face that he had created with his kiss; the beginning of their journey together.

He worked steadily and quietly for nearly an hour. "You must get up now and stretch my love. I have the lilacs and the position that I will place you both in and the preliminary sketches of you both. Let us get the lad to his cot for his nap and you my love to our room for a back rub. We will work out those vexing back muscles Catherine," Cameron said softly.

"I love your back rubs Cameron," Catherine replied holding his gaze with her own.

"So do I love," Cameron said huskily. Jamie looked up at his parents and Cameron grabbed him up quickly and put him over his shoulder, Jamie shrieking with joy at the action.

"You are up so high little one," Catherine said smiling up at the identical set of blue eyes. "Can you believe how he has grown Cameron?" Catherine asked.

"You said he had the whole world to grow in and so he has done," Cameron said. "He is nearly half as tall as you already," Cameron said kissing the top of her head. Catherine carried in the portfolio and another bough of lilac for their room. For a day at least, the war was a very long way away and their garden a hidden bower of peace.

191

*****

The same could not be said for the country as a whole. The war which had begun on June 18, 1812, was now into its second year. Cameron continued to resist pressure by his customers to work on the Sabbath as well as the other six days that his crews labored to outfit privateer ships and keep the merchant fleet in the war. He stated repeatedly that they must seek God's intervention to end this war and that seeking his aid, they must be mindful of his commandments. He would not work on the Sabbath and would not demand that his men work on the Sabbath either. He had no idea how long the war would continue, but he knew that no man could continue to work seven days a week indefinitely. He wanted his men fit and he wanted them to be supported by their own families which must see them just as Catherine and Jamie must see him. Sunday was his refuge with those he loved and he extended that same opportunity to the men in his employ.

*****

By September, the birth of their second baby was imminent. Cameron did not need to argue his case to be part of the delivery process this time as that fact had been established with Jamie's arrival. The fact that Jamie was now in her sphere of concern was but one factor that had not been in their planning process for the first birth. Catherine had a plan to address her concerns about Jamie's welfare during the delivery as well. On the morning of the birth, Catherine shared her concerns with Cameron.

"My love, this time we will have Jamie to be concerned about as well as the delivery of the new baby. I do not want him to worry about Mummy particularly if he should hear any sounds that would cause him to fret. Will you promise me one thing? When the time comes for you to be exiled to the library, will you take Jamie with you to play there or else to take a nap? I do not want him to worry that he doesn't have access to Mummy or that something is wrong with Mummy. He will see us all fine and well and a new brother to play with in short order, but I just do not want him to fret during the process," Catherine said urgently.

"Do not worry Catherine; I will keep the lad occupied. I will give him his first taste of single malt to celebrate the birth of his brother," Cameron said teasing.

"I know that you are not serious about the single malt Cameron but you will keep Jamie occupied so that he does not sense that something is wrong and start to worry?" she continued anxiously.

"Of course my love; I am teasing you and I should not on today of all days when you are worried about me and my exile and about Jamie and about giving birth at the same time. All will be well just as it was the first time. Mrs. Jones will keep Jamie occupied in the kitchen while we walk the halls and you have your soothing bath and back rubs. Then when my exile begins, Jamie and I will pace the floors in the library or more correctly, I will hold his hand while he tries to walk and he will watch me pace until we have the blessed news that his brother has entered the world," he said smiling.

As planned, Cameron was a constant at Catherine's side, walking with her down the upstairs hallway, filling her bath when she needed the relief of the warm waters and giving her back rubs as they walked the halls together. When he was exiled to the library by the ever diligent midwife, he captured Jamie from the kitchen and together they spent the final hours before the new baby made his appearance in the world.

Cameron brought Jamie onto his lap and showed him the surprise that he had prepared for Catherine. The painting had been completed and he would wrap and give it to her as her gift for the baby's arrival. Cameron showed Jamie the portrait and Jamie patted his hands on the desk and said *Mama* for the first time which was a fact that Cameron would be happy to share with Catherine as well. Cameron worked on *Da* while they sat in the library together.

All the memories of the time spent with Catherine in this very room came rushing back to Cameron. Thankfully he had Jamie with him this time to keep his mind occupied and away from the worry that he had experienced whilst he sat in this room during Jamie's delivery. All of his dreams had come to reality in this house with Catherine. Facing a life without her was not something that he could envision and he kept that thought far from his mind on this day. If the baby was a boy as Catherine expected, they would name him Alexander Charles McCullum; Alexander as it was Cameron's Father's middle name and Charles, Catherine's Father's middle name.

During their exile to the library, another letter arrived from Catherine's uncle Jonathan Wentworth. Cameron decided that the policy of avoidance had not been successful to date. He made the decision to open the letter and prepare a draft response that he would review with Catherine to send jointly to her uncle. Obviously the failure to respond originally had continued the charade of marriage negotiations for Catherine's hand and Cameron had had quite enough of that exercise to last him a lifetime. He thought to put an end to that speculation for the last time.

September 12, 1813

"Sir Jonathan Wentworth
Edgewater

Sir:

Your niece Catherine McCullum nee Wentworth is in receipt of your most recent letter. As her husband of two years I am writing to request the cessation of your efforts to negotiate marriage contracts on her behalf. On this day, Catherine has been safely delivered of a second son of our union. He joins our first son James William McCullum who was born a year and a half ago.

Consequently, as I am sure you can gather, she will not be returning to London as she has been warmly received by her adopted town of Lewes, Delaware following her forced marriage at your hands to Mr. Hans Van Ressller now deceased these two and a half years.

I would respectfully request cessation of all marital negotiations related to your niece and my wife Catherine Elizabeth McCullum. I have copied our attorney with whom you will be acquainted Mr. Thomas Wendell, Esquire to attest to the facts of this letter.

Respectfully,

*Cameron McCullum
Lewes, Delaware"*

"There now wee Jamie; I hope that will be that for your Mother's sake and mine. She will have had quite enough excitement for today without having to deal with your great uncle's efforts to see her married again. Your Mummy is not going anywhere, but will be here with us always," Cameron said kissing the top of his head. "What do you have to say about that wee one?" he asked Jamie.

Jamie's response was to pat his Father's desk and repeat his first word *Mama* over again.

"Quite so Jamie; I couldn't have said it better myself; Mama indeed. Now, if I can just have you say Da before the day is out, I will be a happy man indeed," Cameron said laughing.

Shortly thereafter, Mrs. Jones came to the door with her apron to her eyes to announce that the newest baby had made his arrival into the world. "I believe I heard you say *his* arrival Mrs. Jones. Did I hear that correctly?" Cameron asked smiling.

"You did indeed sir. You are safely delivered of a second fine son and the Mistress did remarkably well again. It seems she does well at everything she sets her hand to Master McCullum. Would you like me to see to the lad while you meet your new baby?" Mrs. Jones asked.

"I think it would be best for the young lad to see his Mama and his new brother so that he knows all is well. He has said Mama now twice so far today so I know he will want to see her. I have to teach him to say Da before the day is done and my life will be complete," Cameron replied laughing.

Jamie and Cameron took the stairs two at a time to see Catherine and the new baby brother. Catherine lay radiant but tired with Alexander Charles McCullum in her arms. Cameron brought Jamie to see his Mother and she kissed him and handed Alex to his Father for inspection. As before, she predicted that he was the image of his Father and Cameron continued to wonder how a baby of a few minutes in age could be the image of anyone. Jamie cuddled next to his Mother while Cameron took in the newest lad.

"I brought Jamie with me to check on you as he has said *Mama* twice now this afternoon while we were exiled to the library," Cameron said smiling.

"Did you say Mama my clever boy?" Catherine asked. Jamie looked up at her with Cameron's blue eyes and said it again for good measure.

"We are going to work on *Da* for the rest of the day just so you know," Cameron replied smiling at Catherine.

"Well I do think that only fair Cameron. Can you say *Da* for your Father little one? That would make *Da* so very happy and *Mama* also," Catherine said prompting Jamie.

"Mama," Jamie said and shrieked with laughter.

"If you ask him to say *Da* he will only say *Mama* so perhaps you should just say *Mama* and see if he says *Da*," Catherine said smiling.

"We will work on that after his nap. Speaking of naps my love, I think you deserve one. I will put Alex here in his cot and Jamie and I will retreat to his room and I will be back in just a few moments to hold you. You have done amazingly well again my love. My Father would be over the moon to see his two beautiful grandsons. Thank you so much Catherine for making all of my dreams come true," Cameron said smiling at her.

"We have a wonderful family now Cameron and so much more happiness waiting for us in the future," Catherine replied with her eyes shining with tears.

That evening Cameron came to their room again and took a now sleeping Alex once again from Catherine's arms and placed him in his cot. Jamie had been sent off to bed with kisses from both parents. He had steadfastly refused to say *Da* yet for his Father, but Cameron remained dedicated to the cause. He brought Catherine her uncle's most recent letter to read and a draft of the letter that he had prepared while he waited anxiously in the library with Jamie for the birth of the new baby.

Cameron sat beside Catherine and kissed the top of her head. "Whatever may be happening in the world around us Catherine, our family is strong and growing each year. We are so blessed my love," Cameron said with his arm around her shoulders.

"I hesitate to bother you on this of all days but I have something to show you Catherine. There has been another letter from your uncle and I have taken the liberty to draft a response which I thought we could send jointly to him if it is agreeable to you. I was wrong Catherine to have you ignore his prior letters. He will never stop until we call an end to it once and for all," Cameron said emphatically.

Catherine read through her uncle's letter and Cameron's draft response. She asked for a pen so that she could add her signature and the letter could be prepared for mailing.

"With the unpleasant business out of the way, I have a surprise for you," Cameron said smiling. He went to the room down the hall and returned with a large parcel wrapped in brown paper.

"It is a good thing that I finished this last week," Cameron said smiling. He handed Catherine the parcel and helped her in the unwrapping. Before her was the requested portrait of herself and Jamie in the lilac bower.

"It is so beautiful Cameron; your best work yet. I may not have a portrait of you, but I have your image in Jamie's face and now in the baby's," Catherine replied. "Thank you so very much my love."

"I will do one of Alex when he is old enough to have his own features," Cameron replied chuckling.

"Did I not tell you when I was expecting that Jamie would be a boy and that he would look just like you? Alex will be the same; your mirror image," Catherine replied smiling.

"I shall do a separate portrait with you and Alex when he is Jamie's age and one of the two boys together," Cameron replied.

"You may not do a portrait of yourself for me, but any one with eyes will see you in the eyes of your lads," Catherine said. "Thank you my love for this beautiful portrait," Catherine said with shining eyes.

"And thank you for my beautiful lads," Cameron said kissing the top of her head again.

*****

Weeks later, Jamie woke from his nap and called out to his Mother "Mama, see Da," Jamie cried. Catherine was so excited that he had finally said *Da* without prompting that she failed to see her son's upset face.

"Mama, see Da!" Jamie cried louder a second time.

"You will see him my clever boy as soon as he comes home from the Yard," Catherine said smiling.

"Mama see Da!" Jamie said crying real tears now. Catherine saw the upset and started to become alarmed. She felt his forehead and hands and found him fever free.

"Alright my dearest boy; let me get Alex changed and get my hat and gloves and we will go see Da alright?" Catherine replied cheerily. "Do not cry my little man; we will go see your Da," Catherine said. Jamie smiled then and clapped his hands.

Once Catherine had Alex up and changed and had placed on her hat and gloves, she picked up Jamie who promptly took off for the stairs as she placed Alex on her shoulder. "Mrs. Jones, we are going down to the Yard for a few moments. We will be back soon," Catherine called out. "Jamie, your hand please," Catherine stated.

Off they set for the office and one of the first visits by Catherine out of the house since the birth of Alex. It was a visit out of the ordinary to say the least as they did not disturb Cameron routinely while he was working. It was a beautiful, late autumn day so she decided a trip to the Yard was not totally out of the question. Jamie walked along the path, happy to be outside and on the way to see his Father.

Once they reached the shipyard, the lads waved and shouted out and Jamie continued alternating walking and hopping along to the entrance to the office. Catherine opened the door to the office and Jamie hopped in.

"Good afternoon my love; your lads are here to see you. I hope we are not keeping you from anything too pressing. Wee Jamie here woke from his nap with an urgent need to see Da. His exact words were Mama, see Da," Catherine said smiling. Cameron sat at his desk staring from one to the other of the entourage; Jamie hopping from one foot to another,

Alex wide eyed at his Mama's shoulder and Catherine with a look of amusement on her face.

Cameron stood up then and came to the front of his desk, leaned back and crossed his arms. "So do you have something to say to me my wee lad?" Cameron said smiling.

Jamie leaned back to take in his Father at his full height and promptly fell back on his bottom in the process. He smiled the same heartbreakingly charming smile as his Father and said, "Up Da!" and then laughed.

"Up is it then? You bring your Mama and wee Alex here so you can go up high?" Cameron said laughing. Catherine hid her smile behind her glove.

Cameron reached down then and took Jamie up and placed him on his shoulders and resumed his seat at the desk again. "So you finally decided to say Da did you now?" Cameron said laughing.

"In exchange for going up high apparently," Catherine said giggling. "Did you see that smile Cameron? Did you recognize it by any chance?" Catherine said giggling again.

From his shoulder height vantage point, Jamie looked down and saw the miniature of his Mother on Da's desk. "Mama," he cried pointing.

"That is right Jamie; it is Mama. Isn't she beautiful?" Cameron said picking up the miniature. He handed it to Jamie then who kissed it and handed it back to Cameron.

Catherine came around the desk then looking at the miniature. "It seems like another lifetime Cameron when that was painted," Catherine said smiling. Cameron reached out to take Alex from her arms. Three identical sets of blue eyes looked up at her then.

"Do you ever think of it Catherine; that former life?" Cameron asked.

"Oh no Cameron, I can truly say that I do not. I am a great lady of the Manor House now and of the House of McCullum. The two heirs of the House of McCullum stand before me as well as the Laird of the House. It is a fine house built of love and laughter. I would not trade it for any house in England or for any family for that matter. And when the next baby comes, perhaps this horrid war will be over and I can give the Laird the lassie that he has been talking about," Catherine said smiling.

"Lads, look upon the great lady of the House of McCullum. She makes sure that we have our meals on time and that our house runs like a top; she takes care of the accounts of the House of McCullum; she wipes Jamie's nose and she kisses Alex's toes and no one will ever love us the way that she loves us. We are very lucky lads indeed to have this great lady in our life. And somehow, she is more beautiful today than she was when this miniature was painted and even more beautiful than the day that we married. I am not sure how you manage that my love, but it is true," Cameron said watching Catherine intently.

"Thank you Cameron. That is such a lovely thing to say. On another point, I was wondering my love; . . . how it came to be that Jamie learned to say the word Da with such authority. Could it be that the words *up* and *Da* were said together enough times to lure wee Jamie to say it of his own accord?" Catherine asked grinning.

"The other thing lads that you need to know about your Mama is that she is the smartest one of all four of us. She will always figure it out in the end so do not even try to keep anything from her," Cameron said grinning again. "I believe that the first lady of the House of McCullum deserves a turn down to the shops today and that we her lads should take the rest of the day to show her how much we love her," Cameron said watching Catherine again.

Catherine took Alex back from him and Cameron stood up with Jamie on his shoulders. "I must take you down for a moment my lad as we cannot pass through the door with you on your perch. Do not worry as Da will take you up again as soon as we are outside the door," Cameron said. Cameron took Jamie from his shoulders and placed him under his arm like a parcel which made Jamie shriek even more than when he was mounted on his perch. Outside they went into the beautiful autumn day, walking towards the shops and the promise of treats for Jamie and a walk for the lady of the House of McCullum. All who saw them that day noted the beautiful children of Cameron and Catherine and that the matchmaking efforts by the members of the town were a good day's work indeed.

*****

Within two months of its mailing, a response to the letter directed to Jonathan Wentworth, Baronet was received by the House of McCullum. Catherine saw the customary stationary and seal and sighing placed it to the side of her desk until the arrival of Cameron that night. She had quite put the thought of her uncle and his newest outrage from her mind. The Atlantic Ocean stood between her and his latest plans and schemes. In addition Cameron McCullum stood between her uncle and the Atlantic Ocean. She no longer had worries about the ongoing drama that surrounded her uncle and his efforts to contract marriage on her behalf.

That evening after dinner, Catherine and Cameron read the latest missive from her uncle.

"Catherine Wentworth McCullum
Lewes, Delaware

Dearest Catherine:

I must say that I was astounded by the letter dated September 12, 1813 received from you and your new husband. To have discovered that you have married in America and to a Scot was outrage enough. To learn that you are now the Mother of two sons of this union shook me to my foundations. I wish you to know, however that the action is not irretrievable. You will recall that the agreement with Hans Van Ressller provided you with an outlet from that marriage once the necessary heirs had been provided. Should you wish this outlet to be utilized to exit this unfortunate marriage, I shall endeavor to work with Mr. Wendell to bring about that very conclusion.

You shall be welcomed back to London by your family and friends once this unfortunate period of your life has been placed behind you. I remain hopeful of your rescue and continue to work on your behalf in the completion of highly advantageous marriage contracts. Should I not hear from you in the next two months, I shall have no choice but to engage in marital negotiations for myself during a planned trip to Bath. I assure you that should such negotiations prove fruitful, you will have no expectation of continuing as my heir to the property of Edgewater.

I remain in hopes of your speedy return to London and to your real family.

Jonathan Wentworth, Baronet"

"So which part of your treachery is the greatest Catherine; the fact that you stayed in America or the fact that you married a Scot?" Cameron said with amusement.

"Well perhaps he thinks of you as part of the invading horde that you told me about when first we met. You are as tall as a Viking you know," she replied with mischief.

"Hmm, I have never known a Scot to force himself upon a wee lassie," Cameron replied.

"Well, if my uncle knew you as I do, he would know the good man that you are and would also know how successful you have been in this country. We most definitely need to keep that news from him or he will expect us to pay for the upkeep of Edgewater. He just doesn't understand that I would ever wish to leave London permanently as he considers it the center of the world," Catherine replied.

"The world that I would have lived in there Cameron is so foreign to the life I lead here. Children are taken away and housed on the third floor of most estate houses. They are handed to a wet nurse and their Mothers see them for only a few minutes a day. When I hold my lads and give them their baths each day and feel their chubby arms as they kiss me goodnight, I cannot imagine seeing my children for only a few minutes in the morning and a few minutes before tea in the afternoon," Catherine replied wistfully. "It would have been a completely different life Cameron and not one that would have made me happy for sure," Catherine stated.

"But surely any husband worth his salt would have fought for you Catherine and how you would want to raise your own children," Cameron replied earnestly.

"But you must understand my love any husband that my uncle would have contracted for my hand would have been raised in the exact same way. He would not have fought for me as he would have thought me mad to wish to raise my own children," Catherine replied.

"Perhaps that is why your parents went to the West Indies; they were looking for a new life for you all. If they had not lost their lives, they would have brought you there and you would have had a very different life," Cameron replied softly.

"I did have a new life waiting for me here with you Cameron and the lads and those that will follow," Catherine stated.

"Do you think your uncle intends to marry at last?" Cameron asked.

"Only if he can find a wealthy widow who will accept an inveterate gambler and womanizer," Catherine replied. "Besides Cameron, Edgewater will not survive my uncle's tenure I fear. Between his indebtedness and lack of stewardship, I cannot imagine what will be left," Catherine replied sadly.

"I worry at times that I have taken you away from a life that would have been so different than the one you live here Catherine. Are you truly happy my love?" he asked worriedly.

"I am so very happy Cameron. Everything you told me would come to pass has done so my love. You do not dictate our life together; we decide it as partners. Our children are our greatest joy and our business grows with each passing year as your reputation and skill are known. Besides Cameron, sooner or later I was going to have to actually *live* with one of these men that my uncle continually solicits for my hand. My life would have been quite different and quite unhappy," Catherine replied.

"I only ever want you to be happy my love and to live without regrets," Cameron replied taking her face in his hands.

"My only regret is that I did not meet you sooner so we could have started our wonderful life together then," Catherine replied placing her arms around his neck and kissing him deeply.

CHAPTER THIRTEEN

1814

The year 1814 arrived and the war continued unabated. The McCullum family was strong and continuing the efforts of Lewes and of the country as a whole to fight on to defend their home and the nation.

In the nation as a whole the warfare had mixed results in its successes with many failures on the part of the militia. On the seas and particularly the Chesapeake Bay, the hit and run tactics of the privateers was continuing and the capture of prizes by the merchant fleet meant that Cameron and Catherine's business continued to flourish. Sailed by former navy officers, the statistics told the tale. The American privateers during the course of the war took an estimated 1300 British merchant vessels compared to 254 by the U.S. Navy. The Royal Navy may have had the United States Navy blockaded from Norfolk, Virginia to Havre de Grace Maryland, but the privateers fought on.

Close to Lewes, the worst news of the war came in August of 1814 with the failure of the United States militia at the Battle of Bladensburg and the assault by the British on the nation's capital in Washington, D.C. Fortunately President Madison and the First Lady had sufficient notice to evacuate the capital with some of the prized possessions of the new republic including a portrait of President George Washington by Gilbert Stuart. The burning of the White House, U.S. Capitol building and the Navy Yard by the British was a psychological blow to the American efforts and was felt by all Americans at the time.

Despite the close proximity to Lewes, news travelled very slowly in 1814 and the news of this latest affront did not reach Lewes for nearly two weeks. Attorney Wendell came to the Yard to brief Cameron on the latest papers received from Baltimore.

Cameron quickly scanned the paper provided and looked up from his reading to meet Mr. Wendell's worried frown. "It says here that a storm was responsible for putting out the flames set by the retreating British. We must certainly thank divine providence for sending that storm. I know that this is a terrible blow Thomas, but we must fight on. We have been badly overwhelmed in numbers but look at what the privateers have been able to accomplish on their own? I know in my heart that we will be victorious in the end. Why the British are so terribly stretched with this war against Napoleon it must be the reason for the impressments of our men in the first place. Take heart Thomas, this country won one war that we were not expected to win. Let us hope and pray that this will be the second one. I for one do not intend on returning to the British yoke anytime soon. Any man who came from the Highlands of Scotland in the prior century will tell you the same," Cameron said heatedly.

"You are correct as always Cameron. It is disheartening, but we must fight on. I know that you assist in that effort everyday with the outfitting of the privateers that the Yard has done from the very first," Mr. Wendell stated.

"That is right. We may have to fight our own war against the odds but then from what I understand, that is how America won the War of Independence as well. Highlanders are born to fight and to fight against the odds Thomas; we have had little choice in our history. I know that my fellow Scots will fight on until we can determine our own future once and for all. I will share these newspaper clippings with Catherine tonight if agreeable to you. I need to keep her calm with the new baby on the way, but she must know what has happened as Reverend Clayborne is bound to mention it in this week's sermon and prayers," Cameron stated.

Catherine was expecting their third child now and Cameron longed for a daughter to join their two lads in the nursery. Wee Jamie as Cameron called him was talking up a storm and leading his brother into all sorts of mischief which was to be expected of the two sons of Cameron McCullum. Catherine would look at him disapprovingly on his return from the Yard each night and tell him what *his* two sons had been up to on that particular day. She would always end the report by saying, "but I love them so much that I cannot stay mad at them for long." That he could have ever had such joy in his life was something that he still could not comprehend. As he had said before, the world may be coming apart around them, but their family was strong and growing on a yearly basis. Catherine was the calm center of this storm of domestic life and he could not wait to see her at the end of each day.

When he arrived at the door, Catherine met him with Jamie at her heels and Alex in her arms. She kissed him with mischief in her eyes. "So what have they done today my love?" Cameron asked smiling.

"Oh it will keep Cameron. Come through and wash your face and hands. Boys will be boys or so they say and our two lads are no exception to that rule. You know I would not have them any other way," she replied smiling.

Two high chairs now adorned their dining room. Jamie was seated next to his Mama and Alex next to Da. That Cameron could finally convince Jamie to say Da was testament to his own personal tenacity. He began to think that Jamie could actually say the word for some time and was withholding it out of sheer stubbornness. Catherine agreed with that theory knowing that her lads belonged to Cameron McCullum for sure.

After dinner, Catherine put down the lads and joined him in the library. "I have been provided with some information today Catherine that I needed to share with you. I did not want you to hear about it on Sunday as I am sure that the Reverend Clayborne will mention it in the sermon and in the prayers for the week. It seems that the British made an assault on Bladensburg, Maryland and when that assault could not be repelled by our militia, the British took Washington, D.C. and burned it," Cameron said worriedly.

"Oh my dear Lord Cameron; were President Madison and the First Lady able to escape or were they taken prisoner?" Catherine asked aghast at the news.

"Now you must promise me not to over excite yourself my love. The President and Mrs. Madison are fine. They had prior notice of the defeat by the militia and were able to flee the capital and collect some of the nation's keepsakes in the process. Do you remember the terrible storm that we had about two weeks ago? Well it seemed that it was the day of the assault. I am convinced that we rest beneath divine providence my love because the account in the papers say that the storm managed to put out the fires that were still burning in the city when the British left it," Cameron stated.

"You know that we will fight on Catherine. I am sure that this assault was retribution for some action on our part as that is typically how these things occur. You know that the privateers will fight on. This is a setback, but not the end of the war. That we have survived this long against the finest military in the world is a testament to divine assistance and the pluck and tenacity of our people. Will you promise me that you will not allow this to upset you anymore than it already has? I need to be able to greet my new wee lassie in a few short months and I need her Mama to be well," Cameron said taking her into his arms.

"I know what you say is true Cameron. It is just so very terrible for something like this to occur so close by us and to the nation's capital. We know from experience the terror of an assault such as this one. Thankfully our town was not set aflame, but I just cannot imagine the terror that our poor President and his wife must have experienced," Catherine said worriedly. "Will you ask Reverend Clayborne to preach about this on Sunday Cameron?" she asked.

"I will my love. I am sure that Mr. Wendell will have shared the news with him already, but I will ask him that we all pray for our President, our men in the field and our men on the seas. God give them strength to continue the fight," Cameron replied.

The Reverend Clayborne had been provided the news and prepared an inspiring service designed to keep up the spirits of the townspeople and to focus prayers on the leaders who needed to keep the country together and focused on victory and a cessation to the war.

Cameron, Catherine, Mrs. Jones and the two lads were in their pew. As before during the Ceremony of Thanksgiving, members of the church commented on this day as they had before of the beautiful children of Cameron and Catherine and of the growing brood of the McCullum family. Catherine was glowing again and they must have known that a third member of the clan McCullum was on the way. On this day of all days, good news was being sought by all members of the congregation. The sermon had done its part to uplift all who heard it and the citizens of the town left St. Peter's Episcopal Church with the commitment to continue the fight.

Two weeks later news reached Lewes of another battle and this time the British had not been victorious. As a major base of privateers, the City of Baltimore, Maryland had been a target of the British Royal Navy. The Baltimore privateers had been amazingly successful throughout the war and the Royal Navy had decided to bring the war to Baltimore. On September 13, 1814 an attempt was made to take the port of Baltimore by sea. Twenty-five hours of bombardment, the time period so similar to that experienced by the Town of Lewes but on a much larger scale, would not bring the British a victory. Fort McHenry did not fall on that day and a young lawyer named Francis Scott Key watched the siege from the waters surrounding the Fort that night. He was inspired to write verse which would one day become the Star Spangled Banner as he watched the garrison flag that flew over Fort McHenry throughout the battle.

The British did not take Fort McHenry and were unable to penetrate the Baltimore Harbor. Unlike the news from two weeks before, the people of Lewes learning the news nearly two weeks later were overjoyed that the British Navy had been repulsed. As Cameron had stated, the country was truly tenacious and would fight on as they had so bravely done.

Cameron came home with this news nearly two weeks to the day from the newspaper accounts of the Washington, D.C. siege. He came home early that day just so he could share the news with Catherine. He provided the newspaper accounts to Catherine over the dinner table that night. Catherine's face was alight with the triumph. "Do you remember Cameron when you told us all that we must remain dedicated to an American victory? To think two short weeks later the Royal Navy would have been prevented from taking Fort McHenry. Why this is amazing news my love. It happened one day after our dear Alex's birthday. We shall always remember that date Cameron. Just think of those Baltimore privateers and those who defended the fort. They must be so proud that they could prevent the same thing happening to Baltimore that occurred to Washington, D.C. Mr. Madison must be so pleased my love. We must make sure that Reverend Clayborne knows about this latest piece of news. Perhaps it means that the end is near Cameron," Catherine said with shining eyes.

"We can only pray that is the case Catherine. I pray that our lads never have to fight in their lifetime. This is truly a country that is worth a fight, but I would not wish the worry of the past two years on our lads or any other lads in any other homes in our country," Cameron said emphatically.

"I could not imagine our babies going to war Cameron. Mother used to say that only boys are born during times of war to replace those who die. I hope that the newest baby will be a girl so that we can see that the end of this horrid war is in sight," Catherine replied.

CHAPTER FOURTEEN

1815

The end of the war was in sight, but Catherine was not destined to bear a lassie with the newest baby. The third baby of the house of McCullum was also a son and was named Cameron Robson McCullum for his father. Like his two older brothers he was the image of his Father as Catherine had predicted when first he was born. The war continued so as her Mother had once said, Catherine continued to bear sons.

In January, the Battle of New Orleans was fought and unbeknownst to the participants, the Treaty of Ghent ending the War of 1812 had already been signed in Belgium on December 24, 1814. Because the treaty was not ratified by the United States until February, 1815, the war had raged on.

News of both events did not reach Lewes until March and a Ceremony of Thanks was again scheduled by Reverend Clayborne to celebrate the end of hostilities and an end to fear of British blockade of the Atlantic. All war was not over until the end of hostilities with the French with the Battle of Waterloo in June, 1815, but all Americans could breathe a collective sigh of relief that British warships would not again loom on the Delaware or in the Atlantic. The Town of Lewes, Delaware celebrated along with the country as a whole and nowhere was celebration greater than in the Manor House, now known by Catherine as the House of McCullum.

It was June again and Catherine and Cameron were celebrating their fourth wedding anniversary and the birth of three sons to the family. Their business had not only survived the war but thrived. Captain McEwan was as good as his word and had made Cameron's name known throughout the Delaware and the Delmarva. Cameron would continue to produce ships now that the war had ended, but now for the merchant fleet that would once again ply their trade between the United States and all trading partners including the British and the French.

Cameron and Catherine had decided to remain at the Manor House as it had been the starting place of their married life and in it the greatest events of their marriage had been experienced; their wedding feast, the birth of Jamie, Alex and now baby Cameron and the survival of the bombardment of the Town of Lewes and the War of 1812 as a whole. Its walls would keep the McCullum family safe as it continued to grow in the future. Paintings of Cameron's would continue to grace its walls as he added to the collection on the anniversary of each new birth to the family. Catherine's miniature still serenely sat on Cameron's desk, a reminder to him of the beginning of all of his blessings in this town and the day that he first met his one true love.

Catherine's uncle did find his wealthy widow in Bath but as Catherine predicted, her wealth would not be sufficient to support the ongoing indebtedness of her uncle. Correspondences continued to be received in Lewes by Catherine and Cameron and each one was politely answered with the response that no marriage negotiations were required on the part of Catherine. She had negotiated her own marriage of the heart and had never looked back on the life that she had once led in England.

CHAPTER FIFTEEN

1815

Captain Malcolm McEwan knocked on the door of the Manor House on a fine summer Sunday in 1815. Cameron answered the door himself as it was a Sunday and he was home from his labors. "Captain McEwan; come in man, come in. It is so good to see you. How has life treated you and how is the Rose?" Cameron asked. He showed him into the library and offered him a whiskey.

"I am sorry to visit on the Sabbath but I wanted to see how ye had fared the war Cameron. I see the Yard is busy still and your work has become known the whole length and breadth of the Delaware. How do ye fare then lad?" Captain McEwan asked.

"Oh I am bonny Captain. I have now three sons Captain and the business has run me off my feet for four years now," Cameron replied smiling.

"Three sons did you say? How have ye found the time man?" Captain McEwan said laughing.

Cameron laughed then also and said "You remember my wife Catherine was the model for the Rose masthead? She has not changed Captain. If anything she is more beautiful today than the day of the christening in 1811," Cameron replied.

"Ye are a blessed man Cameron McCullum," Captain McEwan stated.

"Aye tis well I ken it," Cameron replied smiling.

Hearing voices, Catherine came to the door of the library then. "Catherine, come in my love. You will remember Captain McEwan from the English Rose," Cameron stated.

"Captain McEwan how do you do and how does the Rose fare?" Catherine asked.

"She is bonny Mistress and I hear that congratulations are in order to ye Ma'am. Three sons and ye look as bonny as ye did at the christening of yon Rose," Captain McEwan stated.

"Thank you Captain; you are too kind. May we see the Rose Captain?" Catherine asked.

"Aye Ma'am; ye may see her and sail on her if ye are of a mind to," Captain McEwan replied.

"Oh could we Cameron? I would love for the lads to see her," Catherine exclaimed.

"If you go and round them up, we will all go see the Rose," Cameron replied.

Catherine went up to the nursery and roused the three sons of the House of McCullum, grabbed her hat and gloves and descended the stairs shortly thereafter with Jamie at her heels, Alex toddling at her side and baby Cameron in her arms ready for the outing.

"Saints be praised Mistress but ye have three sons of the House of McCullum and each of them the image of himself," Captain McEwan stated. Jamie as usual assumed his perch on the shoulders of his Father, Captain McEwan lifted up Alex into his arms and Catherine serenely carried the newest member of the family baby Cameron, so named for his father.

They all walked to the shipyard and the landing to the Canal and admired the English Rose. "She has seen a lot of action Cameron, but she is a fine ship. Ye built her well lad," Captain McEwan stated.

"Aye she saw you through two years of the war. What is next for you Captain?" Cameron asked.

"I will return to work as a merchant vessel now that the British and French are trading again and we trading with them all," Captain McEwan stated.

Cameron went to see how the figurehead had fared through two years of warfare. Catherine's image serenely looked out from the bowsprit as she had on the day that she had been affixed. "She is a lucky charm is she not?" Captain McEwan called out to Cameron.

"Aye, she is that Captain," Cameron said grinning at Catherine. "As beautiful as the day she was first affixed," he said smiling. "Do you see Mama Jamie? Cameron asked.

Catherine came to his side then to see her image as well preserved as the original. "Da carved that Jamie. Isn't it beautiful?" Catherine said to her wide eyed son.

Alex came next in Captain McEwan's arms, "Mama," he cried.

"It is your Mama my lad, and she has protected my crew for over four years just as she protects you no doubt," Captain McEwan stated to Alex.

"Would you have time for a sail then Cameron?" Captain McEwan asked.

"Oh could we Cameron?" Catherine asked.

"Of course we can my love. When was the last time you have been on a ship Catherine?" Cameron asked.

"It would have been before the war Cameron, on the day of the christening," Catherine replied.

"Of course my love; of course. It is a beautiful day, let us get the lads on board," Cameron said.

The family boarded the English Rose and sail was unfurled. "Look lively there lads. This is the gentleman who designed and built the English Rose and this is his family. This good lady is the inspiration for the name and the image on her figurehead. She is our good luck charm lads," Captain McEwan called out to the crew.

Catherine blushed at the comments and sat down with baby Cameron on her lap and Alex at her side. Being on ship again brought back all of those memories of the first time that she and Cameron had sailed on the English Rose before the war and before the boys had arrived in their life. Today the weather was beautiful, she was on a ship built by the love of her life, the horrid war had ended and she would be going around Cape Henlopen for the first time since the war's conclusion.

"She is so very beautiful Cameron. You must be so very proud," Catherine said grinning up at him.

"Thank you my love; it feels wonderful to be out on the water again. We can do this again now Catherine. There is no fear of a blockade or the British. We are free again my love," Cameron said smiling. Jamie sat on his shoulders, looking up at the sails and the rigging with a look of wonder. His reddish brown hair was blowing in the breeze just like that of his Father's.

"A great deal has happened since the first time I was on a ship Cameron. I have been married, twice," she said smiling up at Cameron, "bore three beautiful sons and survived a war right here in Lewes, Delaware," Catherine said smiling. "We have been very blessed Cameron and there is so much more life ahead of us," Catherine replied.

"That is so true my love. With trade resuming, I will not be outfitting or building for privateers but for merchant ships again. The business will not suffer Catherine, just change," Cameron replied.

"Then there are the Van Ressller holdings also Cameron. We are free to proceed with those as we wish," Catherine replied.

"They do well Catherine and people have jobs because of them. Unless they fail to return a profit, I suggest we hold onto them for our sake and for the town's benefit," Cameron replied.

"I think my uncle may have been correct about your Viking forebears my love. You look very at home on a ship with the wind blowing in your hair and your wee Viking on your shoulders," Catherine said smiling. "You are up very high there my darling boy," Catherine said smiling up at Jamie.

"There is no greater joy than the sun on your back and the wind in your hair and the freedom of the sea my love," Cameron replied, grinning from ear to ear.

They spent the afternoon on the water, enjoying the day, the freedom realized by the end of the blockade and the end of the war and the realization that their family had come a great distance in a very short period of time.

"Catherine, you have given me everything that I could ever wish for in my life," Cameron said watching her intently. "What have I given you in return my love?" he asked worriedly.

"Look before us my love; I see a thousand diamonds on the water. You have given me a thousand diamonds just there for the picking and the three greatest jewels that we hold in our arms. There could be no greater gift to me than your love and my beautiful boys," Catherine said smiling. "And a future with both," she said with tears in her eyes. The English Rose sailed into the Atlantic that day and both the figurehead and its inspiration sailed with her into a bright future.

THE END

NOTES

The English Rose is a work of historical fiction, but many of the events noted in the story were events of history and some of the parties referenced were actual historical figures.

- Captain Sir John Beresford is a historical figure who did pen the letters referenced in the book. He did command the HMS Poitiers and was responsible for the twenty-four hour bombardment of Lewes during the War of 1812. The original letters penned by Captain Beresford are included in the text of the novel in their verbatim context. The squadron that he commanded was required to sail onto Bermuda in 1813 in order to procure the needed supplies for their ships.

- Catherine Wentworth McCullum is a fictional character and the marriage negotiations with she and Captain Beresford were added to the story as a literary device.

- Delaware Governor Haslet noted in the story did own a plantation in Sussex County, Delaware and provided militia to defend the coast against British attack as well as led the actions personally in Lewes during the April, 1813 threat. The parlay referenced in the book is a literacy device, but an actual parlay under flag of truce occurred at the garrison located on the shores of the Delaware prior to the bombardment described. His letter referenced in the book as well as those of S.B. Davis of the Delaware militia are verbatim letters of the incident.

- The bombardment outlined in the book is an actual historical event which occurred on April 6th and 7th, 1813. On April 8th, the British attempted to land in Lewes but were repelled by the militia.

- The burning of Washington, D.C. and the subsequent storm which is now thought to have been a derecho storm are historical facts. The burning of Washington, D.C. occurred followed the routing of the Americans at the Battle of Bladensburg, Maryland as referenced in the story. The storm which occurred the night of the attack is now believed to have been a derecho storm.

- The bombardment of Baltimore, Maryland viewed by attorney Francis Scott Key, the writer of the song which would become the Star Spangled Banner is an historical event and occurred on September 13-14, 1814. The British were not victorious and the Port of Baltimore was not entered by the British fleet.

- There were shipyards located on Shipcarpenter Street on the canal in Lewes, Delaware, near the house referenced in the book which is actually called the Hiram Rodney Burton House. It is located on Shipcarpenter Street, also the location of the fictional cottage which Cameron lived in before his marriage to Catherine and briefly after their marriage.

- There is a Cannonball house in Lewes adjacent to the canal with an unexploded ordinance still in the wall which was a remnant of the April 1813 bombardment of Lewes, Delaware.

- Cannonball Park which is the location of the fictional dance organized by Cameron can be visited today and was one of the scenes of the siege in April, 1813.

- The Capital of Delaware was moved to Dover during the War of 1812 from New Castle, Delaware where it remains to this day in the center of the State of Delaware which consists of three counties of New Castle, Kent and Sussex Counties.

- The Articles of War referenced by Attorney Thomas Wendell were the actual Articles of War in place during the War of 1812.

- The reading of the banns referenced in the novel prior to the marriage of Catherine and Cameron was a tradition of a public statement which announces two people are going to be married. The banns are read in a parish church of the betrothed. The reading was a tradition of the Catholic Church later adopted by the Church of England.

Numerous source materials have been instrumental in the development of the historical background of the book. These include:

1) "Living Lewes", An Insider's Guide by Neil Shister.
2) The Bombardment of Lewes by the British, April 6 and 7, 1813, by William M. Marine, Esq. of Baltimore, Maryland, The Historical Society of Delaware, 1901.

Thank you also to the following parties:

3) The kind assistance of the Lewes Historical Society, 110 Shipcarpenter Street, Lewes, Delaware.
4) Zwaanendael Museum Historical Exhibits.
5) Pam Swartwood and Bill Hammond, beta readers extraordinaire.
6) Moran taing! (Thank you) to my Scot forebears. Thank you for helping to build the United States of America with your ingenuity, skill and tenacity. We your Scot descendants thank you for your many contributions to this nation's history and development. The dialogue between Captain McEwan and Cameron McCullum made use of the word ken a Scots term which means to know. The original language of Scotland was the Gaelic which

though lost to many in the 18th century, is making a
return to usage in Scotland.

Made in the USA
Middletown, DE
10 March 2019